Praise for the Coffeehouse Mysteries

LATTE TROUBLE

"[E]njoy *Latte Trouble*, espresso in hand."
—*Roundtable Reviews*

"A delightful series . . . A captivating narrator . . . Fast-paced [with] a big twist at the end." —*Romantic Times*

"Another delightfully percolating and exciting mystery."
—*Midwest Book Review*

"Intriguing . . . Anyone who loves coffee and a good mystery will love this story."
—*The Romance Readers Connection*

THROUGH THE GRINDER

"Coffee lovers and mystery buffs will savor the latest addition . . . and for those who like both, it's a guaranteed 'Red Eye.' Fast-paced action, coffee lore, and incredible culinary recipes, brewed together with some dark robust mystery, establish her . . . certainly isn't decaf. All . . . *Best Reviews*

"Full of ac . . . thrown in on the sid . . . completely unexpected. . . . *ance Readers Connection*

"A fascinating mystery . . . A brave, quirky heroine."
—*Books 'n' Bytes*

"There were ample red herrings in *Through the Grinder*'s story to lead the reader astray . . . [A] great mystery."
—*Roundtable Reviews*

continued . . .

ON WHAT GROUNDS

"A great beginning to a new series . . . Clare and Matteo make a great team . . . *On What Grounds* will convert even the most fervent tea drinker into a coffee lover in the time it takes to draw an espresso."   —*The Mystery Reader*

"A definite winner! The mystery is first rate, and the characters leap from the page and are compelling, vivid, and endearing. The aroma of this story made this non-coffee drinker want to visit the nearest coffee bar."

—*Romantic Times*

"A fun, light mystery. Recommended."   —*KLIATT*

"[A] clever, witty, and lighthearted cozy."

—*The Best Reviews*

MURDER MOST FROTHY

CLEO COYLE

BERKLEY PRIME CRIME, NEW YORK

THE BERKLEY PUBLISHING GROUP
Published by the Penguin Group
Penguin Group (USA) Inc.
375 Hudson Street, New York, New York 10014, USA
Penguin Group (Canada), 90 Eglinton Avenue East, Suite 700, Toronto, Ontario M4P 2Y3, Canada
(a division of Pearson Penguin Canada Inc.)
Penguin Books Ltd., 80 Strand, London WC2R 0RL, England
Penguin Group Ireland, 25 St. Stephen's Green, Dublin 2, Ireland (a division of Penguin Books Ltd.)
Penguin Group (Australia), 250 Camberwell Road, Camberwell, Victoria 3124, Australia
(a division of Pearson Australia Group Pty. Ltd.)
Penguin Books India Pvt. Ltd., 11 Community Centre, Panchsheel Park, New Delhi—110 017, India
Penguin Group (NZ), Cnr. Airborne and Rosedale Roads, Albany, Auckland 1310, New Zealand
(a division of Pearson New Zealand Ltd.)
Penguin Books (South Africa) (Pty.) Ltd., 24 Sturdee Avenue, Rosebank, Johannesburg 2196,
South Africa

Penguin Books Ltd., Registered Offices: 80 Strand, London WC2R 0RL, England

This is a work of fiction. Names, characters, places, and incidents either are the product of the author's imagination or are used fictitiously, and any resemblance to actual persons, living or dead, business establishments, events, or locales is entirely coincidental. The publisher does not have any control over and does not assume any responsibility for author or third-party websites or their content.

MURDER MOST FROTHY

A Berkley Prime Crime Book / published by arrangement with the author

PRINTING HISTORY
Berkley Prime Crime mass-market edition / August 2006

Copyright © 2006 by the Berkley Publishing Group.
Cover art by Cathy Gendron.
Cover design and logo by Rita Frangie.
Interior text design by Kristin del Rosario.

ISBN: 0-425-21113-4

BERKLEY® PRIME CRIME
Berkley Prime Crime Books are published by The Berkley Publishing Group,
a division of Penguin Group (USA) Inc.,
375 Hudson Street, New York, New York 10014.
BERKLEY PRIME CRIME and the BERKLEY PRIME CRIME design are trademarks belonging to
Penguin Group (USA) Inc.

PRINTED IN THE UNITED STATES OF AMERICA

10 9 8 7 6 5

PUBLISHER'S NOTE: The recipes contained in this book are to be followed exactly as written. The publisher is not responsible for your specific health or allergy needs that may require medical supervision. The publisher is not responsible for any adverse reactions to the recipes in this book.

This book is dedicated with love to
Evelyn Cerasini
and Nana

ACKNOWLEDGMENTS

A *most frothy* thanks to editors
Martha Bushko and Katie Day,
and literary agent John Talbot.

People can't buy a new car every morning, but they can buy a premium cup of coffee that puts a smile on their face. . . . It's the democratization of luxury.

—"$35 a Pound and Going Fast,"
Baltimore Sun, 2004

Coffee is the common man's gold, and like gold it brings to every man the feeling of luxury and nobility.

—Sheik Abd-al-Kadir,
In Praise of Coffee, 1587

PROLOGUE

~~~~~~

AMID the scrub grass of the high beach dune, gloved hands gripped seven pounds of bolt-action. Through the Remington's scope, the shooter scanned the faces on the mansion's expansive cedar deck.

The typical Hamptons crowd was here: Ivy League wives turned interior decorators, captains of industry turned serial cheaters, vapid heiresses turned wannabe celebrities. There were cold-blooded lawyers, eager-to-please newcomers, megalomaniacal executives, and tone-deaf pop singers—all sipping frothy drinks and wearing designer casual with diamonds as big as planets, wrist-watches as pricey as middle-class cars.

Women bared too much or too little, their laughter forced or nonexistent, their attention on each other's cloth-ing, on the faces in attendance, on the host's choice of arti-facts. Men acted too bored or too eager, their focus on networking, for business or pleasure, the mantra always the same: "Close the deal, close the deal."

And, oh, the celebrities. They were here too, looking far less air-brushed than their cover shots on TV Guide *and* Entertainment Weekly. *But those observations would only be whispered after the party or behind their backs during it.*

At last, the shooter located the target—his short, stocky build was unmistakable, his untucked short-sleeved shirt an enormous pink flag. The trigger could have been pulled at that moment. Three rounds were loaded into the Remington's magazine, three seven-millimeter bullets primed for their trip through twenty-four inches of steel and forty odd yards of night air. But the result would have been obvious.

The timing had to be right.

Guests came and went, clustering and dissipating like the tides. Music rolled over the mansion's grounds, across the pool and manicured lawn, down the beach and onto the shoreline. Inside latex gloves, the shooter's hands grew clammy. Behind the shooter's feet, the foamy surf sounded restless, as if the ocean were lapping nearer with every passing minute, closing in with each incoming wave.

Finally, the target stepped away from the crowded deck and into the great room. The place was lit up like a whorehouse. With every shade up and shutter open, every bulb and chandelier blazing, guests could readily see the mansion's splendor—and the shooter could easily track the target's movements down the hallway and into the south wing, up the stairs and toward the master bedroom suite.

Rogue firecrackers had been exploding for some time, a bright bang here, a sharp crack there, just like any other Fourth of July evening, little detonations from god-knew-where. But those stray explosions were nothing. The night's most memorable fireworks were about to start.

Farther down the beach, the patriotic spectacle was finally launched. A succession of roman candles went up amid booms, blasts, and a pumped-up soundtrack. Rockets raced high over the water, bursting with an array of bright red light, trickling down like blood trails against the death-black sky.

Most guests were staring upward now, their blank faces dazzled by the show. The shooter's focus remained far lower. For a few minutes, the target disappeared from view, then reappeared on the mansion's second floor. He had moved to the bathroom window.

A shot rang out and then another. Both missed their target. A third round was fired. It traveled down the Remington's barrel, through the thick window, and into the man's skull.

At the party below, guests were still gawking skyward. They had failed to notice the rifle's discharge. Amid the fireworks, it was just another big bang.

One

꩜꩜꩜꩜꩜꩜꩜꩜꩜꩜꩜꩜꩜꩜꩜꩜꩜꩜

HOURS before I found the body, one of Detective Mike Quinn's pithy comments came back to haunt me: *"You know, Clare, it's a little-known principle of physics, a great deal of money can create a completely separate universe."*

"You were right, Mike," I whispered, taking in my surroundings.

I was standing on the bi-level oceanfront deck of *Otium cum Dignitate*, "Leisure with Dignity," David Mintzer's ten-million-dollar East Hampton mansion, where his annual July Fourth party was in full swing.

Floating candles bobbed in the Jacuzzi like dancing water fairies. Antique porcelain planters sweetened the sea air with rare orchids and night-blooming jasmine. Speakers, hidden in the topiary, accompanied the music of the nearby rolling surf with the majestic compositions of Gershwin and Copeland. And sterling-sliver serving trays overflowed with flutes of obscenely expensive champagne and freshly picked strawberries the size of lemons, dipped in the finest Belgian chocolate.

"East" Hampton, of course, was one of the most exclusive hamlets in the United States. It sat beside Amagansett, Wainscott, Sagaponack, Bridgehampton, Southampton, and a few other quaintly named seaside townships known collectively as "the Hamptons," each with its own set of beaches, permits, and restrictive (some might say fascistically elitist) parking regulations.

East Hampton was also a prime example of my detective friend's theory. For the very wealthy who summered here, from business moguls to movie stars, old money heirs to new money wannabes, the place was a trip back in time, where neon was outlawed, scenic rural landscapes were preserved, and genteel country estates were hidden from public view by towering "stay out!" hedgerows. (Or, as the local gentry referred to them, "privets for breaking the ocean winds," because actually admitting your aversion for allowing the general public to even peek at your property might make you appear a total snob.)

The Hamptons, it seemed to me, were about a lot of things, but mostly they were about being one hundred miles away from the gritty threats and cheap kicks of New York City. Money had carved these people another dimension, an existence of safety and beauty and taste, free of the stench of fear and crime and tackiness.

The villages were located at the end of Long Island's South Fork, a picturesque strip of land filled with ponds, marshes, and hills. Bluewater bays stretched along its north side, the Atlantic ocean along its south.

There were hiking trails here and haute cuisine. Farm stands and a film festival. Bird sanctuaries and built-in pools. Nature preserves and tennis courts. You could find Jackson Pollack's original, unheated studio here, as well as Quelle Barn, Steven Spielberg's multi-million dollar East Hampton summer home, supposedly guarded by retired members of the Mossad—Israel's secret service.

Even the light was special in the Hamptons. Artists claimed it was the peculiar shape of the landscape, the slant of the sun's rays as they bounced off the water. Whatever it was, they could find it nowhere else, which was one reason the area had become one of America's most famous art colonies long before La-La Land's A-list had started driving up the real estate prices.

Hamptons' colors actually appeared richer too (not just the people). One morning when I rose for an early swim, I found myself gaping at an azure ocean so identical to the sky above it that no horizon line presented itself—the blue seemed to go on forever.

At the moment, on the other end of Long Island, the end without pristine white beaches, most of New York City's residents were living on top of each other in cigar-box apartments, rundown rowhouses, and public housing—all of them sweltering in the kind of relentless city heat that liquefied every ounce of energy before sucking it right out of you. Emergency sirens and shouting neighbors routinely punctured any hope of sustained tranquility, and sidewalk garbage, baking in the summer heat, fouled the air with the sort of fragrances that Calvin Klein wouldn't be bottling anytime soon.

Because tempers rose with the temperature, muggings, burglaries, assaults, and murders were now statistically up all over the city. And Mike Quinn had been clocking a lot of overtime at the NYPD's Sixth Precinct.

Here in East Hampton, on the other hand, police work appeared to be limited to public drunkenness, auto accidents, or the occasional actress-turned-pathological-shoplifter. Delicate breezes refreshed the residents with the vigor of salt spray. And the nights were cool, quiet, and dark enough to actually *see* the constellations.

This place was a dreamland, Trump-meets-Thoreau, with an ocean view. And New Yorkers who had no roots in its history bought their way in with oodles of money, staking their million-dollar claims. They had indeed violated the laws of physics, as my friend Detective Quinn had put it, and created a completely separate universe.

So what the heck was I, middle-class working stiff Clare Cosi, doing here? At the moment, I was whipping up frothy coffee concoctions for David Mintzer's illustrious party guests.

I know, I know . . . in America the term "barista" has come to be associated with out-of-work actors and college coeds—never mind that Americans consume half the world's coffee supply, about 100 billion cups a year, and on a typical day seventy percent of the population drinks it. Here barista is not the highly-respected job title it is in, for example, Italy, a country with over 200,000 espresso bars.

The truth is, I'd gotten my coffee start early. My paternal grandmother taught me how. She raised me back in Pennsylvania, where I practically lived in her little grocery, making espressos for her customers and friends with the battered stovetop pot she'd brought with her from Italy. With every cup I poured, there was always a pat on the head, the pressing of a quarter into my palm.

My father, a flamboyant, constantly wired little guy who loved a good cigar and a shot of anisette with his morning demitasse, ran an illegal bookie operation from the back of Nana's store.

My mother never sampled my coffee-making skills. She'd left when I was seven, and although for years I'd thought it was because I hadn't been a good enough little girl, I eventually realized she'd become fed up with my father's running around.

One day when a man from sunny Miami came to our town to visit a friend, Mom ran off with him, leaving nothing but a hastily scrawled note, which made her intentions clear. She wanted to erase her past completely, which unfortunately included me.

That's when my grandmother stepped in. Making espresso in Nana's grocery was one of my fondest childhood memories. So it was no big mystery why I associated the best of things with the rich, warm, welcoming aroma of brewing coffee—the essence of home, of Nana's hugs, of unconditional love in the face of an incomprehensible rejection.

Even after my collegiate studies and successes as a culinary writer, I ultimately decided making the perfect cup time after time for a person who might be tired, weary, thirsty, or down, was not an insignificant thing.

Despite my function at this East Hampton party, however, my job title was not in fact "barista to the stars." My actual occupation was full-time manager of the Village Blend, a landmark, century-old coffeehouse in Manhattan's Greenwich Village, which was where David Mintzer and I had gotten to know each other in the first place.

In his mid-forties, David was one of those men who could be described with a list of features that had "slightly" in front of almost every one: slightly paunchy with slightly thinning dark hair, and slightly bulbous eyes. There were other things about him, however, that were far from slight: his wit for one, which was quick and wry; his business acumen for another.

David was an unqualified genius at whatever he attempted to do. He'd designed successful lines of men's and women's clothing, luggage, shoes, fragrances, and bed-and-bath products that were distributed internationally. He ran three successful magazines, two restaurant chains, and he periodically appeared on *Oprah* to give advice on "seasonal trends" to her television audience.

We had first met at a fashion-week party last fall. David had bought a townhouse in Greenwich Village, and he'd become a regular customer at my coffeehouse. He was so impressed with our exclusive blends and roasts, not to mention my espresso cocktails, that he made me an offer. If I would train and oversee his barista staff at "Cuppa J," his brand new East Hampton restaurant, he would not only pay me a generous salary, he would give me a room in his oceanfront mansion all summer as his guest.

After some persuasion, I'd finally agreed that between June and September, I would split my time between Cuppa J and the Village Blend, using assistant managers to look after things at the Blend while I was gone.

Don't get the wrong idea here. David and I weren't lovers—not even close. At the moment, we had one of those gray-area personal/business relationships. And, frankly, even if I'd wanted there to be more between us, I wasn't even sure it was possible. Sometimes he flirted like a straight man and other times he struck me as, well, slightly effeminate (there's that "slightly" again). In the end, his sexuality seemed ambivalent at best.

The thing is, besides being very wealthy, David was also very sweet—or, at least, he'd been sweet to me. At the start of the evening, for instance, his Cuppa J chef (Victor Vogel) and manager (Jacques Papas) had arrived at the mansion with food they'd prepared at the restaurant. David had made a big fuss about personally serving me two flutes of his imported champagne and an outrageous portion of sixty-dollar-a-pound lobster salad.

For the rest of the night, I continued to remain entranced by the bewitching seaside setting—and, of course, the ever-flowing French bubbles. What can I say? Back in the city, I could barely afford an occasional lobster tail. Out here, sterling sliver serving trays—one of which my daughter, Joy, was now carrying—overflowed with seemingly endless rounds of seafood canapés and miniature French pastries that resembled works of modern art.

David had graciously encouraged all of his servers to eat, drink, and be as merry as his guests, and I most definitely took him up on that offer. While it was true that I was just "the help," and it was also true, when you got right down to it, that this whole Hamptons thing wasn't a whole lot different than your average backyard "kegger," I just couldn't talk myself out of being impressed. I'd never before been to a July Fourth party in the Hamptons (a New York City social accomplishment so noteworthy you'd think it would come with a military campaign ribbon), and I was secretly thrilled.

It's no wonder that violence and decay were the last things I expected to encounter that night. Certainly, they were the last things on my mind before I found the body. The time of death, I would eventually learn, was around the same time the evening's fireworks began. But I wouldn't actually *find* the corpse until long after the show ended. So, at this point in the evening, I was still relatively carefree.

The same could be said of my twenty-one-year-old daughter who had come with me to David's while on summer break from her Soho culinary school (she came at my insistence for reasons I'll get to later). Joy was as thrilled as me about being at this party—but for her own particular reasons.

"Mom, *Mom*, did you see Keith Judd?" she bubbled, rushing over with her empty serving tray.

Joy had my chestnut hair, green eyes, and heart-shaped face, and her father's height. No, she wasn't six feet. But she was four inches taller than my five foot two and had a personality like her father's, with more effervescence than a magnum of Asti. Tonight she was clad in the same Cuppa J outfit worn by the rest of the waitstaff—a salmon-colored Polo knit with the Cuppa J logo embroidered in thread the color of a mochaccino over the right breast. The men wore khaki pants and the females khaki skirts. At the restaurant we also wore mocha-colored aprons. For tonight, however, since we were catering a private party at David's home, he asked us to ditch the aprons.

"Look, Mom, look. See him over by the pool? He winked at me. He totally, actually *winked*. At *me*."

"Uh-huh," I said as I dosed freshly milled Arabicas into the portafilter cup. I tamped the ground beans in tightly, swept the excess from the rim, used the handle to clamp the portafilter securely into the espresso machine and hit the start button to begin the extraction process.

"And why is that a 'good thing'?" I asked Joy.

A number of Famous types—actors, pop stars, writers, television personalities—lived in or near the Village, and I'd served them many a grande latte. But even before my time, the coffeehouse's revered owner and my ex-mother-in-law, Madame Dreyfus Allegro Dubois, had regularly served some of the most famous members of the Beat generation, from Jack Kerouac to Lenny Bruce, Willem de Koonig to James Dean. So I was far more jaded than my daughter about "celebrity sightings."

"C'mon, Mom. Don't tell me you don't know who Keith Judd is."

"Oh, I know who he is, honey. Star of slick spy thrillers, right? He landed a courtroom drama role that got him an Oscar nod this year. Hunk of the moment."

"Hottie, Mom. Hunk is old school."

With a groan, I finished pulling the two espresso shots, dumped the dark liquid into a waiting blender, added crushed ice, milk, chocolate syrup, and a dash of vanilla syrup, then took the whole thing for a spin on high. I poured the "Iced ChocoLattes" (as we called them at the Village Blend) into two glass mugs, mounded the frothy drinks with chocolate whipped cream and chocolate shavings, and waved Graydon Faas over to the outdoor espresso station.

Like my daughter, Graydon was a member of David's Cuppa J waitstaff working tonight's party. A surf-crazy twentysomething with a brown buzz-cut streaked blond, Graydon was the tall, silent type. With a quick, nervous-looking glance at Joy, he picked up the frothy drinks and walked them over to the two waiting guests who'd ordered them.

"Okay," I told my daughter. "Hottie then. What I want to know is why you think I'd be happy to hear that a man at least as old as my ancient forty years, is winking at my twenty-one-year-old daughter?"

Joy rolled her eyes. "Because he's a big star."

"Honey, half the faces here have been on the cover of *Trend* magazine and the other half have been profiled in the *Wall Street Journal*. Didn't you study Chaucer back in high school? The House of Fame has dubious structural integrity."

"I don't care. He's cute."

"Who's cute?" said Treat Mazzelli, walking up to Joy and throwing a muscular arm around her shoulders. "Talking about *moi* again?"

Another Cuppa J waiter, Treat was in his mid-twenties. He had flashing brown eyes, raven hair, and the stocky, muscular build of a weightlifter. He was also an outspoken guy who loved to use his flirty sense of humor on the younger females of the species.

"What an ego," teased Joy. "I wasn't talking about *you*. I was talking about Keith Judd. He winked at me."

I grunted in disgust and shook my head. Treat noticed my reaction. "Relax, Mother Clare," he teased. "I saw the whole 'Keith Judd' incident."

I raised an eyebrow. "It's an *incident*, is it?"

Joy smirked at Treat. "What did you see?"

He shrugged. "Just Joy staring at Judd with naked abandon. Can you say 'obvious'? The guy was clearly shining her on. Apparently, he's used to groupies like her."

"I am not a groupie." Joy's voice held mock outrage, but I could see the little flirty smile forming as she eyeballed Treat. "Yeah, okay, so I was probably staring. But at least I didn't drop the tray, okay? Give me credit for that."

"Okay, sweet thing." Treat laughed. "Here's your credit."

The two were about the same height and he easily tightened his arm around her neck, trying to pull her into a half-nelson so he could buff her head. But Joy was too quick for him. With a squeal, she slipped out of his grip.

"Do not. Repeat. Do not touch the hair!"

Treat rolled his eyes. "What up, princess? It's just a ponytail?"

"A neat ponytail," Joy pointed out. "I don't want you mussing it."

"Check it, baby. You haven't lived till you had Treat muss you . . . just a little, what do you say? After the party?" He reached out to tug her hair.

Joy flipped her chestnut ponytail out of his reach, but I could see she was enjoying the game—a little too much.

So I cleared my throat—a little too loudly.

"You two better get some more trays circulating or Madame may flog you with her Gucci shoe."

"Aye, aye, Barista Bligh." With a salute for me and an exaggerated wink for Joy, Treat headed off to the kitchen, where my French-born ex-mother-in-law was reigning supreme as the "Culinary Queen," as Treat had put it earlier in the evening.

One thing about Madame, whether she was in a vintage Oscar de la Renta or a béarnaise-stained apron, she maintained a regal bearing like nobody's business. And for a woman pushing eighty, she often displayed more upbeat energy than I could muster at the end of the day. I was glad she'd come out to visit me and her granddaughter—and even happier she'd volunteered to manage the mansion's kitchen tonight, making sure our waiters and waitresses properly arranged their trays and kept the prepared food flowing.

Joy watched Treat head back inside the mansion. "C'mon, Mom, give me a chance to impress Keith Judd. Whip me up something extra-special to take to him."

"No."

"Pleeeeeze." Joy tapped her cheek. "How about your eight-layered chocolate-almond espresso!"

The eight-layered espresso was a complicated balance of physics—it required the careful pouring of heavier syrups and lighter liquids to create a beautiful-looking drink. It was my own version of a café pousson, that multi-layered cocktail of liquors of different colors and densities, which originated in New Orleans. Since the French translation of the drink is "push coffee," and since they say a true café pousson separates the men from the boys where bartenders are concerned, I decided to create one using actual coffee. But the last thing I wanted to do was use my talents to help my daughter impress a womanizing thespian.

"That's a hot drink," I told her. "I'm making iced tonight."

"Come on," Joy pleaded. "He'll love a hot drink. The weather's cooling off now anyway."

My daughter's eyes were as wide as emerald moons. Like a little girl she wanted what she wanted when she wanted it. So what did I do? What any self-respecting American mom would do. I sighed, shook my head, and gave in.

"Okay," I said. "But how about a Tropical Coffee Frappe instead?" Rum and coconut had made that one a favorite of tonight's guests.

"No. Not special enough."

"An Amaretto Iced Coffee Smoothie?" Kahlua and amaretto gave that one a kick.

"No."

"Please do the eight-layer thing. He'll love it! *Please*, Mom!"

"Okay, but it'll take a few minutes of concentration. You take over mixing the cold drinks for guests until I finish."

"Deal!"

About fifteen minutes after Joy delivered my "hot" version of a café pousson cocktail to the "hottie" actor, the fireworks began.

I always was a sucker for July Fourth displays. When my ex and I had been happily married—for a few years there, when Joy was still very young and things hadn't gone totally to hell yet—we would put Joy in a stroller and go over to the FDR drive in Manhattan. The city closed the highway off so residents could line the East River from Harlem to the South Street Seaport and watch the most spectacular fireworks display in the country. The rockets would shoot off from barges floating in the river. Ice cream, hot dog, and shish-kabob vendors would supply the crowd with delicious street fare, and portable radios would provide broadcasts of synchronized music.

I remember Joy clapping happily in her stroller, Matt putting his big, strong arms around me and telling me to just lean into him. If only we could have stayed that way, never left the FDR, kept the fireworks going forever.

Tonight's display had been privately arranged by David, who was a newcomer to East Hampton. This was only his third annual Fourth party. Two brothers from Manhattan's Chinatown, who had long ago worked out the pile of permits needed from the local authorities to create private fireworks for Hamptons parties, set their rockets up down the beach and angled them to fall over the ocean.

Now colors bloomed in the evening sky, painting the starry canvas with flickering lights that trailed like wet diamonds down to the black surf. We all stopped to watch the spectacle, then the party cranked up again, one last burst of energy before the guests, like the flickering lights of the expended rockets, trailed off into the night.

The fairly speedy exit of the partygoers was not surprising. Clouds were moving in fast from over the ocean—a flash of distant lightning and a rumble of thunder had been the equivalent of a Broadway curtain call. With smiles and waves, and calls goodnight to each other, the friendly, happy throng filed into the mansion and out the front door like a human commuter train.

As the last of the guests trailed off, I quickly directed Joy and Graydon Faas in a cleanup detail on the large outdoor deck. There were cups, cocktail glasses, and napkins all over the joint. Lounge chairs, antique benches, and other furniture had been scattered across the deck and lawn as well. And with the storm moving in, all of us had to work fast to get the valuable pieces inside before the skies opened up.

"Clare, what do I do with these fabulous strawberries?" Madame asked me as I moved the espresso machine back onto the kitchen counter. "There's not one egg of caviar left and the prawns are long gone, but I have about ten quarts of fresh strawberries left over here. I can package them up for the restaurant or place them in bowls for David's personal use."

Even after a long night, Madame was looking as put-together as ever. Her blunt-cut, shoulder-length gray hair, dyed sleekly silver, had been twisted into a neat chignon and her sleeveless fuchsia blouse and black summer-weight slacks were protected from spills by a still nearly-spotless white chef's apron.

"I think David better make the decision on the strawberries," I said, snatching a plump one to nibble on. "Where is he, anyway? I haven't seen him since before the fireworks."

Joy overheard us. "Maybe he's out front with the last of the guests."

"No, no. He wasn't feeling well earlier," said Madame. "He mentioned to me that he had a migraine coming on with a vengeance, said it felt like a food allergy reaction, although he was certain he hadn't eaten anything to induce it. In any event, he went upstairs for some medicine and to lie down. He asked me to make his apologies to any guests that might leave before he came down again. Do you think he's fallen asleep?"

I checked my watch. "If he took migraine medication, I'm betting the man's down for the count."

"Perhaps you better check on him," Madame suggested. "See if he needs anything."

"Good idea."

"Oh," she called after me. "If you see that young man Treat, would you send him my way? That boy went off to find a free bathroom some time ago—the first floor bathrooms were constantly in use all night—and I believe he's been shirking work ever since!"

I raised an eyebrow at that. It wasn't like Treat Mazzelli to shirk work. He was a good, dependable waiter at Cuppa J. Nevertheless, he did seem to have a penchant for flirting, and the party atmosphere may have given him license to indulge himself. I figured I'd find him in a secluded corner with a willing female on our wait staff—and only hoped it wasn't more than a few kisses he was stealing. David would have an absolute cow if he found out Treat was using one of the mansion bedrooms to seduce a co-worker.

"Don't worry," I called back to Madame. "I'll throw a rope around him and drag him back."

Thunder rumbled in the distance as I left the large gourmet kitchen. Still nibbling the giant strawberry, I entered the great room—a spacious salon filled with goosedown sofas, overstuffed armchairs, and dozens of gorgeous antiques. A large fireplace dominated the room on one end, and the wall parallel to the deck and beach had been made transparent by a line of tall palladium windows, closed up tight now because of the coming storm.

David's bedroom suite was on the south end of the sprawling mansion. He'd shown it to me once, during the "grand tour" of the entire estate on the day I arrived.

I climbed a set of stairs tucked between the great room and the library. At the end of the hallway on the second floor of this wing was a set of mahogany double doors that led to David's master bedroom suite. The doors were shut, and I was about to tap them lightly when I heard water running.

The sound came from behind a single door along the hallway, which stood perpendicular to the double doors. This door, I remembered, led to David's private bathroom—a huge, sleekly modern affair with a Jacuzzi, mood lighting, a towel warmer, and satellite television.

David would, of course, typically enter his bathroom from inside his bedroom. This hallway entrance was for Alberta Gurt, the housekeeper. It allowed her to enter the bathroom from outside the bedroom suite and clean it without disturbing him. Of course, with the water running, I assumed David was now in there, and I lightly knocked on the bathroom door.

"David?"

No answer.

I knocked louder and waited, finished the last bite of my huge strawberry and licked my fingers.

"David! It's Clare. Do you need anything?"

Still no answer.

I pounded as loudly as I possibly could.

"David are you all right? David?"

I turned the knob and realized the door wasn't locked.

"David, I'm coming in!"

I slowly cracked the door, giving him time to protest. Peeking inside, I saw the pool of red on the ivory marble. Then I swung the door wide—and screamed.

Two

∿∿∿∿∿∿∿∿∿∿∿∿∿∿∿∿∿∿∿∿

"MOM! Was that you screaming? Are you okay?"

Joy was the first one down the hallway, Madame right behind her, a little slower than her granddaughter, but hustling nonetheless.

"Clare, what's wrong?!"

"It's David . . ." I whispered, feeling numb.

His face was turned away from the bathroom doorway, but I could see he'd been shot in the head. His body was still as a stone, the skin of his arms a waxy blue-gray, his fingernails colorless.

"Joy, what's going on?" Graydon Faas came down the hall next, his lanky form striding with urgency. Two more members of the wait staff followed—Suzi Tuttle, a Long Island native, and Colleen O'Brien a young Irish immigrant.

The entire group formed a huddle around me. I pointed, and they turned to see David Mintzer lying face down on his imported Italian marble floor, a pool of red staining the ivory stone.

"My god," Madame murmured.

"Jesus, Mary, and Joseph," Colleen whispered.

"No," Graydon rasped. "It can't be."

As we all stared in shocked silence, a male voice spoke up from behind us—"Was I dreaming? Or did I just hear Clare scream?"

We turned. David Mintzer was standing right behind us. Then we all screamed.

David had just stepped out of his pitch dark bedroom, bleary eyed and squinting. He was only a few inches taller than my five-two, and I spontaneously threw my arms around his neck.

"Ohmygawd, David," I cried. "You're alive!"

"Clare?" David's bulbous brown eyes blinked at me in puzzlement. "What in the world is—"

He stopped talking, having finally noticed the wide open door and the tragic, bloody mess in his custom-designed bathroom. "Oh my lord . . . who *is* that?"

Everyone was still staring in shock through the doorway. I gently pushed past them. Careful to avoid the blood, I walked into the bathroom and crouched down next to the body, felt the waxy blue-gray skin. I gently turned the head so that we could all see the corpse's face.

Joy gasped, Graydon cried out, and Colleen screamed.

By this time, I'd already guessed who it was by a process of elimination. When I saw the features of the young man, my fears were confirmed. The corpse on the floor was Treat Mazzelli.

By now, I also knew why I had made the mistake of misidentifying the body. Both David and Treat had short, black hair, stood under five seven, and were wearing short-sleeved shirts. Sure, David's Ralph Lauren linen number was 300 dollars more than the "Cuppa J" Polo that Treat was wearing, but the pinkish/salmon colors were nearly identical and so were their khaki slacks. Because the shirts were worn loose and untucked, it wasn't immediately apparent that

Treat's form was that of a muscle-bound weightlifter in his twenties and David's that of a middle-aged foodie. From a distance, both men appeared to have the same hairy arms and stocky builds.

As the crowd at the door reacted with distressed exclamations, my mind began to race. Awhile back, I'd solved the murder of a Blend employee—a case on which a certain tall, attractively rumpled NYPD detective had been assigned. After that, Mike Quinn had become a regular Blend customer. As I routinely foamed up his grande lattes, he'd share details about his homicide cases (not to mention his rocky marriage, which was still bordering on divorce).

I was far from a pro at detective work, and I'd made plenty of mistakes in my subsequent attempts. But there were a few things I'd learned from listening to Michael Ryan Francis Quinn. In fact, I could almost hear his advice now—

Think objectively, Clare, not emotionally. Start by simply looking around. What do you see?

I glanced around the bathroom floor, near Treat's blue-gray hands and saw no gun. Then I took a closer look at his skull. There were no sooty smudges or burns around the wound. No gunpowder particles were visible. That meant Treat hadn't been shot at close range. And, of course, he hadn't shot himself.

I turned and scanned the large bathroom window.

"There it is," I whispered.

At about the height of Treat's head in a standing position was a single bullet hole in the glass. I knew next to nothing about ballistics, but it seemed obvious the glass would have slowed the velocity of the bullet. I looked for an exit wound in his skull, but saw none, and I knew the medical examiner would have to retrieve the bullet from inside his brain during the autopsy.

I gently lifted one of Treat's arms. It wasn't stiff, but I wasn't surprised. I had seen Treat alive less than two hours before and it took longer for rigor mortis to set in. The skin still felt warm. The parts closest to the floor appeared purplish, but when I touched the purple areas, they blanched.

"Clare, what are you doing?" asked David. He was about to step inside.

"No, don't!" I warned. "Don't come in. This is a crime scene."

I rose and carefully left the bathroom, closing the door behind me.

Treat had been a considerate young man, personable, with a buoyant sense of humor. He'd been a good worker, always on time, amazingly even tempered, even in the hot house of Cuppa J's East Hampton kitchen. In fact, he was one of the few people who could make Victor Vogel, the relentlessly intense chef, laugh. For that we were all grateful.

So who the hell would want to shoot a good-natured young man like Treat in the head? I asked myself.

Nobody, I silently answered.

The shooter must have made the same error I had, mistaking Treat for David.

Standing around me now in the hallway were the members of Cuppa J's wait staff. They had been working closely with Treat for more than six weeks, and I noticed their reactions.

Colleen O'Brien was sobbing uncontrollably.

Joy, teary-eyed, was trying to comfort her.

Graydon Faas looked totally stricken as he stared at the corpse, slack-jawed and dumbfounded.

Only Suzi Tuttle looked unaffected. She simply stood there with arms folded, a look of ennui on her attractive features.

I made a note of Suzi's reaction (or lack thereof) before I pushed through the group and walked into David's bedroom. The large space was pitch dark, but there was enough light from the hallway for me to make my way around his divan and over to his king-size bed.

"Clare, where are you going?" asked David. He followed me into his bedroom while the others waited in the hall.

"I'm going to call 911."

As I removed the wireless receiver from its base on the carved mahogany end table and dialed the emergency number, David clicked on a few of his Tiffany lamps. When the operator picked up, I explained the situation, gave my name, and David's address and phone number.

"Did you hear anything while you were in here, David?" I asked after hanging up. "Anything at all?"

"Nothing."

"How long were you up here?"

He checked his wristwatch. "About two hours I guess. I came up to lie down just before the fireworks. I must have fallen asleep. My god . . . I still can't believe this . . . what do you think happened to Treat? An accident?"

An accident? Yeah, right. One of your guests just happened to be cleaning a gun on your back grounds, and it just happened to go off and accidentally pop through your private bathroom window at exactly the right time to take down a man close to your height and dressed just like you.

I said none of this, of course. With the exception of Ted Ammon's tragic fate, homicide was unheard of in this burgh. (Ammon had been an upstanding financier until he was brutally bludgeoned to death in his East Hampton mansion by his estranged wife's electrician, who also happened to be the woman's lover.)

Okay, so the locals referred to Ammon's old Middle Lane address as "Murder Lane," but until that specific crime, there hadn't been a homicide out here in years. The last thing an East Hampton resident expected was a real murderer to squeeze through their impenetrable privets— and I could see it was going to take a little time for David to accept that a homicide had just taken place in his own house.

"I'm not sure what happened," I told him carefully, "but, David, back up a minute. Tell me exactly why you left the party."

He shrugged. "I felt a migraine coming on. They're allergy induced and I know exactly how to treat them—a cold, dark room and my prescription medication. I popped two pills and came straight to the bedroom. Didn't bother turning on any lights, just turned up the air-conditioning and lay down. I heard the fireworks going off, but I couldn't even bear to watch them. I dozed off and the next thing I remember is hearing you scream."

"Clare, what's going on?" called Madame from the doorway. "Did you call the police?"

"Yes," I replied.

I could hear Colleen's sobs hadn't subsided and the others were still huddled around the bathroom doorway like witnesses of a traffic accident who weren't sure whether they should leave the scene.

I glanced at David. This was still his house and I didn't want to sound obnoxiously bossy, so I tried to pose my directive as a question. "Maybe we should all go downstairs? To the kitchen? I'll make us some coffee and we can wait for the police together?"

"Okay . . . all right . . . sure . . ." Everyone mumbled and began to wander back down the hall and toward the stairs.

"Wait for me," David said as I swiftly walked away. "I'm certainly not staying up here alone!"

THREE

∿∿∿∿∿∿∿∿∿∿∿∿∿∿∿∿∿∿∿

"DEAD bodies freak me out."

Graydon Faas's hands shook as he lifted his mug of coffee.

"It's all right," said David, patting the young man on the shoulder. "They aren't a barrel of laughs for me either."

I had brewed a twelve-cup drip carafe of our medium roast Breakfast Blend and was just finishing gradually and evenly filling seven mugs. (I never pour one cup at a time out of a pot. I always pour a little into each cup until they're all filled. That way, if there are any inconsistencies in the suspension—too strong at the bottom of the pot, for instance, and too weak at the top—no one cup will suffer from the extreme.)

As David splashed cream into his coffee, I gulped mine black, barely tasting the nutty warmth. Adrenaline wasn't a problem at the moment, but I feared my energy levels would spike and then fall, which was why I'd chosen the Breakfast Blend. I had many other more complex and robust-tasting blends on hand, but the medium roast had more caffeine than the darker Italian or French roasts, and I wanted to be alert for the next few hours.

Everyone was drinking their coffee now, except Colleen, who was still sobbing into a series of Kleenexes. The girl's loose auburn curls had begun slipping from their ponytail, and her usually ruddy skin looked pale as a shroud, making her dusting of freckles appear as if someone had roughly grated a cinnamon stick across her barely-there nose. An Irish immigrant here in New York on an education visa, Colleen had just turned twenty. From the age of eight, she'd worked in her family's Dublin pub/restaurant and her experience as a waitress showed in her efficient, earnest, unflappable service.

I sat down at David's seven-foot-long kitchen table directly across from Colleen and Joy. Madame sat next to me. Around the rest of the table sat David, Graydon, and Suzi. For a minute, we all listened to Colleen's sobs in the huge gourmet kitchen—that and the dishwasher's rhythmic swishing next to the Sub-Zero fridge.

Joy reached over, stirred cream, then sugar into Colleen's warm mug and gently pushed it into the girl's shaking hands. Colleen swallowed with difficulty, then began to take small sips.

We all silently watched.

Obviously, Colleen had something very personal going on, but no one said a word. Normally, I would have given the young woman her privacy, but if she knew something that would help the police, I wanted to know it too.

"Colleen," I carefully began, "we're all upset about Treat, of course, but you seem really undone. Is there anything you want to share with us?"

"Ohhhhhh!" she wailed, then began bawling again.

Damn. Now everyone was staring at me as if I'd just kicked the poor girl. Everyone except Suzi Tuttle.

"Oh, for god's sake, Colleen," she snapped. "He's not worth it."

Suzi, the Long Island native, was twenty-five, but she'd been bartending and waitressing since high school. She had triple-pierced ears and (apparently) more piercings elsewhere on her body, or so she liked to brag. The hard-partying image was deliberately played up with short-cropped hair dyed white blond and black eyeliner as thick as Cleopatra's.

Suzi's tough attitude actually worked well in David's East Hampton restaurant. Cuppa J's customers weren't exactly known for being passive and polite. They were wealthy, elite, famous people who were used to having their whims and demands satisfied with a finger snap. One thing you could not have in that environment was a thin skin.

Still, Suzi's hardness at this moment seemed out of place—until Colleen blew her small, pug nose and, in a mild Irish brogue, announced with great profundity: "You all might as well know. Treat and I, we were . . . we were close."

"He was banging you," Suzi said flatly.

Colleen's eyes narrowed. "We were lovers."

Suzi waved her hand. "Treat didn't love anyone but himself."

"You raccoon-eyed witch! How can you say that? With him lying upstairs like that and all . . ." Colleen's sobs began again.

"I can say it because I know exactly how he operated," Suzi calmly replied. "He told you to keep your relationship quiet, right? So there wouldn't be any 'funny vibes' at the restaurant."

Colleen stopped crying. Her jaw dropped. "How did you know? Did he tell you about us?"

"Girlfriend, get a clue. Treat told me the same thing when he was sleeping with me. And I found out why. Before me, he was hooking up with Prin!"

Madame put down her coffee cup, leaned toward me and whispered, "Sounds like the boy was sampling David's restaurant staff like a box of chocolates."

Prin Lopez was a model-gorgeous Hispanic girl with sleek, dark brown hair down to her hips and long-lashed copper eyes. She'd grown up in a rough part of the Bronx, the poorest borough in New York City, but had worked her way into waitressing at a popular Upper West Side bistro, where David and Jacques Papas (Cuppa J's manager) had met her. Both had been impressed with her service as well as her ability to speak fluent Spanish—always handy in an industry that consistently employs kitchen workers from Mexico and Latin America.

According to Jacques, Prin had left the South Fork abruptly for a family emergency and wouldn't be around to help with the July Fourth weekend crowd, which was a shame, because this weekend was bound to be the busiest of the season.

As I made a mental note to ask Prin about her relationship with Treat when she returned to work, I noticed Joy, across the table, squirming uncomfortably and gnawing her lower lip. I wasn't going to press her now, but I was praying that Treat Mazzelli hadn't also started sleeping with my daughter. From the way the guy had been flirting with Joy earlier this evening, it seemed apparent he was already making plans to dump Colleen.

It also seemed apparent that Treat had been racking up conquests. But not just any conquests. The Hamptons were always packed with single, available women. If Treat had wanted to bed a string of willing young females, he could have driven just a few miles over to Sagaponack. "Sagg Main" was the most active singles beach scene in the Hamptons, full of gym-toned bodies looking for true love—or a weekend simulation of same.

Obviously Treat had preferred to seduce a succession of

young women in close proximity to one another, bedding each one while pretending he could keep them all from finding out. It was the sort of pattern set by a guy who obviously got off on high-risk living, maybe even thrived on a situation that could, at any time, blow up in his face.

If that were the case, I wondered: were there other parts of his life that were just as high-risk? So high-risk that someone would want him dead? Had the shooter hit the right target after all?

Graydon interrupted my thoughts with a sudden sigh of agitation. Running a strong hand through his blond-streaked buzz cut, he self-consciously announced, "You guys, I barely knew Treat. I mean, I'm sorry for what happened to the dude, but I don't know anything that can help and I really . . . I'm really wrecked. I'd like to go home and hit the sack. Is that okay?"

Suzi again waved a dismissive hand. "You just want to catch your waves at the crack of yawn."

"So?" Graydon folded his arms. "I said I was sorry about the dude, but do you really think he's in a position to care one way or the other?"

Suzi looked away.

Colleen began to cry again.

"There, there," said Madame, reaching across the table to pat Colleen's hand. "You know Ms. Tuttle may not have said it in the kindest way, but I do believe you've shed enough tears for the boy upstairs. Take it from a woman who's been around the block a few times, my dear, men are like buses—one may throw you off unexpectedly, but there'll always be a new one coming right behind you, inviting you to climb aboard."

For a second there, we all stared at Madame, a little shocked at her suggestive phrasing. She simply blinked at us, either completely oblivious to the unintentional double entendre or appalled at our provincial reaction to it.

"What?" she finally snapped. "What did I say?"

Joy put an arm around Colleen. "My grandmother's right. In fact, how's this for something to cheer up about. I've got Keith Judd's phone number, and I'll bet we could both party with him—"

"What?" I interrupted with alarm. "Joy, you're kidding, right? That actor didn't actually give you his phone number."

Joy nodded excitedly. "He did. Look."

From the pocket of her khaki skirt, my daughter pulled out a cocktail napkin.

"Let me see that," I said.

She handed it over, sliding it across the kitchen table as she explained, "He gave it to me after I brought him your café pousson."

I examined the napkin. On it, the slick, forty-year-old Hollywood actor had scrawled his name. Below it was a cell phone number. I stood up, tore the napkin in two, pushed the autograph back toward my twenty-one-year-old daughter and shoved the piece with the man's phone number down the garbage disposal.

"Mom!" she cried. "What are you doing?!"

With the determination of a mother on a mission, I flipped on the disposal. "Sorry, honey."

Joy leaped to her feet and banged the table with her fist. "I can't believe you did that!"

"Believe it."

"You had no right!"

I could see she was just getting started.

It wasn't the first time she and I had faced off. The entire reason Joy was out here was because of my playing protective mom.

Less than a year before, I'd caught her doing cocaine with her friends in the bathroom stall of an infamous nightclub. (I know, I know—what was I, myself, doing in an infamous nightclub, right? Trust me, there was a good reason, and when I stumbled upon Joy, she had insisted what she was doing was none of my business. But I begged to differ.) I asked her father to have a long talk with her. God knows I'd had enough of them with her when she was in high school, but now she was a young woman, living with a roommate her age. I knew she needed to hear some straight talk from the horse's mouth (so to speak—and I'm being kind). Matteo Allegro had become an addict during our marriage and it was one of the reasons our wedded bliss ended long before our ten-year union did. (It was also the reason I used to refer to Matt as a "horse's other end").

Matt well knew what could happen to a person who thought he or she could handle casual drug use: impaired judgment, pouring money into the habit, becoming unreliable, lying to and hurting loved ones. In Matt's case, this included the habit of cheating on me, which, as far as I was concerned, was as much an addiction as his chemical dependency and sprang from the same "self-medicating" issues.

In any event, Matt's "horse's mouth" talk seemed to work, and Joy had buckled down with her culinary school studies for the rest of the year. Then, one day near the start of spring, she came running into the Village Blend waving a local magazine.

At the time, David Mintzer had been sitting at my espresso bar, reading the *Wall Street Journal* and sipping a doppio espresso. He had already asked me to work for him. And I had already declined. "I work for Madame," I'd told him with a shrug. "Managing the Blend is a job I love, and I'll be taking over as co-owner in the future. I'm not looking for a change."

But when Joy burst into the coffeehouse with her "big plans for the summer," which included an illegal Hamptons share, my outlook changed. Joy had circled five possible share houses listed in the local magazine. She just needed a "teensy-weensy loan" from me to get into one of them.

Now I knew perfectly well that Hamptons' officials had set up codes limiting the number of occupants in rental houses. I also knew that hundreds of entrepreneurs routinely violated those laws by running illegal shares all season long, cramming up to thirty or forty people into one house. This was the way twenty- and thirtysomethings without Hilton sisters-level loot could afford to "summer" in these exclusive seaside towns.

A decade ago, this share thing seemed like a good idea. I'd been around thirty at that time, Joy around eleven. When she'd gone away for two weeks of Girl Scout camp, I gave in to a girlfriend who'd insisted that a "wild" week of meeting men, dancing, drinking, and sunbathing was exactly what I needed after my divorce from Matt.

I decided to give it a try, shelling out 1,500 dollars for one week of a South Fork summer by the sea. Typically this was how it worked: a three-or-four-million-dollar house would rent out for 100,000 dollars or so for the season. In order to cover that cost, the people running the share would cram each bedroom with multiple mattresses. For your share price, you got the mattress, toilet paper, paper cups, and the use of the house's kitchen, pool, hot tub, and bathrooms.

On the face of it, the idea seemed good. It was the "democratization of luxury," I'd told myself. But the reality wasn't so good. Frankly, I'd hated it. The house was a 24/7 party. Jello shots, cocaine lines, naked orgies in the hot tub.

Hey, I like a good time as much as the next person. But I'd never been a hard partying girl. My ex-husband would have loved it. Not me. I did my best to get into the spirit of the house. Then, near the end of the week, one of the men

I'd gotten to know pretty well began kissing me in a hot tub of a dozen people and, before I could stop him, removed the top of my two-piece swimsuit. When a second guy I'd never even seen before that night tried to join in the "fun," I suggested to the first, as I frantically tied my top back on, that if he wanted to go further we should find some privacy.

He took me to the only private place in the huge house—a mattress placed in a walk-in closet. He said this was the spot for anyone who needed to "spend time alone." I looked at that bare mattress on the floor of that closet, a naked light bulb above it, and spontaneously threw up. Suffice it to say, the "ambiance" of the place didn't do it for me, and the next morning, I packed up and left a day early.

I didn't want Joy to go through that—or worse. And I certainly didn't want her to be exposed to drug use again or excessive drinking and partying in a wannabe Animal House.

Joy was livid. She did not share my attitude toward illegal share houses and found my point of view hopelessly clueless and unhip. We faced off.

Wanting to make her happy (without making me crazy worried), I came up with a compromise. I proposed a deal to David. I'd work for him part-time over the summer in his East Hampton restaurant, set up all his coffee selections and a dessert pairings menu, and train his staff in barista skills, as long as he'd agree to employ Joy and allow her to stay with me in his mansion, and allow me to continue overseeing the running of the Village Blend.

David happily agreed to my terms and everything had worked out superbly . . . until tonight, of course.

Joy was once again furious with me for being clueless, unhip, *and* interfering in her private life. Treat's body was temporarily forgotten in the heat of the moment—or maybe it was the stress of that discovery that made our stand-off all the more emotional.

"That phone number was mine," she shouted. "You had no right to destroy it!"

The people around the table had gone dead silent watching us, but I wasn't backing down.

"Joy, don't you understand? You're my daughter. If I see you throwing yourself in front of a truck, I'm going to do everything in my power to push you out of the way—even if it means I get run over in the process."

Joy frowned and folded her arms, glaring in silence. I glared back. Surprisingly enough, it was Graydon Faas who broke the tension.

"You know, Joy," he said after clearing his throat, "I think your mom's sort of right about that actor dude."

Joy shifted her gaze to Graydon. He shrugged. "Keith Judd, like, gave his number to every cute girl at the party." Graydon scratched his head. "You've got a lot going for you, you know? A guy like that . . . he wouldn't appreciate you."

"Oh," Joy said in a small voice. Clearly dying of embarrassment, she sank back down in her chair, refusing to look at me.

I sat back in my own chair, too. Nothing like having co-workers witness an intimate family squabble. I sighed, hearing a distant rumbling rolling in off the ocean. *The coming storm. As if there wasn't already a tempest in here.*

The police had yet to show. I checked my watch. It had been almost twenty minutes since I'd called 911, and I was used to New York City's lightning-fast response times—usually somewhere between three and eight minutes.

I began to worry. Surely there would be evidence outside, but if the rain came before the police showed, would some of that evidence be washed away?

"I wonder where the police are?" I fretted aloud.

David shook his head. "July Fourth in the Hamptons is the craziest time of year and the village police force isn't very big."

Suzi agreed. "There are probably major problems all over town tonight."

"Traffic will be horrendous," David added. "There'll be accidents, DUIs, and drunk and disorderlies on top of what will surely be a few requests for ambulances."

"I guess we were triaged," I speculated aloud. "I mean, they did ask what Treat's condition was, and I did tell them that he was . . . you know, already gone."

Colleen began crying again.

I stood up. "Everyone stay here."

"Where are you going?" David asked.

"I'm going to check on Alberta."

This was the truth, just not the whole of it.

I moved through an archway and entered a long hallway. A large garage sat at the far end. In between were doors to the laundry room and the servants' quarters.

I passed by the first door, which was the bedroom shared by the cook and butler. I knew it would be empty. Kenneth and Daphne Plummer had been married for twenty years. They'd worked for David more than six. Daphne was the cook, Kenneth the butler. For the long Fourth of July weekend, Daphne had traveled to Indiana for her niece's wedding. And Kenneth was in the city, taking care of some utility issues at David's Greenwich Village townhouse.

When I came to the second door, however, I lightly knocked.

"Alberta?" I called.

David's fifty-seven-year-old housekeeper was the only staff member he'd asked to work over the weekend. She'd declined an invitation to the party, so David gave her the night off, knowing we, the restaurant staff and Madame, would handle any post-party cleanup duties.

I knocked again. This time I was sure I heard voices on the other side of the door. I just couldn't tell if it was two people talking or Alberta's television set. Then there was some scrambling movement and the door opened.

Alberta Gurt's quarters consisted of a bedroom, sitting room, and private bath. David had mentioned this to me the day I'd first arrived in the mansion. Her front door wasn't open very far at the moment, but I could see the bedroom door was closed and a single dim lamp was all that illuminated the sitting room. The TV set was off.

"Alberta," I said, "I'm sorry to bother you, but something happened during the party tonight."

"Oh?" she asked, blinking. "What's that?"

Alberta had pale blue eyes and light brown hair sprinkled with gray, which she wore in a short, neat cut around an attractive face. She had the full shape of a woman in her middle years, not slender, but not heavy either, and at the moment she was wearing a deep violet nightgown with pink lip gloss and pearl earrings. It was strange seeing her like that. I was so used to her crisp housekeeper's uniform of sky blue slacks and matching tunic. But it was her evening off, so more power to her.

"Did you happen to hear or see anything that may have seemed out of place?" I asked.

"What do you mean?"

"I mean, did you hear something that may have sounded like a gunshot?"

"What? Like the fireworks? I heard them, all right. How could you not?"

"But you didn't come out to see them?"

"Oh, no. I was watching my favorite TV show, enjoying the night off. You've seen one fireworks display, you've seen them all," she said with a wave of her hand. I noticed some pretty rings on her fingers.

There was a silent pause. It seemed odd to me that she

didn't ask why I was asking about a gunshot. "All right, Alberta. Thanks. Sorry I bothered you."

"That's all right, Clare."

She seemed in a hurry to shut the door. Nevertheless, I quickly asked, "What is your favorite TV show, by the way?"

"Oh! . . . you know, that new reality show everyone's watching, *American Star*."

I raised an eyebrow. "Really?" Alberta wasn't exactly in the demographic for a show like that, which took a pool of unknown young singers and had them perform every week until the audience voted them down to one winner, presumably America's next pop diva.

"Oh, yes," Alberta said quickly. "Talent scout shows aren't new you know, I grew up on Ed Sullivan. Is there anything else, Clare?"

"No," I said. "Good—"

I never got "night" out of my mouth. Alberta was already shutting the door with a hastily called "G'night!"

As the thunder rolled again, louder than before, I proceeded down the hallway until I reached the door at the very end. I turned the knob, entered the dark space, and flipped on the light.

There were a few flashlights on a shelf in David's ten-car garage. I grabbed one and resolutely headed out the side door. It was late, it was dark, and it was probably dangerous, but I intended to have a look around the grounds for myself.

FOUR

~~~~~~~~~~~~~~~~~~~~~~~~~~~~~~~~~

I clicked on the Maglite and began to walk the perimeter of the building, sweeping the milky white beam back and forth. At this time of night, the lane at the end of the long drive was country dark. There were no streetlights, not even any passing headlights.

When I first arrived here as a houseguest, I asked David about privacy and security issues. Unlike most of the residents of this area, he had elected not to place walls of privets around his property or a gate on his drive. He said it was because he didn't want to feel hemmed in. But I suspected it was because he was a showman at heart, and he enjoyed the idea of people gawking at his property, although he claimed the location was remote enough that trespassing tourists hadn't posed much of a problem. (Obviously, a trespassing shooter was another matter.)

An alarm system had been installed on the mansion's doors, but not its windows. And there was no outdoor lighting, a decision I certainly regretted at this moment. The darkness felt eerie as I moved along. The coming storm had brought thick cloud cover and a hovering mist, making the night feel close. The temperature was also at least ten degrees lower than the day's high of seventy-six, and I shivered a bit in my khaki skirt and short-sleeved Polo. To be completely honest, however, part of that shiver was from apprehension.

Don't get me wrong, I wasn't afraid. If I had been, I would have stayed inside, because believe me, I'm no daredevil—not like my adrenaline-junkie ex-husband, who routinely got his kicks from rock-climbing, cliff-diving, and scouting out the most dubious dive bars in the Third World.

(In addition to being my ex, Matteo was an astute coffee broker, who traveled the world's coffee plantations in search of the finest cherries. He was also the Village Blend's coffee buyer, and therefore my business partner. As I already mentioned, during our marriage, in addition to becoming a drug addict, he'd also been a serial cheater who'd had less trouble giving up the cocaine than a variety of "inconsequential female conquests," as he put it. The *inconsequential* was supposed to have been enough of an excuse for me to forgive him. It wasn't.)

In any event, Matt recently accused me of having a Nancy Drew compulsion. He claimed it was a wish-fulfillment impulse carried over from all the mystery novels I'd read in my formative years. He asserted this was my own personal version of an adrenaline rush.

Maybe Matt was right. Maybe he wasn't. One thing I knew, however, coming out here to have a look around was my choice, whether smart or stupid. That's why I kept my destination from David, Madame, Joy, and the rest of the crew. At this point in my life, I was through letting other people's doubts, fears, and worries make my choices for me. And, anyway, there was a very logical reason why I was out here—

Because the police weren't.

Thunder rumbled again and I felt moisture suffuse the air. The scent of sea salt was strong now as I moved along. My ultimate destination was the back of the mansion, but I figured it wouldn't hurt to sweep the grounds as I went.

I wasn't sure what I was trying to spot in my Maglite beam—pretty much anything suspicious before the rain or wind had a chance to drench it or blow it away. Maybe something out of place . . . like a piece of clothing or a dropped personal item. (A stray hunting rifle was probably too much to ask.)

As I came to the end of the mansion's front facade and started moving around the corner of the south wing, I found myself observing how much work had gone into the stunning grounds, from the fully-grown topiaries and blazing blossoms to the gigantic shade trees. According to David, none of it had been here a few short years ago, just scrub grass, weeds, and rocks.

This acreage had originally been part of a larger estate. When the owner died, the estate was broken in two. David bought the land with one goal in mind: to make his brand new *Otium cum Dignitate* look like something Stanford White might have left to a great-grandson.

Apparently, this was one of the latest Hamptons trends: using a variety of tricks to make a brand new mansion look like a weathered heirloom that you'd just inherited. David settled on the Shingle Style, which was a popular Hamptons design in recent years precisely because it was all the rage in late-nineteenth-century New England.

Frankly, after my own modest study of historical styles, from Beaux Arts to Bauhaus, it was hard to believe that today's structural designers weren't banging their heads against the wall in frustration. Instead of giving them the chance to create something wholly new, the Hamptons' new money was forcing them to recast the all-over-shingle idea for the third time in three centuries, and in supremely larger versions—sort of like architectural deja vu supersized.

David's approach was extreme but not atypical. Once he'd bought the property, a pneumatically inflated dome had been set up so that his construction crew could work through the winter months. The vast bi-level sundeck alone had cost a half-million because the architectural firm had hired a restoration contractor to scour the country for cedar planks that had been uniformly weathered like those of an "old money" beach house.

To encourage the growth of moss, mixtures of yogurt and buttermilk had been smeared onto the gray fieldstone foundation. Super-fine mud, dredged from a Maryland bay, had been rubbed onto the shingles to give them a worn look. And in the spring, fully-grown plants had been imported to establish grounds that looked as if they'd been thriving for decades. Deep green topiaries, blue hydrangeas, and beds of burnt-orange and crimson tulips had been planted around the building.

Using a super-speedy type of horticulture called "ivy implantation," the gardener had even affixed thick coats of English ivy up the mansion's sides, giving it a decades-old look before the front tire of David's Jag even touched the driveway.

David's absolute pride and joy, however, were his trees—hundred-year-old oaks and sycamores from upstate and weeping willows from south Jersey. These beauties had been pulled from their original roots and shipped on huge flatbeds (root balls wrapped for replanting) so instant shade would be available at the front and sides of his house.

According to David, two of the largest trees, which I was now moving toward, had root balls so large a toll booth had to be temporarily removed on the George Washington Bridge in order for the flatbed trucks carrying them to pass.

In the end, this was just one more contributor to the multi-million dollar price tag on David's estate.

The excess was truly hard to fathom for someone like me, who'd been financially struggling for years to raise a daughter and now put her through school. On the other hand, I knew David was simply being canny. In his neck of the business world, you weren't keeping up with the Joneses, you were keeping up with the Hiltons, Trumps, and Bloombergs. David wanted an impressive presence here to continue the kind of networking with CEOs, celebrities, and media types that kept his projects and product lines thriving.

As I moved along the south wing's side, the wind quickly intensified, whipping my chestnut ponytail loose. I put the flashlight between my knees and retied my tangling hair. As I was finishing, however, the Maglite slipped and fell. The beam arced wildly and I heard the sound of twigs snapping a few yards away.

I immediately bent down, grabbed the flashlight, and frantically shined it in the direction of the noise. The sallow beam illuminated rubber-soled boat shoes and a pair of black Capri pants.

"Party over?"

The words spiked angrily through the darkness. I swept the beam higher to shed light on a woman about my age in an exquisite black camisole and black cashmere half-sweater. She had straight blond hair, parted down the middle, and cut into fashionable layers. The woman was smoking a cigarette and sneering at me like a female wasp looking for a place to sink her stinger.

"W-who are you?" My nerves were momentarily rattled, and I failed to control the waver in my voice. "What are you doing here?"

"I might ask you the same question."

For at least thirty seconds, Wasp Woman and I faced off in silence. Finally, I caved.

"I'm a guest of David's. My name is Clare Cosi."

"Pleased to meet you, I'm sure," she said, although her tone said she was not. "I'm David's neighbor."

In terms of an ID, that statement actually didn't help much. East Hampton residents valued their privacy more than anything. They kept to themselves, and since I'd arrived here six weeks ago, no "neighbor" had ever before walked down David's driveway. Still, the woman did look familiar, and, for David's sake, I didn't want to unnecessarily offend an acquaintance.

"Sorry, uh . . . which neighbor?" I meekly asked.

"Across the lane," she said with a you're-so-tiresome sigh.

That's when I realized. This woman was Marjorie Bright, the granddaughter of Elmer Bright, founder of Bright Laundry Detergent. The heiress had been in Cuppa J a few times as a customer. David had pointed her out to me. He'd also told me he was surprised to see her in his restaurant because they weren't exactly "on good terms."

At the time, I'd asked David what he'd meant by that.

"Well," he'd answered, "I'd say we haven't yet reached the level of Hitler and Churchill. I'd put us more in the realm of Reagan and Gorbechev."

According to David, Marjorie had always enjoyed an unobstructed view of the ocean from her large, old estate. For almost two decades, her entire decor and entertainment plans had been built around the spectacular vista from her second floor. She'd even had a custom-made loggia constructed for this purpose. But David Mintzer had utterly ruined her view when he'd brought in his giant, hundred-year-old oaks and weeping willows.

She demanded he cut down the trees. He refused.

She complained to the local zoning board, most of whom were regular (and very happy) customers of Cuppa J. They backed David.

She offered him money. He rejected it.

Clearly, this woman was at war with my friend. I folded my arms and narrowed my gaze, any pretense of politeness over as I asked in a cold, hard voice, "What are you doing here, Ms. Bright?"

The woman's smirk faltered. Now that her haughty demeanor had stopped cowing me, she seemed less sure of herself. Taking a dramatic drag on her cigarette, she appeared to be stalling for time to think. Finally, she released a long, white plume of smoke. The whipping wind instantly shredded it.

"Just tell David I'm not through suing him," she responded at last.

Before I could ask another question, she wheeled on the heel of her rubber-soled boat shoe and marched off toward her home, her black-clad form quickly disappearing in the thickening dark.

By now, my pulse was racing. Marjorie Bright's presence was both creepy and suspicious. It reminded me of something Detective Quinn had said about particular kinds of murderers, how they got off on seeing the results of their acts, something akin to arsonists sticking around to watch the sirens, the activity, the fiery destruction.

My mind began to turn this idea over and over. Was that what Marjorie had been doing? Was she the shooter? Or had she been checking on an accomplice? Clearly, she was no friend of David's. But was an obstructed ocean view a reason to shoot your neighbor to death in cold blood?

Before I'd left the mansion's garage, I'd pretty much convinced myself the killer had either slipped away or disappeared back into the crowded party the moment Treat had hit the floor. Now I wasn't so sure. And the uncertainty unnerved me.

Still, I had come out here with a specific goal in mind. I hadn't accomplished it yet, and really hated the idea of letting my fears get the better of me. So I gritted my teeth and moved on.

At the rear of the house, I circumvented the cedar plank deck and walked down the lawn, toward the ocean. About halfway there I stopped, turned, and gazed up at the sprawling mansion. I easily located David's master bedroom window, a huge palladium number that matched the design of windows on the first floor. Next to David's bedroom was the square window to his private bath.

I lined myself up with the bathroom where Treat's corpse now lay. Then I walked away from the mansion again, sweeping the flashlight beam back and forth along the lawn. At the end of the grass, a narrow pathway of smooth white pebbles had been used to define the end of the manicured grounds and the start of the beach. I stepped across the pebbles and onto the sand.

As I glanced back at the mansion to check my position, I realized I'd strayed from the intended line of sight. I adjusted my position about two yards, aligning my body up once again with the south wing's second floor bathroom window. Then I turned my gaze back towards the water— and saw I was lined up with a series of beach dunes.

I climbed the closest one, finding high scrub grass on top.

What an effective spying place this would be . . . that is, for anyone wanting to spy on David's beach house.

Every room in his home with a light on was transparent. I could see the people assembled around the kitchen table on the first floor as well as David's Tiffany bedroom lamps, shining on the second.

This dune could have been the very place where the shooter had taken a shot at Treat, I realized. Without moving my feet, I shined the flashlight beam around every inch of the dune, the high scrub, the sand, the stray gray rocks.

Behind me, the surf had become wild, the waves crashing with unnerving intensity. A sudden, earsplitting crack of thunder nearly stopped my heart. I jerked in surprise and the beam shot across a section of sand a foot away. That's when I noticed a glimmer of something metallic.

I swept the light back again and moved closer. The pasty spotlight illuminated three brass-colored cylinders on the sand. I didn't want to touch them, so I crouched down over them as close as I could and sniffed. The smell of gunpowder was unmistakable.

Bullet casings.

I knew very little about guns, ammunition, or caliber, but I could see these shells were long, at least two inches. Obviously, they would not have come from a small gun; more like a hunting rifle, for *distance* shooting.

This was it, I realized, the evidence the police could use to catch the killer. The rush of excitement was hard to suppress. Consequently, Matt's accusations about me becoming a risk junkie came back with a vengeance.

Okay, I told myself, so it felt good to find something like this, to play detective and succeed. That didn't mean I was happy about a young man's life cut short. Pushing aside the memory of Matt's words along with my fleeting high, I tried to calm down and decide what to do next.

If I left these casings here much longer, the coming storm and resulting high tide could easily wash them away. But if I disturbed them, I'd be messing with crucial evidence.

With another glance toward the mansion, I could see there was still no sign of the police. So I decided to compromise. Digging into the pocket of my khaki skirt, I came up with a lip balm and a few unused cocktail napkins. I shoved the balm back and used the napkins to carefully pick up one of the bullet casings, leaving the other two where I'd found them. Holding the single casing carefully in one hand, I used the other to sweep the flashlight beam around the area in wider and wider arcs.

If the shooter had used this dune, I figured there might be other clues around. I searched the sand for footprints, but if there had been some, the killer must have covered or obscured them. I walked closer to the water, then paralleled the breakers. About twenty yards away, I noticed something in the damp sand, not footprints but flipper prints. Diver's flippers were leading straight into the surf.

I shined my light out over the water, but saw nothing. Just black waves. They were high now, roiling ashore with the froth of maddened animals. Lightning flashed, and I felt a few drops of rainwater on my head. On the next disturbing crack of thunder, I shuddered and gave up.

I jogged back across the dry sand, the lawn, the cedar plank deck. As I stepped through the mansion's glass patio door, the rain began to fall, and I heard voices coming from the front foyer. At last, the police had arrived.

THERE were two units, four uniformed officers from the local force. To a man, they were nice and polite, but it was obviously the end of a very long day for them, and they were all looking pretty drained.

The oldest officer, a sergeant, explained what had taken them so long—a major auto accident with critical injuries had occurred on the other side of town. There'd been crowd control issues all night, as well as drunken brawls and disturbances ending in arrests. As a result, every unit had been occupied when my call came. Just as David and Suzi had predicted, the craziness of July Fourth had stressed the small local force to its limits.

"The Suffolk County detectives and their forensic team will take over the investigation in the morning," explained Sergeant Walters, a fortyish balding officer with a friendly, round face. "We'll take care of the basics tonight."

He took the bullet casing I'd found and bagged it up. While his partner took statements from David, Madame, me, and the rest of the Cuppa J staff, he supervised the two younger officers in the bathroom.

They took photos of Treat, placed tape around his body, and when the ambulance arrived, helped the paramedics remove the deceased young man. Finally, they closed the bathroom door, crisscrossed it with crime scene tape and asked us not to enter.

By the time I took the sergeant and his two younger officers out back to show them the dune where I'd found the bullet casing, the storm was really raging. The officers were dressed in raingear. I was attempting to hold tight to a flimsy umbrella—a laughable sight in the face of the pelting water and blowing wind.

I pointed out the other two casings, and the officers picked them up and bagged them. Then they began to sweep their flashlights over the dune, just as I had done.

"I didn't find anything else over there," I called to them over the roar of the surf. "But I saw flipper prints over here."

I waved them over to the shoreline, and swept my flashlight along the sand to show them the set of diver's flippers leading into the water, but in the dark and the rain and the rising surf, I couldn't find even one.

The sergeant patiently watched me flail around with my flashlight for a few minutes before he pulled the plug. "Ma'am, we'd appreciate it if you'd go on back to the house now!" he called. "Whatever you saw has probably washed away!"

As his officers attempted to rope off the high dune in the pouring rain, I walked back into the mansion looking like a drowned rat. Madame toweled me off in the kitchen.

"Where is everybody?" I asked.

"The staff gave their statements and left. Joy went to her room. And David's up in his master bedroom throwing some things into a gym bag. He's moving into the guest wing with us."

"There's no way I'm sleeping next to that bathroom!" David told us when he came back downstairs. "At least, not until all that blood is cleaned up!"

Frankly, I was happy to have a man nearby, even one who wasn't exactly Braveheart.

FIVE

~~~~~~~~~~~~~~~~~~~~~~~~~~~~~~~~~~~~

I must have fallen asleep at some point during the night, because when I opened my eyes again, the morning sun was lasering through the curtains. I rolled out of bed with the dull throb of a headache, no doubt induced by the tight, airless space, and opened two large windows. A stiff breeze streamed into the second-floor guestroom, fluttering the diaphanous saffron and refreshing the stale air with the vigor of ocean salt.

Outside the storm had passed, the sun shone brightly, and the nearly cloudless sky looked like an artist's rendering in cerulean blue. The rain had cleansed the air, and the surf had transformed from a roiling black cauldron into a gently lapping sea of tranquility. The morning, in fact, was so dreamy I almost forgot that a man had been shot and killed on the other side of the mansion. *Almost.*

Before another night came and went, I was determined to convince Joy and Madame to leave this house. I knew this would not be easy. For twenty years, I'd butted heads with one pigheaded male member of the Allegro family.

Two generations of its women working together might utterly defeat me.

I decided it would be best to approach Joy and Madame separately. After that silly disagreement with my daughter the night before over that actor's phone number, I figured it might be wise to give her a little more time to cool off.

First up would be my ex-mother-in-law—*after* my morning swim, which I prayed would relieve my throbbing headache and fortify me for the inevitable argument.

I ran a brush through my hair and donned my red suit, a no-nonsense one-piece that probably looked like I'd stepped out of *Baywatch* lifeguard training. Of course, my breasts weren't even close to Pamela Anderson's monumental assets, although they were enough to make me self-conscious in anything without an underwire, and ever since that hot tub incident ten years ago in that awful share house, I'd dumped bikinis from my wardrobe for good.

I wrapped myself in one of the thick, white terrycloth robes David provided for all of his guests (part of his spa product line), and with a pair of decidedly retro rubber flip-flops on my feet, I was good to go.

Halfway down the back stairs, I caught the scent of something wonderfully enticing. With one whiff, I knew someone was brewing a fresh pot of Summer Porch, a seasonal blend I'd just invented about a month ago to showcase the Bagisu Sipi Falls beans—Matteo's latest amazing find on Uganda's Mount Elgon. The pull of the heady roast was too powerful to pass up, and I lurched instinctively toward the kitchen like a George Romero zombie.

Mount Elgon is one of the tallest mountains in Africa, and the terrain is steep and treacherous with thick forest cover. According to Matteo, roads were less common than dirt tracks, which were often washed away during rainy season when gullies overflowed. Nevertheless, the Bagisu tribesman who lived near the Sipi Falls had become experts

at coffee farming, and they had a foolproof method of trans-
porting their cherries, even amid the challenging terrain.
No, they did not use Hummers. They used donkeys.

"Good morning, dear," said Madame, her eyes full of
energy, despite the hour. Her silver hair was down this
morning, sleekly combed into a pageboy. Her erect, elegant frame was wrapped in a white terrycloth robe identical to mine. She handed me a freshly-brewed cup of the
Summer Porch blend. I accepted it with a nod and a grunt.

"Drink up," Madame advised. "This is my second pot.
A few cups of this and I guarantee your disposition will
improve."

My mood-altering drug of choice, I thought as I shuffled
over to the kitchen table and plopped down with a weary
sigh. *But at least it's legal.*

Still bleary-eyed, I wondered for a moment what
made Madame choose the Summer Porch this morning. I'd
placed twenty different types of coffee in David's kitchen
cupboards. It was the same selection I'd put on his tasting
and dessert pairings menu at Cuppa J. When I saw what
Madame had placed in middle of the table, however, I
didn't have to ask why. A selection of last night's strawberries sat mounded inside a Waterford crystal bowl like a
lush ruby mountain.

The hint of strawberry in the finish of Sipi Falls was
rare and surprising; and since the Sipi was the star coffee
in my Summer Porch blend, it was the perfect pairing for
the fresh Long Island fruit. I sipped the coffee black and let
the flavors wash over me like the warm sluicing water of a
Jacuzzi.

A coffee taster trains the tongue and the nose to detect
the faintest traces of every flavor. There were hints of star-
fruit, pear, and red cherry behind the Jasmine tealike flavors of the Sipi Falls. And I'd roasted it light to really bring
out the strawberry flavor (a darker roast produced a sort of

black tea finish to the cup). The coffee was sweet in the mouth and I'd balanced the blend to make sure the Sipi Falls shortcomings were diminished in the taste profile. The problem with this unique Ugandan coffee was that, unlike its East African neighbors, it lacked acidity.

In the coffee world, acidity was not a bad thing. It actually referred to a brightness or pleasant sharpness in the mouth, and you definitely wanted it in your taste profile, or your coffee would come off as flat.

Since a good blend's three elements are acidity, aroma, and body, I remedied the low acidity of the Sipi Falls by blending it with Kenya AA beans. To boost its body, I used a Costa Rican bean. But the Sipi Falls itself was the star of this trio, providing delightful aromatic notes.

I sipped the coffee again and sighed. As it cooled, it actually gained rather than weakened in its rustic intensity. I reached for a strawberry, took a bite, then another sip. The strawberry flavor in the coffee was now enhanced a thousand percent, practically exploding in my mouth.

This was indeed a cheerful, uplifting coffee to wake up to—a bright country morning in a cup, a coffee to disperse bad dreams.

"What are you up to today?" Madame asked with an amused smile at my obvious return from the dead.

"I'm going for a swim," I replied as she slipped a bone china saucer under my cup. "Then I'm going to check on David. After that, I'm going to help you pack and drive you to the train station."

"Nice try, my dear," Madame said.

"But—"

"Don't waste your breath. I'm not leaving," Madame pronounced with a regal wave of her hand.

"But—" I tried again.

"Drink up, Clare. You don't want to waste your husband's—"

"My *ex*-husband's."

"*Matteo's* latest find in your latest blend, because you still don't have your wits about you if you think I'm going back to the city and leaving you to play detective all by yourself."

I opened my mouth to reply, but was interrupted by a series of electronic musical tones, a snippet from Vivaldi. Madame reached into the voluminous pocket of her terrycloth spa robe and found her cell phone.

"Matteo! You're home," she cried upon answering.

"Speak of the devil," I quietly muttered and gulped more coffee.

"Oh, no. Everything's fine. Just fine," Madame chirped, rather like her phone, before changing the subject. "How did things go in California, my boy?"

Matteo's latest trip was not to a Third World coffee plantation, but to a series of First World shopping Meccas. David Mintzer had become one of Matt's biggest backers in a financial plan to expand the Village Blend business via coffee kiosks in high-end clothing boutiques and department stores worldwide. This last trip of Matt's was to the West Coast, where he was overseeing Village Blend coffee kiosk installations in Marin County, Rodeo Drive, and Palm Springs.

Madame spoke with her son for a few minutes, while I finished my first cup and poured another.

"Yes, she's right here," Madame finally said, passing the phone to me.

"Hello, Matt," I said on a yawn.

These days, our relationship was actually pretty good. Like it or not, we were stuck with one another as business partners in the Blend, not to mention parental partners in the raising of Joy. Parenting, as I'd often lectured Matt, was not only a full-time job, it was a lifetime appointment, sort of like a judgeship on the Supreme Court, but with far less influence.

"What's wrong out there?" Matt asked, his voice had gone low. "Mother sounded strained."

"Everything's fine. Just fine," I chirped, rather like Madame. I could almost see Matteo's eyes squinting with suspicion.

"Whatever," he said at last. "I just phoned to tell you I'm at La Guardia waiting for a taxi. I'm heading over to the Blend to check things out."

Good, I thought, *Tucker can use the extra pair of helping hands.*

"After that, I'm hitting the sack in the duplex, catching a few hours sleep. I'm wasted. Totally jet lagged."

So much for the extra helping hands.

Tucker Burton was my assistant manager, an actor-playwright whom I could always rely on to handle the Blend when I was absent. Tucker certainly wouldn't require Matt's help to keep things running, but it would have been nice.

"How's my pride named Joy?" asked Matt, the smile evident in his voice, as it always was when it came to his little girl.

I glanced at the digital clock on the microwave: 7:02 A.M. "Still sleeping, I suspect."

"Don't wake her. I'll try to see you both before I leave for Central America. Give Joy my love, tell her I'll see her soon. Oh, and I bought her a present. Damn, my ride's here. Gotta go."

The line went dead. I handed Madame her phone and cradled the warm mug of coffee in my hands.

"Do you think Matteo suspects?" Madame asked.

"Suspects? Whatever is there for him to suspect?"

"That the game is afoot, of course."

"Madame, for heaven's sake, it's not a game. I'm not getting involved in this murder investigation beyond what I helped to discover last night. I'm going to let the police handle it. And stop channeling Arthur Conan Doyle. I think maybe you've been spending too much time with Dr. MacTavish." (Madame had been dating the distinguished St. Vincent's oncologist for some time now, a Scottish stud on a par with Sean Connery.)

"I assure you, Clare, Gary and I are not reading Sherlock Holmes stories to one another," she sniffed, "and don't change the subject."

I sighed. "Look, even if I do stick my nose in, it'll only be to see that David gets some proper security in place around here."

"Of course," said Madame in a tone that sounded more like "of course not."

"Besides," I went on, "you've had your turn at playing detective. Don't forget, you helped me clear Tucker of murder."

"Pooh!" Madame replied. "I was so worried about our dear Tucker, I hardly enjoyed the experience. This time it's different. I'm terribly sorry about what happened to that young man, but I hardly knew Mr. Treat Mazarrati—"

"Mazzelli. Treat Mazzelli."

"There you are! I didn't even know the victim's proper name. Without a personal stake in the crime, I am free to be objective about the hunt. I'll just put on my figurative deerstalker's cap and—"

"Except," I interrupted, "I don't think Treat Mazzelli was the intended target. I believe the killer was after David."

Madame paused, considering this. "Mistaken identity?"

I nodded. "The shooting occurred in David's private bathroom."

"But the men are twenty years apart. How could you mistake one for the other?"

"From a distance, do you really think that would be apparent?"

Madame tapped her chin. "Yes . . . yes, I see what you

mean. And the two are about the same height . . . with the same color hair . . ."

"And clothing."

Madame shook her head. "There I have to disagree with you. While they were both in khaki pants, David's shirt was a linen Ralph Lauren. How can you compare that quality to Treat's Cuppa J Polo?"

"No comparison for a fashion layout, I grant you. But both shirts had short sleeves and the same loose, untucked shape. And they were very close to the same color."

"Yes, my dear, of course, you're right. And you're very good at this—"

"Thank you."

"All the more reason for you to continue investigating and me to help," Madame replied resolutely.

"Madame—"

"I may just learn a thing or two from you, and, besides, if the true target was David, the least I can do is aid our host in his time of need. I'm not the sort of person who deserts a vessel when the captain's in need of hands!"

"You win." I took a sip from my china cup and set it down on its matching saucer. "Stick around if you want. But in an hour or so I'm going to talk to—"

"Joy?" Madame finished for me.

"What? Are you reading my mind now?"

"She's already gone for the day," Madame warned. "She left exceedingly early. To catch the sunrise wind."

"Excuse me?"

"Joy went kite surfing with that waiter from last night. Graydon is his name, I believe."

"Graydon Faas?"

Madame nodded.

"Joy went off with Graydon this morning?" I had some trouble wrapping my mind around this development.

Madame nodded again. "She and I have connecting

rooms, you know. So I heard her rising and speaking to him on her cell phone. I made her coffee before the boy beeped his horn out front. What is this world coming to when a young man simply beeps for his date?"

"It's a *date*, is it? And to do what, did you say? Kite surfing? How are we supposed to know what kite surfing is?"

"Actually, Clare, it's more defined by what it isn't," Madame levelly informed me. "It's not wave surfing, you see. Nor wind surfing. And it's not kite flying, either. It's really a fusion of these sports. The surfer catches the wind with a kite and uses it to race across the ocean's waves." Madame sighed. "It sounds absolutely marvelous."

I shook my head. "Where do you pick up this stuff?"

"Oh, I keep my mouth closed and my ears open. You can learn a lot from the leisure class—a lot about leisure, anyway. And to be perfectly frank, a percentage of them aren't much good for anything else."

I stood and drained my cup. "On that note, I'm heading for my swim. Now I really need it."

Outside, the wind had dried up most of the night's rainfall, but the air was still damp and salty. I flip-flopped down the lawn, across the white pebbles and onto the beach, then I kicked off the rubber thongs and let the wet white sand squish between my toes.

Sunlight sparkled on the green-blue water. I reached the edge of the surf, dropped the flip-flops and the towel I'd draped around my neck, slipped out of my robe, and waded into the surf.

The chilly water was a shock, but I soon got acclimated. I swam around a bit to stretch my limbs. Then I turned over on my back and floated, letting the lapping Atlantic sooth the edges of my dulled but still throbbing headache.

The cool waves and the warm sun worked their magic, and I imagined myself tethered to a kite, racing across the rocky surf as swift as the jetstream. I wondered what Mike

Quinn was doing at the moment and tried to imagine what the lanky, broad-shouldered detective would look like stripped to the waist on the back of a surfboard, his sandy hair slicked back, his pasty skin tanned golden, his perpetually weary, wrungout expression rejuvenated by the ocean wind.

This pleasant image had barely formed in my head before it was interrupted by a booming declaration, echoing across the waves. "This is the Suffolk County police," announced the amplified voice. "Please come out of the water now. We need to speak with you."

Startled out of my wits, I splashed out of my floating position and abruptly sank. My mouth gaped like a fish and I swallowed salt water as I flailed downwards. My arms thrashed and I surfaced once again, gasping and spitting. I spied three police officers pacing along a stretch of David's private beach. A fourth man—the heaviest of them—wore a suit and tie, not a uniform. He stood with a bullhorn clutched in his fist.

"I'm coming!" I called.

Doubting the man had heard me, I swam toward the shoreline, cognizant of the fact that my robe, towel and flip-flops were at least twenty-five yards from the knot of policemen. I emerged a few moments later, sopping wet. As I moved across the sand, a cold gust breezed by, raising goose bumps on my arms and legs. Suppressing a shiver, I faced the heavyset man with the loudspeaker.

"Are you Mrs. Cosi?" he asked, this time without the bullhorn.

I nodded. "*Ms.* Cosi."

"I'm Sergeant Roy O'Rourke, here to investigate last night's shooting death. You were the one who found the shell casings? That's what the old lady inside the house said."

The voice was surprisingly high, almost reedy for such a big, wide man. Sergeant O'Rourke regarded me through fading gray eyes that matched the thinning hair on his head. His complexion, too, seemed faded and gray—astonishingly tan-resistant despite sun and surf.

"Yes, I found them," I stammered, certain my lips were turning blue.

"Here you go, ma'am."

A young policeman—barely older than my daughter— had retrieved my robe. I accepted it with a nod of thanks, slipping the thick terrycloth over my wet body. O'Rourke waited impassively. Behind him, another man crossed the beach. He was not in uniform, either, wearing a gray suit and blue striped tie almost identical to O'Rourke's.

"This is my partner, Detective Melchior. He's going to interview any witnesses, put together a timeline while I examine the physical evidence."

"The local police bagged the shells last night—" I began.

"I know, Ms. Cosi," said O'Rourke, cutting me off. "I'd like to see the spot where you found them."

"Of course."

We crossed the flat sands and entered the dunes, where I told Sergeant O'Rourke about the tracks I'd discovered and how I could not locate them again last night in the storm, after the local police had arrived.

"Don't worry, if there are tracks, we'll find them."

I'm sure Roy O'Rourke meant to sound competent and reassuring, but to me he sounded tired and dulled by routine. I wondered where he'd gained his world-weary manner. Thinking of Quinn, I took a guess.

"Were you, by any chance, an officer in the NYPD, Sergeant O'Rourke?"

The man's head dipped slightly. "Twenty years," he replied. "I worked homicides in South Brooklyn, Washington Heights, the Bronx. Gang and drug violence, mostly."

"Those are tough areas."

"I've solved more than a few murders, ma'am, if that's what you're asking."

"I'm just wondering . . . aren't the cases out here different? Different than the crimes in the city, I mean?"

"Every case has its own rhythm, but the work's the same. Find the weapon and you'll find the killer."

I blinked. "It's that simple?"

O'Rourke sighed. "Finding the weapon isn't so simple, Ms. Cosi, believe me. But when you find it, the DA's office usually has what it needs for a conviction. You follow, don't you?"

"Yes, Sergeant. I follow."

I halted just then. We had come to the spot. There was no longer any crime-scene rope around the scrub grass. The storm had blown it down, which wasn't surprising.

"I found the shells right here," I told the Sergeant, pointing to the spot. With a gesture, O'Rourke's men fanned out, no doubt to seek out more clues.

"No sign of tracks here," the man noted, looking around the dune.

"They weren't here," I corrected. "They were twenty yards down. But I'm sure the storm and the tide washed them away."

"Maybe. Let's see what the others find," he replied. Ten minutes later, Detective Melchior sidled up to his partner. He was a foot taller and a decade younger than O'Rourke. Thin to the point of consumption, Melchior possessed a prominent cleft chin which jutted from a head seemingly too large for his scarecrow frame.

"Good line of fire from these dunes," the detective observed, pointing to David's bathroom window, clearly visible almost forty yards away.

O'Rourke squinted against the glare. "You said you saw tracks, Mrs. Cosi? Big shoe prints or little ones? Or were they bare feet?"

"Well, actually, Sergeant," I replied. "I believe they were made by *webbed* feet."

"Webbed feet?" O'Rourke repeated, a bit taken aback.

I nodded.

"What do you mean?" he said. "Like a *duck*'s?"

I instantly regretted my choice of words. "Like scuba diving gear," I corrected. "You know, the webbed flipper fins divers' use?"

O'Rourke exchanged an unreadable glance with his partner.

"Maybe I should draw you an example," I quickly suggested. "You know, in the sand?"

"Good idea," said O'Rourke.

I set to work, crouching down and using my finger to recreate the tracks I'd found. Soon all the officers gathered around to watch. I was lost in concentration, searching my mind in an effort to recall the image. Were there three toes, or four? How big were they exactly? And how far apart? I made a few marks in the sand, erased them and started again. Halfway through the exercise, I looked up to find the policemen clearly suppressing laughter.

"Looks like we've found our culprit," Sergeant O'Rourke quipped, folding big arms over his barrel chest. "The Creature from the Black Lagoon."

Everyone laughed. Even the polite young policeman who'd brought me my robe couldn't suppress a chuckle. I rose to my full (albeit rather puny) height.

"A decent clue is no laughing matter," I snapped.

"No it isn't, ma'am," Detective Melchior said, obviously stepping in quickly to sooth my ruffled duck feathers. "So why don't you take me back to the house. You can help me put together a list of everyone Mr. Mazzelli worked with and who you saw him conversing with last night. Let's see if we can't narrow down some clues the old-fashioned way and find out who may have had a beef with the victim."

"But that's just it," I said, hands on hips. "Treat Mazzelli wasn't the intended victim. I believe that the shooter was after David Mintzer."

O'Rourke and Melchior exchanged glances again. This time I didn't get the impression they were amused.

"Ma'am, if you know something, it's important that you tell us," O'Rourke replied.

"I agree."

We entered the kitchen a few minutes later. David was awake and completely pulled together. Clearly he'd had a good sleep. His color looked good, a deep tan against white teeth. And, as usual, he was dressed impeccably: tailored ivory slacks, a pale olive shirt, and Italian leather sandals. With a smile, David shook Sergeant O'Rourke's hand.

"Some coffee? It's a very special blend, truly delightful. Please help yourselves," David gestured. Behind him, Alberta Gurt had set up the large table with a pot of Summer Porch, mugs, and a basket of warm croissants next to a replenished bowl of strawberries. Madame hovered nearby. I could see her peeking around the corner, pretending not to eavesdrop.

Without preamble, Sergeant O'Rourke bluntly declared, "Mr. Mintzer, Ms. Cosi tells us that you were the real target of last night's killer. She believes Mr. Mazzelli's murder was a case of mistaken identity." O'Rourke shifted his pale gray eyes in my direction. "Would you care to elaborate, Ma'am?"

"It makes perfect sense," I began, covering the exact same ground I had done with Madame an hour earlier. "David left the party before the fireworks display and went to his bedroom with a migraine. Anyone would have expected him to be using his own bathroom—not Treat. Both men are about the same height. Both men have short black hair, and both were wearing the same khaki pants and short-sleeved, untucked shirts of nearly the same pinkish color."

"So are you accusing someone who attended the party? Or perhaps one of Mr. Mintzer's business associates?" Detective Melchior prompted.

"Oh my god," David said on an outraged exhale.

"Hold off, Mr. Mintzer," said O'Rourke. "We want to hear everything Ms. Cosi has to say."

"Thank you," I said, relieved the initial flippancy I'd experienced over the flippers had changed into serious consideration. "Remember the tracks I found among the dunes?"

O'Rourke's brow wrinkled unhappily. "The webbed feet, from the 'Creature'?"

"Oh my god," David said again.

"From a swimmer wearing fins," I quickly corrected. "I believe those tracks were made by the shooter."

Melchior scratched his chin. "Wait a second, Ms. Cosi. We thought you knew something specific. A threat perhaps?"

"Well . . . I did encounter Marjorie Bright on the property after the party was over. She threatened David."

"Threatened him how?" Melchior asked. "What were her exact words?"

"She said, 'Just tell David I'm not through suing him.'" David snorted.

O'Rourke turned to him. "You don't consider that out of the ordinary, Mr. Mintzer?"

"A lawsuit? In this town? Puh-leeeze. If there's a Hamptons pastime more common than suing your neighbor, I don't know what it is. People file in civil court as often as they file onto tennis courts. Look, Ms. Bright's already taken local action against me once over my trees being too tall, and I've already assumed her lawyers and mine will be playing footsie for some time before our issues are resolved."

"But, David, what was she doing on your property?" I demanded. "Don't you find that suspicious?"

"She has no direct access to the beach now that I've built on this land," David replied with a shrug. "Maybe she simply took a walk along the beach and was returning through my property when you caught her. No big deal."

"If she was on the beach last night, we should interview her," said O'Rourke, glancing at his partner.

Melchior nodded. "I'll make a note."

But that wasn't enough to satisfy me. Marjorie Bright had been *loitering* on David's property, smoking, and stewing, not just passing through. I was sure something was up with her, something bad—and although I couldn't very well testify to seeing her there for any length of time, I felt in my gut that she meant harm to David.

"What about the diver's fins," I argued. "How can you explain their appearance just twenty yards away from the bullet casings on the same night as the shooting?"

"Ma'am, this is a resort area," said O'Rourke. "Diver's flippers in the sand aren't exactly bloody fingerprints on a rifle stock."

"But I swim or walk every day on that beach. I've never seen tracks like that before."

O'Rourke folded his arms. "And what's your explanation?"

"It's possible Marjorie, or another enemy of David's, paid for someone to do the shooting. The shooter had an employer."

"So we're looking for two killers now," said O'Rourke. "A trigger man and the person who paid for it?" He faced David. "What do you think of Ms. Cosi's theory, Mr. Mintzer?"

David shifted his surprised gaze from me to the Sergeant. "Why, I think it's absurd. Ridiculous," he replied.

It was my turn to be shocked. "David! I—"

"No, Clare," he interrupted, directing his words to me.

"I'm sorry but I have to say this now, because I don't want any misunderstandings."

He paused. When he spoke again his tone was measured, his words carefully chosen. "No one is trying to kill me. I completely dismiss the notion that I am a target. No one has threatened me, I have no mortal enemies, nor am I involved in any illegal activities that might provoke the interest of some kind of professional hit man." David faced the policemen. "I shall cooperate fully in your investigation. I and my staff are available for interviews if you care to speak with us."

"I'll need a statement from everyone," Melchior said.

"And I shall also provide you with a guest list from yesterday's event."

"Good," O'Rourke said. "That would be helpful."

"I only ask that you not bother my party guests unless you absolutely feel it is necessary to approach them. That said, I want you to do all you can to apprehend the person or persons responsible for this terrible crime."

"I understand, Mr. Mintzer." O'Rourke nodded. I promise you we'll proceed with great discretion."

"Thank you," said David. "Now let me take you upstairs and give you my version of what happened last evening."

As they spoke, David steered O'Rourke and Melchior out of the kitchen and presumably toward the bathroom where Treat had been shot. I peered out the tall kitchen windows at the uniformed officers still pacing the dunes. When I turned around again, Madame was in front of me.

"David was certainly adamant in his denial," she remarked quietly.

"He protested too much," I replied, rubbing my forehead.

"You still think he was the assassin's target?"

"Now more than ever."

David appeared thirty minutes later. I braced myself, ready for him to unleash another wave of righteous outrage. Instead, he took my arm and steered me back toward the kitchen table.

"Listen, Clare. I'm sorry about doing that to you in front of the authorities, but you have to understand my position."

I might have been humiliated but I wasn't stupid. "You're more concerned with bad publicity than the fact that someone may be trying to murder you, is that it?"

David sighed. "Please, Clare. No one is trying to murder me. But even if someone wanted me dead, I could never admit it publicly. I have multiple businesses. Partnerships all over the world. I frankly loathe the comparison, but, like Ms. Stewart, I *am* my companies. They do not function without me. I can't afford for anyone—not my associates, not my partners, investors, customers, or clients—to entertain the notion that I'm involved in something shady enough to invite a murder attempt. Millions of dollars and thousands of employees livelihoods are at stake. I have responsibilities."

I wanted to speak, but bit my lip and nodded instead. "I understand."

David slumped down in a seat in front of the table. "In any case, there are obviously gaps in my home security system—"

"Didn't I tell you that the first day I came?"

"Indeed you did. *That* you were right about, Clare."

"It's time you got a serious alarm system," I told him, "installed outdoor lighting—"

"I shall make the call just as soon as the police leave my house."

"Not just alarms and motion detectors, okay?" I said. "Real security guards, around the clock. You don't have to hire Spielberg's ex-Masaad agents, but for god's sake get some Pinkertons, at least until Treat's murder is solved and the murderer caught."

David smiled. "Very well, but on one condition."

"Yes?"

"I want you to drop the notion that I'm the real target for murder—pronto."

After a beat I nodded. "Okay. Agreed."

"Good." David rose. "Now I'll rejoin those detectives, before there's any more damage done to my imported Italian marble bathroom."

Six

~~~~~~~~~~~~~~~~~~~~~~~~~~~~~~

CUPPA J was a short ride from David Mintzer's beach house, but, typical of a sunny summer day in the Hamptons, traffic was horrendous.

Democratic, too.

Late model BMWs, Ferraris, Mercedes, and Jaguars inched along with the same egalitarian sluggishness as my lowly Honda. A ten-minute drive became forty minutes of start-and-stop frustration.

When I finally left "Leisure with Dignity" around eleven-fifteen, the Suffolk County police were still going over details of the shot in the dark. I could tell David was losing patience in discussing details of the party, what he knew of Treat's background, how it might be related to his fellow employees or David's guest list. Through it all, David's facade probably appeared as charming as ever. But I had gotten to know him pretty well by now, and I recognized the cracks forming at his edges.

I'd promised him that I'd stay out of it ... but how could I keep my promise? While I tried to tell myself that the police were on the case and that was enough, in my gut I knew they were on the wrong case. And what good would that do David?

In the bumper-to-bumper traffic, I contemplated what O'Rourke and Melchior would do next. They'd probably want to know the results of the autopsy and whether the bullet in Treat's skull actually matched up with the shells I'd found. I'd bet a forty-pound bag of Jamaica Blue Mountain that they would.

They'd also be conducting interviews with people who knew Treat, trying to dig up some significant vendetta or grudge. But it was the people around David who needed to be interviewed as far as I could see.

Well, I thought, *at least they're going to talk to Marjorie Bright.*

Certainly, she was at the top of my suspect list. But as I inched along in traffic, I rethought the theory I'd hastily blurted out to the Suffolk County detectives. Cringing, I realized there were holes in my hypothesis through which I could probably drive a Hummer (much like the bright yellow one hogging part of the shoulder in front of me).

For one thing, why would Ms. Bright have fouled up her alibi by hanging around the crime scene? Unless she fell into that category Mike Quinn had once mentioned— pathologically wanting to see the results of her bought-and-paid-for crime—which I myself didn't wholly buy.

And for another, if a paid assassin had been involved in the crime, then why did I find bullet casings? A true professional would not have left shells behind. It smacked of amateurish carelessness . . . so . . . did that mean the shooter was actually an amateur?

"Clare! Hey, there, Clare!"

I peered out my open window to find Edna Miller waving at me from her roadside farm stand. Around her, wicker baskets displayed the colors of summer—red tomatoes, green-husked corn, plump white cauliflower, purple eggplant, and quarts and quarts of those lush, Long Island strawberries.

"Hi, Edna!" I called back.

My first week in the South Fork, I had befriended Edna and her husband, Bob, with a two-pound bag of Kona, that sweet, smooth coffee with buttery characteristics and hints of cinnamon and cloves, grown in the volcanic soil of Hawaii. (Many coffee roasters offer Kona blends, but for my money the single-origin experience is the way to go.)

The Millers had been running this farm stand of impossibly fresh vegetables and fruits every summer for the last twenty odd years—and before that, Bob's father had run it. They were "Bonackers," part of the local families that had been living out here for generations.

(At one time, "Bonacker" had been a pejorative term like hick or bumpkin. Its etymology was Native American, from the word "Accobonac," which roughly means "place where groundnuts are gathered." Such was the naming of nearby Accobonac Harbor and, consequently, the people who lived around it. These days people wore the name with pride. The East Hampton High School sport teams had even adopted it as their nickname.)

The Miller's land was located on the unfashionable side of the highway—the side away from the ocean—yet they'd been able to sell off just a portion of it for a small fortune. They'd kept the rest in the family and continued to farm it, just as they had for hundreds of years.

"You want anything today?" Edna called, striding quickly out to the road. She was in her usual worn jeans and large tee-shirt, a half-apron wrapped around her waist.

"No, I'm heading over to work at the moment," I replied, as the car inched along. "Did you have a nice Fourth?"

"Yes, but what's this I hear about yours?" Edna was pacing the Honda now, slowly moving along the shoulder of the road as I rolled along.

"My Fourth?"

No way, I thought. *There's no way she could possibly be referring to the shooting. All of the guests left before I discovered the body. So who could have told her?*

"My daughter-in-law's sister is married to Park Bennett," she explained. "And he lives next door to John King. And his son's on the local police force. He said his boy was at that mansion you're staying at . . . David Mintzer's place. And he said a young man was killed—"

"Yes, yes, I know all about it. But we don't know very much at this point. David's a little touchy so maybe you could, you know, keep it quiet." *Right. That'll happen.*

"Oh, surely, surely!" said Edna. "Of course!"

Behind me, the platinum blond on her cell phone laid on the horn of her Mercedes convertible so loud and so long that I thought I'd lose the ability to hear higher decibels. When I looked ahead, I saw the yellow Hummer in front of me had pulled away about a grand total of four car lengths.

"Whoa," I said. "I guess I better speed up a little, sorry, Edna!"

"No problem, Clare. People are really touchy this weekend. You should have been here an hour ago. Two corporate attorneys got into a punch-out over the last honeydew melon!"

"See you soon!" I called, my car speeding up.

"See you, Clare!"

Edna waved and turned back to the farm stand. I considered what she'd just said—not the story about the honeydew punch-out. That was actually on par for how bad things could get during the crowded summer season. Wealthy Manhattan people came out here to relax, but far too many of them packed their sense of entitlement and city impatience along with their toothbrushes.

"The people out here are competitive and ambitious," David had warned me when I first came. "They're killers on the job. That's how they got out here in the first place. And people who spend Monday through Friday screwing over people aren't going to stop acting that way on Saturday and Sunday."

The local paper was full of incidents like shoving matches over parking spaces and restaurant tables. Just last week there was an assault charge filed after a few haymakers were thrown in a health food store. (One can only presume it took place in the stress reduction supplements aisle.)

Anyway, I began to consider how Edna had heard about Treat's death. Obviously news traveled fast in this small enclave. And I doubted a murder in East Hampton would be treated like one in the city, precisely because murder was so rare.

This small village fussed over the color of the awnings on Main Street for god's sake. They cited you for tacking up a yard sale sign. The last thing they would tolerate was an unsolved murder in their midst. The guilty party would have to be found and successfully convicted or the competency of the authorities would be loudly and continually questioned by the powerful, opinionated people who summered here.

In a place like this, the only sure way for the murderer to escape detection would be to pin the crime on someone else . . . that's why the bullet casings could have been left. Sure, it *could* have been a careless amateur, or it could have been a cunning assassin setting up a frame job. To do that, the shooter would have to plant the weapon somewhere the police could find it . . . say, on the premises of someone who might have had a motive. Then the cops would have their conviction, and the shooter would get away with murder.

The permutations of this theory were still bouncing around in my head when I turned into the shaded driveway of Cuppa J.

Seven

~~~~~~

My grandmother grew up in a world of straightforward sensibilities, when things were labeled simply and clearly. You said what you meant, and you meant what you said. But that was a long time ago, before SNL, MTV, metafiction, *The Daily Show*, and the saturation of practically every aspect of contemporary culture with irony.

Sure, "Cuppa J" sounded like a casual, unassuming joint, but those were hardly the adjectives for David's tony East Hampton cafe. Of course, he wasn't the first to apply paradox to a restaurant name, not by a long shot. Chef Thomas Keller's lowly sounding "French Laundry" was the most acclaimed gourmet restaurant in Napa Valley, if not the most highly regarded eatery in the country. And the Brooklyn Diner, just a few blocks away from Manhattan's Carnegie Hall, was actually a four-star restaurant with linen tablecloths and a stellar wine list.

Cuppa J offered eclectic, upscale bistro fare, with the flavor of coffee infused into many of the main dishes (coffee can be used to great effect in meat dishes as a subtle flavoring agent, tenderizer, or marinade). The restaurant served wine and cocktails, but the star of the culinary show was the array of expensive after-dinner coffees and dessert pairings. Consequently, this season we'd become *the* place to book an after-dinner, pre-clubbing table. While most restaurants wound down by ten in the evening, our place was still hopping with many tables booked right up until midnight.

The two-story restaurant, with its red brick exterior, had been a Chinese restaurant before falling into foreclosure a year ago. This past spring David redid the surrounding grounds with topiaries, flowerbeds, and shade trees. He'd cleaned the brick, repainted the peeling white trim, and replaced the first floor windows with white french doors.

I drove through the customer parking area, framed with ivy-colored trellises, and around to the back of the restaurant where the employees parked. It was just past noon when I walked through the kitchen door. The waitstaff would be arriving in a few hours to prepare for dinner service from four until midnight—and I expected finally to see Joy, who I hadn't heard from the entire day. Clearly, she was ignoring the five messages I'd already left on her cell phone's voicemail.

"Hi, Carlos." I waved at the restaurant's reliable sous chef, Carlos Comacho. He was busy, cutting up onions and carrots, preparing for Executive Chef Victor Vogel's arrival. He gave a quick smile and went back to his work.

The next person I encountered was Jacques Papas, who stuck his head out of his office at the sound of my voice. Papas acted as the restaurant's manager, maitre d', and sommelier. Half-French and half-Greek, Papas was in his early forties, swarthy, with dark eyes and ink-black hair (which I assumed he had dyed, because the only thing that occurred in nature that dark was a celestial black hole). We stood nearly eye to eye, but what the man lacked in size he made up for in belligerent energy. I had yet to see him smile. His usual demeanor was one of mild disdain mingled with boredom—either that or a sneer.

"Good afternoon," I said.

The manager offered me a sour look, then crisply turned and disappeared back into his office.

Living in Manhattan, I was no stranger to divas of all stripes in the upscale restaurant game. But Papas had attitude beyond reason. At least he was consistent, I thought, shrugging off Papas's chilly snub. He treated employees and guests with equal contempt.

After walking through the spotless, stainless steel kitchen, I strolled by the staff's break room and pushed through the burgundy leather double-doors, which took me into the two-story dining room.

While the exterior of Cuppa J was as unassuming as its name, the interior was another matter. David had taken great pains to model the decor after a pair of famous Paris coffeehouses—the traditional Café Marly, designed in the 1990s by Oliver Gagnére and Yves Taralon, and the more modern Le Café Costes designed in 1985 by Philippe Starck.

The Marly's influence was evident as soon as you stepped into the breathtaking room. Dark burgundy-hued walls were gilded with art deco flourishes and lined with cherrywood wainscoting that perfectly matched the sixty-two cafe tables. Forest green velvet couches and low-backed ivory armchairs were interspersed with freestanding antique *torchiers* (a practical replacement for the Marly's iron incense burners). A staircase of emerald marble framed by twin cenotaphs was situated on the south side of the dining room. And the brass-railed stairs led to an upper mezzanine fronted by more brass rails.

At the top of the staircase a massive clock was set into the wall. This mosaic timepiece, fashioned from sheets of translucent quartz and colored stones, was a homage to the central motif of the now defunct La Café Costes, right down to the movement of the clock's arms, which spun around twenty-four times every hour.

David assumed this bizarre *Alice in Wonderland* feature was a nod to the surrealists. To me it seemed a fairly obvious statement about the nature of caffeine.

The narrow mezzanine circled the entire restaurant. Along with additional seating, the upstairs featured a cherrywood bar, a spectacular view of the main dining room below, and an eye-level view of the huge brass-and-glass chandelier that dangled from the high ceiling.

Crossing the dining room, I walked over to the first floor's open coffee bar.

Over the years, the crimes I'd seen upscale restaurants commit against the bean truly made me shudder. Leaving pots to simmer on burners until the liquid had the consistency of muddy tar. Serving customers espressos in cold cups. Frothing cappuccinos with steam wands that hadn't been properly cleaned. Filling stacks of paper filters with pre-ground coffee and allowing it to sit around aerating for hours before brewing. (The moment you grind your beans, they begin to lose their freshness.)

As Cuppa J's barista manager/drill sergeant, I'd pretty much browbeaten every waiter and waitress into following the holy rituals of high-quality coffee service.

With my clipboard in hand, I was very pleased to note that the area had been left shipshape by the previous evening's closers. The espresso machine had been properly cleaned, demitasses neatly stacked on top; the coffee canisters were left tightly sealed; and the French presses were lined up in formation on the cherrywood shelves like good little soldiers of sparkling glass.

I checked the contents of the coffee canisters. There were twenty in all, each holding a different blend or single-origin coffee featured on our menu. Back in the city, we did micro-roasting daily in the shop. In my weekly trips back to the city, I'd create the roasts needed at Cuppa J, then transport the whole beans back here in vacuum-sealed bags.

I began making careful notes on the levels in each canister. Which ones needed replenishing? Which ones weren't moving? This data would be fed into the computer where I'd created a program to track customer favorites.

"Ms. Cosi, will you be finished soon?"

I let out a reactive yelp of surprise. Papas had crept up on me. There was no other way to describe it. One second I was alone, the next he was there, right next to me.

Others had joked about this phenomenon. Colleen O'Brien likened him to the ghost of Squire Malone, a legendary Irish haunter from her home county. Graydon Faas, a fan of Anime, maintained that the manager's ability to spring upon an employee the moment he made a mistake must mean he's housing a secret teleportation device in that office of his that he seldom let anyone enter. I could believe it.

"I'm almost through," I told Papas. "We're really low on the Mocha Java. Probably because it's a dark roast, so I'm pairing it with the chocolate soufflé and the flourless chocolate-kahlua cake, and chocolate's the most reliably popular dessert flavor. I have more MJ in the basement, but not enough to get us through Sunday brunch. I guess I'll call the Blend and have Tucker send some through our delivery service."

Thinking out loud was something I did when nervous and Papas was a guy who made me very nervous. He stared at me for a long silent moment. This was an annoying habit of his: you spoke, he stared, answering in his own good time.

"Very well then, call your people," he replied at last. Then he checked his watch. "I must run an errand. I will be gone for an hour, no more."

"That's fine. When the wait staff starts arriving, I'll put them to work dressing the dining room tables. By the way, have you heard from Prin about her family emergency? Do you think there's a chance she'll be back before Monday?"

The man's frown deepened. "No."

Poor girl, I thought, assuming the worst. "Is there a death in her family? Is that the emergency? Maybe I should give her a call and ask if—"

Papas cut me off. "That won't be necessary. Prin won't be back."

I blinked. "Really? What happened?"

Jacques Papas looked away. "David Mintzer happened. He personally fired the young woman a few days ago. Gave her the boot without even a letter of recommendation. Left me short of help, I can tell you. And in the middle of the season."

"But two days ago you yourself told the staff she'd left on a family emergency. We assumed she'd be back."

Papas shook his head. "That was a lie that David made me pass along to everyone because he didn't want anyone else in his employ to know he'd fired her. David loves to be loved, you know. But at times he can be an indiscriminate bastard."

It was now my turn to fall silent and stare. "Do you know the reason for Prin's dismissal?" I finally asked.

The manager shook his head. "No. David doesn't like to be questioned, Ms. Cosi—surely you've seen that side of him."

With that, I couldn't argue.

"I have worked for two decades in restaurant management," Papas continued. "And I do find that the stick gets much better results than the carrot. But I would never have fired Prin. Not when we're so shorthanded."

I nodded, not quite sure what to say.

"I'd appreciate your remaining discreet with this information," Papas pointedly added. "The only reason I'm telling you is to stop you from wasting time pursuing Ms. Lopez. Now you know there's no reason to call the girl." Papas glanced at his Rolex. "I have to go."

After the manager departed, I took a deep breath and made use of the espresso machine in front of me. What I badly needed at the moment was a shot (excuse the pun).

Last night, I found out that Treat Mazzelli was secretly bedding every girl on the Cuppa J wait staff—Prin Lopez being one of the first to get shagged and dumped. Now I find out she's been dumped a second time in the middle of the busy Hamptons season by David Mintzer himself.

If that wasn't enough to make a girl a little angry, I didn't know what would be. But how angry? As I sent whole beans of our espresso blend through the grinder, then tamped, clamped, and extracted the essence of the beans into a shot glass, I considered this question.

I'd found Prin to be a consummate professional on the job. But Suzi Tuttle maintained the girl had one hell of a temper off it. I remember an animated story Suzi had told in the break room about how Prin "went totally postal" at a Hamptons nightclub. A pretty hostess from a Southampton restaurant dissed Prin in some way at the crowded bar. The fight escalated from verbal to physical, with Prin pulling handfuls of the girl's hair out. The bouncer had to be called in to stop it and ejected them both.

It was very hard for me to believe that Prin herself would have gone "totally postal" by stalking and shooting Treat Mazzelli—whether she'd been trying to get revenge on Treat himself, or David, or both of them. It was equally hard to believe she may have persuaded some gangbanger friend from her South Bronx neighborhood to do it.

But Prin's firing was unexpected, and I wanted to talk to her. I downed the espresso, absorbing the rich, warm, nutty essence of the darkly roasted Arabica beans in one fortifying hit. Then I dried my hands and went back to the break room. An employee schedule was posted on the wall next to the door. Next to Prin's name was a cell phone number. I dialed it and got a voicemail message.

"Prin? It's Clare Cosi, from Cuppa J. Would you please call me? It's a matter of extreme importance." I left the number of my own cell phone and hung up, wondering if Prin would even bother to return my call.

While I was in the kitchen, I decided to get started restocking the milk, cream, and half-and-half at the coffee bar. I checked the standing refrigerator near the dessert prep area and saw three gallons of milk, two of cream, and no half-and-half. I headed for the walk-in stainless steel refrigerator. I opened the thick, insulated door and stepped into the chilly steel box, which was nearly as large as a bedroom in my Manhattan duplex above the Village Blend.

A single bare bulb illuminated the interior, which smelled like a butcher shop—a not-unpleasant mixture of cheese and preserved meat. Shanks of dry-aged beef hung from hooks in the ceiling above, wheels and squares of imported and domestic cheeses. Boxes of green leafy vegetables, all of it produced locally, were stacked in the corner next to bags of onions, shallots, and several types of potatoes. Bundles of garlic hung from hooks on the wall, near slabs of bacon, aged prosciutto, and chorizo.

Several stacks of plastic containers stood in the corner—all of them empty. Clearly, David's July Fourth party had drastically leached the restaurant's supplies. Unless we got a hefty delivery of dairy products in here, pronto, our impressive array of latte drinks would be off the evening's menu.

Rather than wait for Papas to return, I headed for his office. The manager's inner sanctuary was untidy, but the vendor list was where I remembered seeing it a week ago, when Papas last called me in for a micromanagement session.

I found the number for Cream of the Lakes Dairy and used Jacques Papas's phone to make the call.

"Dairy. This is the dispatcher," a male voice said gruffly.

"Hi. I'm calling from Cuppa J in East Hampton, on—"

"Sure, sure. I know the place," the dispatcher said, suddenly friendly.

"I was wondering if you'd made our dairy delivery for today?"

"Let me check . . . Ah, here it is. My guy was there at nine. Mr. Papas ordered three gallons of milk, two gallons of cream, and sixteen dozen eggs."

Great. "Look, apparently there's been a mistake. We've got no inventory here on dairy for the weekend and we need a lot more. At least twenty more gallons of milk, ten of half-and-half, and ten of cream."

"No problem, Ma'am. We'll get it out there in an hour."

"Thank you so much."

"Not a problem. You want me to bill this on the fifty-ten plan, too, right?"

"Excuse me?"

"The extra ten percent. We take fifty percent up front for deliveries, and we get the other fifty percent—plus ten—at the end of the season."

"I, uh . . . suppose that's . . . okay," I replied, not knowing what else to say.

"Great. Just ask Jacques about it if you have any questions," he added, clearly sensing my confusion. "He's the one who worked it out."

I hung up, even more confused.

Why, I wondered, would David Mintzer sign off on such a terrible arrangement? He had more than enough capital to pay for all of his deliveries on time. Even if he'd wanted to delay payment via a credit plan, there were certainly better interest rates out there than ten percent.

The more I thought about it, the fishier the deal sounded. David would not have signed off on such a deal, but the man at the dairy didn't mention David. "Ask Jacques," he'd said.

Clearly Papas was up to something—but what? Embezzlement?

I checked my watch. Papas had been gone only thirty-five minutes, so I figured I had time to do a little sniffing. I began searching through the mess on his desk, hoping to find the blue book he constantly carried. I fumbled through a week of piled up newspapers without success. Next I decided to go through the drawers in the man's desk.

The first one I opened contained personal items—toothbrush and toothpaste, several bottles of very expensive cologne, a hairbrush, and so many men's hair care and styling products I expected to find a tiny Vidal Sassoon in there with a pair of scissors. The second drawer contained stationery, envelopes, pens and pencils, and a stapler. The third drawer was locked.

Before I could look any further, however, Papas's angry voice shattered the silence.

"What are you doing in here?"

"Oh, hi, Jacques, I, uh—"

"Who gave you permission to come in here?"

"I had to call the dairy. We were out of half-and-half, and far too low on milk and cream."

Jacques Papas's nostrils flared as he stared at me, obviously seething.

"Since you weren't here, and we needed the supplies, I found the dairy's number and placed the order myself," I continued. "The dispatcher was very nice. The truck will be here within the hour."

My words seemed to calm the man. He nodded. "You should have told me you needed supplies before I stepped out. I would have placed the order."

"I didn't know until I checked the walk-in. And I didn't want to trouble you."

Jacques nodded again. "Fine. I shall be here to meet the delivery man."

"Great," I said. Then I slipped by the man and out of his office.

EIGHT

~~~~~~~~~~~~~~~~~~~~~~~~~~~~~~~~~~~~~~

AFTER being jolted into near-drowning by a Suffolk County Police bullhorn and uncovering a possible extortion scheme by a workplace colleague, I didn't think anything else could surprise me today, but that evening something managed to do just that—or rather someone.

Madame glided into Cuppa J in an elegant chartreuse sundress, on the arm of an elderly man I'd never seen before. His gray beard and tweedy blazer gave him the air of a professor, but his short, white ponytail, French beret, distressed jeans, and trendy rectangular glasses made him look more like a patriarch of West Village pop artists.

"Clare, you look so stressed," Madame told me as I walked up to her cafe table. "Perhaps you should call it a night."

Madame's suggestion was kind but impractical. From five o'clock onward, the restaurant had been packed. It was now ten in the evening and most of the customers were here for coffee service and dessert. That may have slowed things down for Victor and Carlos in the kitchen, but not for me in the dining room. Because we were understaffed, I was pulling double duty, managing as well as waiting tables.

"We're far too busy for me to ditch early," I told my ex-mother-in-law with a patient smile. "Besides, I'm not at all tired."

From her seat on one of the first floor's green velvet couches, Madame raised a silver eyebrow. "I didn't say tired, my dear. I said *stressed*."

Sitting cozily beside Madame, the bohemian-looking senior stroked his neatly-trimmed beard and remarked, "I think perhaps your daughter-in-law has been spending too much time on the 'fashionable' side of the highway."

I might have taken more offense at the man's familiarity, if his bright blue eyes hadn't been sparkling attractively with humor as he said it.

"And you are?" I asked.

Madame's date stood up, clicked his heels, and extended his hand. "Edward Myers Wilson."

I placed my hand in his. "Pleased to meet you. I'm Clare—"

"Allegro," the man replied. "I know. Blanche has told me much about you already and your . . . shall we say *very interesting* Hamptons summer."

I bristled at both points. Firstly, my surname was no longer Allegro. I had gone back to Cosi after the divorce. Madame knew this, of course. She just didn't like it and, obviously, had misinformed Mr. Wilson.

"Clare, I can't believe your giving up your married name," she'd said to me years ago when I'd first told her. "Your daughter's last name is Allegro. That's never going to change. Why don't you consider keeping it?"

"Because," I'd answered, "your *son* is never going to change."

Ever since, Madame would occasionally "forget" that I took back Cosi, an act of total passive-aggressiveness as far as I was concerned. But then, what else could I expect from Joy's grandmother? Like my own daughter, Matt's mother could be as stubborn as she was effervescent; as reckless as she was adventurous; as contentious as she was understanding. Also, like Joy, Madame wanted to see Matt and me get back together. In the past she'd even tried crazy schemes to achieve this goal. My greatest fear was that, one day, she might actually accomplish it.

For the moment, I silently shrugged off the Allegro surname error. I'd never seen this Wilson character before and I didn't expect to see him again, so who cared if he got my name wrong? What I couldn't let go, however, was Madame's apparently telling this perfect stranger about the shooting at David's party.

Hoping I was mistaken about his pointed implication, I went fishing. "Yes," I replied to Mr. Wilson. "Working here has been very interesting."

"I'm sure it has," he said, easing back into his green-velvet seat next to Madame. "But not as interesting as trying to track down a murderer, eh?"

I sent a three-alarm glare my former mother-in-law's way. She responded with a wave of her hand.

"Don't worry so much, Clare," she chirped. "Edward's here to help."

"Help?" I whispered, glancing around me to make sure no one in the crowded dining room was listening. "How can a perfect stranger help?"

Edward Wilson appeared amused at that. He turned to Madame. "Blanche, I think perhaps you're right. Clare does appear rather stressed this evening."

Madame laughed.

With two fingers, I massaged the bridge of my nose, feeling the edges of a headache beginning. It was bad enough that my daughter and I weren't talking at the moment. Now I had to put up with Ma and Pa Enigmatic.

"Edward's not a perfect stranger," Madame informed me.

"Although some of my colleagues have accused me of being perfectly strange," he quipped.

"Only when the moon is full," Madame retorted.

"And I'm out of single-malt Scotch. Either that or every last tube of 538."

"Oh, that's right," Madame said. "You *are* obsessed with Prussian blue, aren't you?"

"Not the color, love. The sky. Matching its palette out here has been a lifelong obsession." He put his arm around Madame's shoulders. "One of them anyway."

I raised both eyebrows at the old guy's smooth move, wondering whether or not Mr. Wilson knew (or cared) about Madame's ongoing relationship back in the city with Dr. Gary MacTavish.

"So you two are old friends?" I prodded, expecting them to amplify the subject.

"Well, we are *friends*," said Edward, stroking Madame's bare shoulder. "And we are *old*. Aren't we, Blanche?"

"Speak for yourself."

I couldn't believe both Joy and her grandmother seemed set on testing my nerves this evening.

My daughter had done it earlier, when she'd shown up late to work, in the company of Graydon Faas. I'd jumped down her throat the minute she'd walked in the kitchen door. We'd had a furious fight about where she'd been all day and what she'd been doing, but she refused to answer any of my questions, or apologize for ignoring my many worried cell phone messages.

All night, I couldn't help noticing how Joy and Graydon kept lightly brushing against each other, exchanging subtle touches. With alarm, I realized just how little I knew about this surfer-waiter "dude." Graydon was a good worker and a quick study with the barista techniques. But I could have described Treat Mazzelli the same way, and he'd ended up being a systematic womanizer. (I couldn't very well blame him for the bullet in his brain since I didn't even believe it was meant for him. Nevertheless, where my daughter's happiness was concerned, I considered womanizing bad enough, thank you very much!)

At the moment, I couldn't discuss my thousand-and-one worries with Joy, but, considering the way Treat had ended up, I felt I had a right to butt in and grill her about her relationship with Graydon. When we finally had some privacy, I intended to do just that. I also intended to quiz Joy's grandmother. Here she was, flirting shamelessly with a man about whom I knew even less than Mr. Faas.

"Why don't I take your orders?" I suggested, glancing over my shoulder to make sure my other customers weren't getting antsy. "We can chat again when I bring your food."

"Very good," said Edward with a smile.

"We're just having dessert and coffee tonight," Madame said. She pulled a delicate pair of vermilion reading glasses out of her clutch, balanced them on the end of her nose and looked over my pairings menu.

"Very nice selection, my dear," she said after a minute.

"Thank you." I replied, trying not to blush. A "very nice" from Madame regarding coffee was akin to a grad student finally earning that Ph.D. The woman knew more about beans, blends, microclimates, harvests, processing, roasting, brewing, and serving than any professional I'd ever met in the food and beverage trade.

Edward glanced over Cuppa J's coffee selections, as well. "Estate Java, Costa Rican Tres Rios, Kona, Ethiopian Harrar, Kenya AA, Sumatra," he recited. "My goodness how do we choose what coffee?"

Madame and I exchanged little smiles. "Well, lucky for you my daughter-in-law here is Cuppa J's coffee steward."

"Excuse my hearing," said Edward, "did you say *coffee steward*?"

"Indeed I did. It's a delightful notion of Clare's that every fine restaurant should have someone on staff who knows how to buy, store, and properly serve a large variety of coffees and can knowledgeably recommend them to customers."

"Ah, I see," said Edward, "like a sommelier only with coffee?"

Madame nodded. "Turn the page on your menu and you'll see that she's suggested pairings with tonight's dessert selections."

Edward turned the page. "Ah! Yes, yes . . . and you give a little description of how each coffee tastes—"

"The flavor profile," Madame informed him, with a wink for me.

Edward stroked his gray beard. "Well, I must say, it's still difficult to decide."

"Do you enjoy chocolate?" I asked, trying to help.

"Not really," said Edward.

"Why don't we go for something a little more subtle," Madame suggested. "Edward, I wonder, do you still have a passion for . . . figs and almonds?"

Still looking down at the menu, Edward smiled. "Oh, yes, Blanche," he replied, covering Madame's hand with his own. "That afternoon on my porch? Indeed I do."

Madame looked up at me, but I'd already guessed their order.

"Spanish fig cake," I said. "And the almond torte. Both pair nicely with the Sul de Minas."

Customers who knew a little about coffee sometimes raised an eyebrow at putting a Brazilian on the menu. But a little knowledge sometimes can be as worthless as none at all.

Yes, Brazil is the largest coffee producer in the world, and much of it comes from lower-grade Arabicas and Robustas grown on massive plantations. And, yes, these coffees are flat and average, many of them ending up in mass-marketed blends—the kind you find canned on grocery store shelves. But Brazil is a huge country with a wide spectrum of conditions and quality. In recent years, its growing associations have been working to re-create the image of its coffees. Small farms, like the one Matteo found in the south of Minas Gerais, use higher quality harvesting and processing methods to produce specialty-level coffees that really sing in lighter and medium roasts.

I was surprised to see Madame, of all people, raising an eyebrow at my recommendation. But then she smiled and said—

"The Brazilian is the ideal choice for passion, isn't it?"

"Passion," Edward said, seeing Madame's little smile. "Let me guess why? It reminds you of an old Brazilian beau?"

"Oh, yes, he was Brazilian, but he wasn't *my* beau," said Madame. "He was the lover of the French governor's wife."

Edward's look of curiosity turned into one of confusion.

Madame laughed. "It's a very old story."

"Go on," Edward said.

"Well, you see, ages ago, when coffee plants first came to the New World, they were limited to certain regions. French Guiana and Dutch Guiana both grew coffee, but they jealously guarded the export of their seeds. Then, during a border dispute between the two colonies, Brazil sent a diplomat to help settle it . . . now what was his name? Clare, help me?"

"Francisco De Mello Peheta."

"Oh, yes! That's right. Francisco was a dashing Brazilian, you see, and the wife of the French governor fell for him. They had a passionate affair, and afterward, she sent him back to Brazil with a bouquet of flowers. Buried inside was her real gift to him—clippings from a coffee tree, including fertile coffee cherries. Voila! The Brazilian coffee industry was born."

Brazilians in the coffee trade loved to repeat the story Madame had just told, which claimed their entire billion-dollar coffee industry had emerged from a love affair. I knew the legend had very little credibility. Madame knew it, too. But, clearly, tonight she was having too much fun seeing the world through her rose-colored reading glasses.

"Shall I bring separate presses?" I asked flatly. "Or just the one pot for the two of you?"

"Make it for two, dear. We'll share," she replied.

Of course, they'll share, I thought, heading back to the coffee bar to prepare their order. *They're sitting so close to each other, they're practically sharing each other's laps!*

Needless to say, I was less than thrilled to see Madame with a new man. Dr. MacTavish had been her steady beau for over a year, and I had become used to that . . . comfortable with that. She hadn't broken up with the good doctor, of that I was sure. Yet here she was tonight practically giddy over Edward.

Part of me knew I was being way too harsh. At her age, Madame had a right to enjoy happiness wherever she found it, whenever she found it, with whomever she found it. But another part of me felt she was betraying her friendship back in the city.

As I told myself (or at least tried to) that it was really none of my business, I began to prepare their order at the coffee bar.

"Who's that man with Grandmother?" Joy whispered.

It was the first time Joy had spoken to me in six hours, ever since we'd had that fight at the start of dinner service.

"He's her date," I replied. "His name's Edward Myers Wilson. That's all I know."

"What do you mean that's all you know?" Joy hissed. "They're all over each other. Where did she meet him? Does he live around here? Don't you know anything else?"

I put my hands on my hips and stared at my daughter. "No, I do not know anything else," I told her. "In fact, I know as little about Mr. Wilson as I do about Graydon Faas."

"That's not fair," Joy snapped. "You've been working with Graydon for over a month—"

"I could say the same about Treat."

"Graydon's not like Treat. And, anyway, it's my private business whom I see."

I folded my arms. "Just like it's your grandmother's private business whom she sees."

Joy's mouth moved but no words came out. Knowing she was trumped, she frowned, wheeled, and slammed through the leather padded doors to the kitchen.

nine

~~~~~~~~~~~~~~~~~~~~~~~~~~~~~~~~~~~~~

AFTER checking my other tables, I returned to Madame's and found the happy couple had moved off the topic of romantic coffee legends and onto a discussion about the restaurant's decor.

"Quite a delight," said Edward, gesturing to the mosaic clock at the top of the staircase. "I mean, just look at that surrealist piece up there. It gives the impression of an actual timepiece, yet its arms are turning, turning, turning, so quickly, as if its gears were caffeinated. Perfect!"

Okay, I thought, begrudgingly impressed, *give the man points for noticing.*

I transferred the contents of my silver tray onto the marble-topped cafe table: the four-cup French press, the Waterford crystal timer for the brewing process, and the slices of fig cake and almond torte on hand-painted plates.

Edward shook his head as he continued. "Touches of artistic whimsy like that timepiece . . . you just don't see much out here anymore. It's all gone vague and predictable. They're razing our brilliant, off-beat architectural history like Motherwell's Quonset hut, and replacing it with mock shingle-style cottages, for god's sake."

Despite my determination to find fault with Mr. Wilson, I couldn't help seriously considering his observation. The Quonset hut he'd mentioned was one I remembered from my architectural history classes.

"Did you actually see it?" I asked Edward, unable to curb my curiosity. "The Quonset hut."

Madame chuckled softly.

"Yes, my dear," Edward answered. "I've seen it."

The Quonset hut represented an important era of Hamptons' history. If this man had taken the trouble to see it, I knew he at least cared about that history.

The avant-garde structure had been built in the 1940s as an East Hampton home and studio for the artist Robert Motherwell. Motherwell had come out to this area with the wave of artists who'd followed the world-renowned Abstract Expressionist painter Jackson Pollack. He needed a place to live and work, so he hired the modernist architect Pierre Chareau to design it. Chareau had been an accomplished architect in France until Hitler's forces invaded and he'd fled to America. Just like Madame, who'd fled occupied Paris with her family when she was just a young girl, Chareau had left in a hurry, carrying no possessions and hardly any money.

Motherwell didn't have much money either, so for cheap building materials they purchased two war surplus Quonset kits. Then they scrounged, adapted, or invented features to complete the structure. I still remember the photos of the home's exterior in my college textbook: the long curving roof of the half-cylindrical building, the wall of windows.

"I've always wondered what it would be like to live in a house like that," I mused.

Edward took it as a question.

"It was an open and free-flowing space," he informed me, his bright blue eyes animated. "It was futuristic, a subversive challenge to conventional floor plans. There was a wonderful freestanding brick fireplace at one end of the living room and a small open kitchen at the other. Above you, the ribs of the building were exposed, those wonderful curving steel crossbeams that supported the roof, and Motherwell had painted them with a bright red lacquer so you felt as if a giant mobile was dangling high above you. The natural light was marvelous. Thirty-six feet of windows, salvaged from a commercial greenhouse. In the dead of winter, there was enough heat from the sunlight to keep the space fairly warm—they'd actually created solar heating without intending to. And when it rained, the water would flow over those overlapping panes of glass in a mesmerizing waterfall."

The way Edward spoke, with such deeply felt passion, I could see how easily a woman might find herself swept away. Even now, Madame was gazing at him with what appeared to be her own deeply felt passion—which, I had a hunch, had very little to do with Motherwell's Quonset hut.

"It sounds amazing," I told Edward sincerely. "I had wanted to see it with my own eyes when I came out here. But when I asked around—"

"You found out it was bulldozed in 1985," Edward finished for me. "You know why? The new, wealthy owner wanted a more conventional structure for his summer weekends."

"It's so strange what's happened out here," I said, thinking of what my dear old bookie dad might have said. "It's money laundering in reverse. The new money is attempting to look old."

"It's a bankruptcy of creative design is what it is," said Edward in disgust. "Most architects are sick about it, but they want to be successful, and these people with money don't have the sense of adventure the modernists did. They're simply desperate to fit in. 'Build me something that looks like it's been around for one hundred years. And make it really, really *big*.' "

"This generation supersizes everything, darling," Madame replied with a dismissive shrug. "Get used to it."

"Ah, but that's the beauty of old age," Edward countered. "I don't *have* to get used to anything. I'll be checking out of this daft hotel soon enough."

"Don't be morbid," Madame scolded, then she smiled up at me. "Clare, I think my friend needs a jolt of caffeine. What do you think?"

I nodded and checked the crystal timer. The last grains of sand were just running out. I gently pushed down the plunger on the French press, forcing the coarsely ground Sul de Minas to the bottom of the glass cylinder.

"There, you see, pointless ends are everywhere," said Edward. He gestured to my press with a grave little sigh, his elderly frame sagging a bit, as if the draining sand of the timer had just defeated everything he held dear. "Those beans have just gone the way of Motherwell's Quonset hut."

"On the contrary," I replied, pouring out their cups, a little in Edward's, a little in Madame's, until both were equally filled. "Those Brazilian cherries have just spent the last fraction of their lives infusing the hot water around them with their essence, a memorable burst of flavor that will bring joy and energy to those who drink it. In the scheme of things, I'd say that's not a pointless end at all."

Edward's face slowly brightened. He turned to Madame. "My goodness, you didn't tell me I'd get philosophy with my coffee service."

"We aim to please," I said.

"You did, my dear." Edward clapped his hands. "Very good."

"Didn't I tell you my daughter-in-law was something?" said Madame with a wink for me. "Well, she isn't finished yet, so settle down, Edward."

As the couple picked up their cups and sipped, I continued. "This Sul de Minas comes from a family-owned farm. In this medium roast, you have a flavor profile of a mellow, low-toned coffee with dry-yet-sweet, almost sugary figlike characteristics. The finish is sweet, rich, and long with a hint of cocoa and dry fruit notes."

Edward smiled as he sipped. "That's the finish I'd like, come to think of it. Sweet, rich, and long."

Madame laughed. She dug into the Spanish fig cake and presented a forkful to Edward. "Taste a bit of this, then sip again."

Edward's eyes widened as he obeyed. "Fig! I taste it in the dessert, of course. But now I can really taste it in the coffee."

I politely stated the obvious. "That's why they're paired."

"Oh, but, Clare," said Madame, "you have them paired with the almond torte as well, don't you?"

"Yes," I said slowly, worried she was about to disagree with the combination. "And? What are you getting at?"

"Just this: *one* coffee can be paired quite naturally with *two* sweet things, depending on the situation."

She glanced at Edward, then back at me, as if I were so very thick-headed I'd need help figuring out her analogy. *Don't worry, I got it. Loud and clear.*

After excusing myself, I went to check on my other customers, then returned to Madame's table to see if they needed anything more.

"Clare, didn't I ever tell you how Edward and I met?" asked Madame. "I'm sure that I did."

I shook my head. "No."

"We met in Greenwich Village, at the Village Blend . . . a very long time ago."

Edward sighed. "A lifetime ago."

"Edward used to come in with a few friends of his," Madame went on. "There was Alfonso Ossorio, Willem de Kooning, Lee Krasner, Truman Capote, Jasper Johns, Robert Motherwell, and, of course, Pollack."

My mouth went dry. *Good god, no wonder he knew what the inside of Motherwell's Quonset hut looked like!* "So, Mr. Wilson . . ." I said after clearing my throat and regaining my equilibrium, "you're a painter too?"

"Not like Pollack, not in the same league," Edward replied. "Pollack was a genius. He was also a degenerate drunk. Then, Lee—Lee Krasner, who ended up marrying him—dragged him out here to East Hampton, got him away from the demons of the city. It sobered him up being out here. Of course, back then East Hampton was a lot different. Untouched by time, quiet, pastoral . . . *sane*. Now Pollack's buried in Green River Cemetery over in Springs. Can't miss his grave. It's marked by a fifty-ton boulder."

"But you still paint?" I asked.

"Just for myself now. It's something I thoroughly enjoy. Of course, back then I was completely consumed by it. And, oh, I thought I was hot stuff."

Madame laughed. "You did indeed."

"We all did. There were hundreds of artists who moved out here after Pollack in the forties and fifties. Prices for land were dirt cheap then. And we were all rivals of Pollack's, secretly seething with jealousy over his success and fame. But, after he flipped his car at ninety on Fireplace Road and died at forty-four, I found that though I still loved the art, I'd lost my taste for the competition."

"Edward became a professor," Madame informed me.

"I started writing first," Edward corrected. "Then teaching—art history, criticism. Of course, the others

I knew continued to stay in the game. There's an old joke about de Kooning looking out his window every morning at the Green River Cemetery, just to make sure Pollack was still under that fifty-ton boulder!"

"You see, Clare," said Madame. "Edward's been around here forever."

"Nearly," said Edward, interlacing his fingers with Madame's and bringing her hand to his lips.

"That's why I thought he could help us with David's little, shall we say—" Madame glanced to the full tables to her left and right—"*problem.*"

Problem, I thought. *Yes, I'd definitely characterize a sharpshooter trying to turn you into a live target at your own party as a 'problem.'*

Madame turned to Edward. "Tell Clare what you told me . . . about the foreclosure and the town trustees."

Edward nodded, leaned close and motioned me to bend toward him. "This place wasn't sold in the regular manner."

"What do you mean?" I asked.

"What Edward means is the previous owner closed the place last summer during a messy divorce," Madame quietly informed me. "Because of tax delinquencies, this property ended up in the hands of the town itself."

"O-kay," I said slowly. "So how is that important?"

"How much did you tell me a single chair in a Hamptons' restaurant makes in one season?" Madame asked.

"On average, about 180,000 dollars per chair."

Edward gave a low whistle.

"Well," Madame said, "don't you think that's enough of a reason to be fairly angry if your dream to open a restaurant here was thwarted?"

"But David did open a restaurant," I pointed out.

"No, Clare, you're not following me," Madame said. "Edward told me that someone else wanted this place, too."

"It was in the local papers over the winter," Edward interjected. "There was a war, a bitter one over this place. It came down to two proposals. The town trustees chose David's."

"But what's the big deal?" I said. "So the other bidder lost this place. It happens every day in Manhattan. Why not just move along and buy another building?"

"Edward, tell her," Madame prompted.

He shrugged. "Here in East Hampton, you don't just buy a building and open a restaurant. This is the Land of No, my dear. It's governed by very strict rules to keep commercial growth down. If you're an aspiring restaurateur, you must wait for one of the existing restaurants in the area to close, then you must outbid others for the property, and gain the approval of the myriad planning, zoning, and design appeals boards for the town."

"Oh," I said. "David never mentioned any of that."

"Of course he didn't," Madame said. "Apparently, things got pretty ugly during the fight for the property. And David doesn't like ugly."

"So . . . who was the other bidder?" I asked.

"Bom Felloes," Edward replied.

"That famous TV chef?" I said. "The one with the Good Felloes restaurant chains all over the country?"

"The very same," Madame said. "Apparently, he'd been chomping at the bit to open an East Hampton Good Felloes restaurant like his others."

"But the town trustees practically retched at the idea of a chain restaurant coming into this tony area," Edward said. "And, quite frankly, the name didn't help his case much."

I could see what he meant. "Good Felloes" was a play on the celebrity chef's name, of course, but (as my dear old dad once told me) "goodfellows" was one of the ways Mafia "wise guys" referred to each other.

"Oh my goodness," Madame said. "The very idea probably made the East Hampton officials turn green."

"It's absurd when one contemplates the fact that something as historic as Motherwell's home and studio can be demolished, yet a new restaurant cannot be built," Edward said with another grave sigh. "But in any case . . . they rejected Bom's proposal and approved David's. I can see why they were impressed. Just look around you. Mintzer clearly spent a great deal of time and effort on designing the decor alone."

"Not to mention a small fortune," I added.

"You've got to spend it to make it," Madame pointed out.

"So, what else do you know about Felloes?" I asked Edward.

"Not really much more. Just that he's a single man, young and good looking, and he bought The Sandcastle about three years ago."

I frowned, not liking that news. "The Sandcastle? That's right near David's place. And it sounds like he bought it the same time David bought his land out here."

Edward nodded. "The original Sandcastle grounds were huge. When it fell to a younger generation, they broke it into two pieces. The acreage with the residence on it was bought by Bom. David Mintzer bought the plot of land next to it and built from scratch."

I'd never seen The Sandcastle. It was completely surrounded by a wall of high green privets, and the ornamentation on its wrought-iron front gate was so Byzantine, I couldn't see beyond it. Certainly I was aware The Sandcastle abutted David's property. But I didn't know that Bom Felloes was the owner. David had never mentioned Bom— I would have remembered if he had.

I tapped my chin with my ordering pencil. "David obviously has a serious rival. But I don't doubt the man has serious rivals in all of his businesses."

"You think Bom wouldn't mind seeing David under a fifty-ton gravestone?" asked Edward.

"I hope Bom isn't the one trying to put him there," I replied. "But I need to know more about him . . . a lot more."

"Well, my dear, never fear," chirped Madame, the caffeinated sparkle in her gaze making me understandably nervous. "Edward and I are on the case!"

ten

∽∾∽∾∽∾∽∾∽∾∽∾∽∾∽∾∽∾∽∾∽∾∽∾

It was close to midnight when I finally returned to David Mintzer's oceanfront mansion, dead tired from hours on my feet and emotionally drained after my latest, unhappy confrontation with Joy.

I'd had no luck convincing Madame to move out of David's because of the shooting, but I'd hoped I could at least pull rank on my own daughter. So after we closed the restaurant, I'd waved Joy into the empty break room and tried to convince her to leave East Hampton and go back to the city.

She flatly refused.

"Look, Mom," she said. "I was ready to go into a share house, but you stopped me. I need this job, and I need the money. I'm really, really sorry Treat got shot, but it's obvious that bullet was meant for him. He's dead now, and it's over. If you force me to leave David's house, I won't go back to the city. All the share houses are full up by now, so I'll just move in with Graydon. And if you get me fired from Cuppa J, I'll just find another job out here—I hear cocktail waitresses make much more if they wear a little less."

I was flabbergasted. I stood in front of my daughter speechless. I may have trumped her earlier, but now she was trumping me, and needling me with that last comment. She had cast me as a prude and herself as a slut, just to win her point. It wasn't fair to either of us. But that's the trouble with children—they know just how to twist your guts.

Joy sighed. "I'm twenty-one, Mom. Stop treating me like a child."

"You know very well why I'm worried," I calmly reminded her. "The shooting aside, moving in with Graydon's hardly a solution. He's even less of an open book than Treat. What do you really know about him?"

"I know what counts. He's sweet. He's fun. He likes me and he treats me like I'm beautiful."

A chill went through me. She sounded as naive as yours truly when I'd first met Matt. I'd been around Joy's age at the time, studying art history during a summer break in Italy. My guard had been down when Matt and I had first encountered each other on a sun-drenched Mediterranean beach. He'd been warm and giving and handsome as hell, his young body tanned and hard from his typical athletic antics, sculpted as perfectly as the Renaissance statues I'd been studying, his ink-black hair, worn down to his shoulders, constantly slipping out of its ponytail.

Being in such a heavenly, exotic location, I'd found it far too easy to dreamily fall into bed with Matt over and over again. But I'd come home to America wide awake, pregnant with Joy, and agreeing to marry the absolutely wrong man.

"You're being naive," I told my daughter in a tone more harsh than I intented. "If you want me to see you as an adult, then you should start acting more responsibly."

Joy's reply was to storm off again. This time when she marched into the restaurant's kitchen, she continued moving all the way through it and out its back door. Graydon had been waiting for her in the parking lot and together they drove away in his Mini Cooper.

By then I was totally depleted. Despite my spent spirit, however, I refused to call it a night. With my daughter and ex-mother-in-law refusing to leave David's house, I was more determined than ever to get to the bottom of Treat's murder. As soon as I got back to David's mansion, I intended to ask him about Bom Felloes as well as that suspicious "ten percent deal" with the local vendors Jacques Papas had cooked up. (Pardon the pun.)

Giving my Honda more gas than necessary, I turned off the dark lane and swung onto David's long driveway. I quickly realized something was different—a tiny gold flame was flickering inside a newly installed gas lamp. It cast a pale light on the stone path that led up to David's front door. I rolled up to the house, staring with disbelief . . . and a slowly building anger.

The lamp was a genuine antique, complete with leaded glass and a blackened cast-iron post. The design perfectly suited the shingle-style beach house, but a feebly flickering gas lamp next to a footpath was not what I had in mind when I told David Mintzer that his home needed security lights!

Obviously, the man had not taken me seriously.

Okay, I admitted to myself, so I hadn't taken him seriously either. He had asked me to drop the idea that he was the murderer's target, and I obviously hadn't. And wouldn't.

David's driveway looped in a racetrack-size circle in front of his large house. I parked near the front door, right behind the man's small convertible sports car, noting with annoyance that the meager illumination from his quaint choice of lighting didn't even reach the front door area.

Luckily for me, there was a nearly full moon and the stars were providing significantly more glow than the pathetic flame in the gas lamp. Still, I had trouble locating the front door key in my large handbag—something I wasn't used to doing. Usually David's butler, Kenneth, let me in, but he was gone for the entire weekend.

I decided simply to use the key to the kitchen door instead. I'd kept that key handy on my car keyring for convenience because that was the door I used to take beach strolls at all hours. With a shrug, I started to walk around the dark grounds to the back of the mansion.

By the time I reached the pool and deck area, my eyes became accustomed to the celestial light, and I could easily discern the outlines of the Adirondack chairs on the lawn and the frothing surf of the rising tide along the empty shoreline.

As I moved across the cedar deck, I heard someone coming towards me with heavy footsteps. If it had been David, I realized, he would have called out by now. I lunged for the back door, then nearly screamed when a gruff voice demanded—"Who are you?"

Reflexively, I lifted my hand and squinted at the blinding white beam directed at my face. Just as reflexively, I began to shout in my best aggressive, pissed off New Yorker tone—"Who the hell are *you*? You have no right to be here! This is private property! Get that flashlight out of my eyes!"

The blinding beam was redirected toward the heavens. I saw a shape in the shadows. I made out a dark uniform and silver badge.

"S-sorry, ma'am," said the man with the badge. "Your name please?"

"Cosi. Clare Cosi."

"Okay, your name's on the list."

"List? What list?"

"Mr. Mintzer's personal list of who's allowed to enter."

"And who are you?"

"I'm a security guard from Shield Security Services. I'm making my rounds."

He couldn't have been more than twenty-five, bulky, with a large round head under a blond crew cut. His half smile told me he was as nervous about this unexpected encounter as I was.

"That's all right," I replied with extreme relief. "I'm glad David hired security. Better safe than sorry."

"Yes, Ma'am. Someone from Shield will be here around the clock, twenty-four seven."

"That's good to know." I unlocked the door and pushed it open. "Well, goodnight."

The youth touched the brim of his hat. "Goodnight, Ms. Cosi."

He watched until I was safely inside with the door relocked, then he left, I assumed, to continue his rounds. Mouth dry as the Gobi, I dropped my purse on the counter and went to the refrigerator. I unscrewed a small bottle of ice-cold Perrier and gulped it down, hands a little shaky. I poured a second and pressed the bottle's cold, frosted glass to my forehead.

I searched the house next, starting with the rooms in the guest wing. I discovered I was alone. Madame was still out with her gentleman friend and Joy was, too. Obviously, Graydon hadn't given her a ride directly home. I was surprised to find David out—especially since I saw his car parked in the drive.

Then I realized David might have decided to move out of the guest wing and back into his own room. So I went back down the steps to the first floor and crossed over to David's wing on the south side of the mansion. As I approached his second-floor bedroom to knock, I stopped at the door to his private bathroom.

The crime scene tape was gone now, and the door was ajar. I couldn't resist pushing it further, flipping on the light. The last time I'd opened this door, I'd found a bloody corpse. This time there was not one sign that a crime had been committed. The formerly bloodstained marble was pristine again, the holed window pane replaced with a sparkling new sheet of glass.

Suddenly the door on the bedroom side opened, and I prepared an apology to David for invading his privacy without knocking. But it wasn't David. Pale blue eyes stared at me. Alberta Gurt's alarmed gaze. She held an armful of dirty laundry.

"Oh!" we both cried. Then we nervously laughed.

"Couldn't resist taking a look at the marble, eh?" Alberta said, dumping David's clothes into a wicker hamper. The woman wore her maid's uniform and her brown, gray-flecked hair was pinned up. There was no sign of the makeup and jewelry she displayed last night when I'd questioned her.

"Oh . . . yes," I stammered. "The marble is spotless."

"The stonemason did a fine job of restoring the finish," Alberta said, regarding the work. "David had a car service drive the craftsman here from Hoboken. The fellow was working in here for hours. Now it's as good as new."

Wish I could say the same for Treat.

"I thought maybe you were David," Alberta said with a sigh. "He's had a stressful two days, what with the Fourth of July party and all that's happened afterwards. Arranging for security, getting the stonemason and the lamp installed . . ."

"I saw."

Alberta shook her head. "Now he's off gallivanting again. He needs his rest, that boy. He's already had one migraine this week. If he's not careful, he'll be courting another."

"Where did he go, by the way?" I asked. "His car's still parked outside."

"He's gone to another party, just down the beach. He walked there around sunset."

"Walked? Alone?"

Alberta nodded.

Now I was really annoyed with David. The lack of proper security lighting was bad enough. I'd told him about the flipper footprints in the sand! Didn't he realize what an easy target he was making himself?!

"When did the security people arrive?" I asked.

"Soon after the detectives left. David arranged everything with a few phone calls."

Alberta carried the wicker hamper out the bathroom's hallway door. I followed her downstairs, to the laundry room, where she methodically separated the clothes by color.

"You've known David a long time," I said.

"Too long, according to David. He tells me I treat him more like a son than a boss. It's true I guess. When you see someone every day for fifteen years, it's like they're family."

I tried to imagine what David Mintzer was like fifteen years ago. He would have been around thirty, I knew, but I couldn't form a picture in my mind of him looking any way but how he looked today.

"I can't complain," Alberta continued. "David's treated me like family, too."

"Really?" I fished, thinking of his abrupt firing of Prin. "He can be a pretty demanding boss. Doesn't like to be questioned."

Alberta gave me a funny look. "Well, to me, he's been good. He put me in his will so if something ever happened to him I'd be taken care of. He even included my nephew, too. How many people would do that for an employee?"

This was the first time I'd heard Alberta mention any other member of her family. "Your nephew?" I asked.

Alberta nodded. "My sister's boy. Thomas got into some gang trouble in Buffalo a decade ago, when he was still a juvenile. After the justice system was done with him, Thomas came here to live with me, to get away from that environment. David helped Tommy get his G.E.D. After that, the boy enlisted in the Army."

"He's still a soldier?"

"Not anymore. He finished his enlistment last year, got an honorable discharge and landed a nice security job over in Hampton Bays. That might not have happened without David's help."

Of course I wondered if that security job involved carrying a gun. Certainly, the army would have given the guy training in target shooting. I also wondered if he knew that David had included him in his will—and if the amount of his inheritance was worth killing for. The hairs on the back of my neck began to prickle.

I was glad Alberta Gurt was feeling talkative. Perhaps it was the isolation that came with working on a property like this one. Although a whirl of social activity suffused the Hamptons, folks like Alberta weren't part of that lifestyle. For them the Hamptons was a very different place.

"David seems like a very complicated man," I said after a pause. "Over the years, you've watched him rise to the top of his game. It must have been an interesting sight."

Alberta nodded. "I remember when David sold his fashion line to the Unity department store chain, and the first time he was on *Oprah*, too. I was sitting in the audience that day. He introduced me to Ms. Winfrey herself after the taping."

"That must have been exciting."

"David knows all sorts of people. He's made so many friends over the years."

"I suspect he's made a few enemies, too?"

"That's the funny thing about David. Even his business rivals come around. David finds a way to make things work out for the best, especially when he turns on that charm of his."

I thought about his firing Prin and instructing Jacques to lie about it to the Cuppa J staff. Then there was that neighbor of his across the lane, the heiress in black, smoking among the trees.

"His charm certainly hasn't worked on Marjorie Bright," I pointed out to Alberta. "She told me she's suing David."

Alberta frowned and shook her head. "That woman is a piece of bad road, I can tell you. All her threats and raging over a few silly trees that only partially block her view from one window. But then people get riled up easily out here. Egos and money make for a bad mix."

Alberta didn't talk much more after that, just checked her watch and said she had to finish up her work for the night. I followed her down to the first floor, then bid her goodnight as I stepped into the kitchen to pick up my handbag. That's when I heard my cell phone chiming.

"Hello, Clare. You needed to speak to me?" The voice was female, familiar, and blunt as a kitchen mallet.

Prin Lopez was returning my call.

Eleven

~~~~~~~~~~~~~~~~~~~~~~~~~~~~~~~~

"Prin," I said, sitting down at the large table, "thank you for calling back." On the other end of the phone, I could hear clattering sounds, the familiar noises of plates rattling in a busy restaurant kitchen. "I found out what happened to you, just today," I told her. "Jacques informed me. I'm so sorry . . ."

There was a pause, followed by a cutting laugh. "Does that bastard want me to come back? Too late, I got my old job again, and with a raise, too. Tell that pompous pig I'm staying in the city."

Okay, I thought, so there's no love lost between Prin and David. Or was she referring to Jacques?

"Prin, I'm sorry to be nosy but . . . why were you let go?" I asked carefully. "Jacques either didn't know or didn't want to tell me."

"Screw his so-called propriety. What do I care? I'll tell you why I was fired. I 'imposed' on one of David's precious guests."

"I don't understand."

"I've been trying to make it as a singer for a couple of years now. I even recorded a demo, but I haven't gotten much traction with it. Then, last week, Big D came into Cuppa J."

"I'm sorry. I don't know who that is."

Prin sighed. "Big D? Devon Conroy? Among other things, he's the host and producer of *American Star*—"

"Oh, right, right. Like that *Star Search* show from the eighties with Ed McMahon."

"Ed McWho?" I could practically hear Prin rolling her eyes.

"Forget it," I said, feeling my age (and for a moment there, I actually felt good that I didn't have to go all the way back to Ed Sullivan for an example!) "Go on."

"Well, Big D was having lunch with some television people. I saw him sit down at one of Graydon Faas's tables. So I pulled Graydon aside, begged him to switch with me, give me the chance to wait on them. You know that prick Faas actually made me pay him a Benjamin to trade tables?"

I was sorry to hear that bit of the story. Obviously, Graydon wouldn't be the first young man interested in making a buck (or a hundred) where he could. But it didn't speak very highly of his character to charge a fellow worker for a favor.

"So you waited on Big D's table?" I prompted.

"Yeah, I did. And along with the check, I slipped Devon my demo CD."

"Ohhh . . ." I groaned, finally understanding why David had fired Prin. She'd broken his first commandment of working at Cuppa J.

"Remember that celebrities are here on vacation," David had lectured the staff at the beginning of the season. "My guests do not want to be harassed, photographed, or hounded. And while they're under my roof they won't be.

No one is ever to do anything but wait on them. No fraternizing, asking questions, requesting autographs, ever. On grounds of immediate termination."

"Fine, so I knew it was against the rules," Prin went on. "But it's not like rules can't be bent a little. And Big D was totally down with it. He didn't complain. David wasn't even there to see me do it."

"You mean someone ratted you out?"

"Nobody had to. Jacques caught me in the act and fired me on the spot."

"*What?* It was Jacques who fired you?"

"Yeah. Who do you think fired me?"

"Jacques told me it was David."

Prin laughed. "Mintzer was nowhere in sight. I pissed Jacques off so he got rid of me. And let me tell you, he was looking for a way to get rid of me, so he did."

I wasn't so sure Prin was telling the truth. "But David hired you," I argued. "And he owns the restaurant . . ."

"I'm sure Jacques got David to see things his way. Based on what I actually did, it wouldn't have been too hard. It doesn't matter anyway. I'm glad to be back in Manhattan. *Madre Dios,* I thought people on the Upper West Side had attitude, but they've got nada on the 'I'm all that' divas out there."

"Prin, back up. You said Jacques was looking for a reason to fire you." One particular reason suddenly came to mind. "Did it have something to do with the suppliers?"

Prin laughed again, sharp and cynical. "You're talking about Jacques's ten percent deal, aren't you? I found out about it, and I figured he was up to something shady. I never said a word, but he knew that I knew, which is really why that bastard wanted me out. I don't know what's going on, but you better watch your back, Clare."

"What do you mean?"

"I mean Papas is a prick. But I always liked you. You

know, before you got ahold of me, I thought a can opener was the standard tool for coffee prep! Anyway, Clare . . . guess I'm trying to say thanks for everything you taught me and always being so patient and sweet, you know?"

"Oh, Prin, you're welcome—"

I was about to ask Prin about her relationship with Treat Mazzelli, but I never got the chance. Someone on her end called her name, and Prin told me she had to get back to work. I wished her luck and said goodbye.

I stood in David's kitchen a moment, gazing at the glowing display panel on my cell phone and thought about the one person I could talk to right now, the one man who would understand my dilemma—and not just because it was his job. Without hesitation, I toggled to the fourth number on my speed-dial list and pressed.

On good days, I liked to think Detective Mike Quinn's attraction to me was genuine and based as much on my ability to listen as my big green eyes and sense of humor (and take it from me, a weary, grim-faced New York cop is one tough comedic audience). On bad days, however, I chalked up his regular appearances at the Blend as a simple case of his addiction to my barista skills. Upon meeting the man, I'd single-handedly converted him from a drinker of stale, convenience-store swill to an aficionado of rich, nutty, freshly pulled Arabicas. And, for sure, once you're hooked on that perfect cup, going without can make you homicidal (well, figuratively anyway).

Whatever the reason for Mike's friendliness toward me, however, I was glad to hear him answer my call on the first ring.

"Clare? Are you back in the city?"

Mike's voice was as difficult to read as his features. By now, however, I had trained my ear to detect his subtlest change in tone—not unlike picking up the faintest traces of exotic fruit in a hard-to-cultivate coffee. In this case, the almost inaudible rise in Mike's deadpan pitch told me the NYPD detective was, in fact, delighted to hear from me.

"No, Mike, I'm not back yet," I replied. "I'm sorry to tell you I'm still stuck on the balmy beaches of the Hamptons."

"Poor kid."

"I hope I didn't wake you."

He snorted. (I always could make him laugh.) "I'm on duty," he informed me.

"So what are you doing? Right now."

"Why? This isn't one of your phone sex calls is it?"

A male voice in the background laughed.

"I'm serious, Mike. Tell me."

"I'm sitting in an unmarked car parked on Houston Street, waiting for someone to rob the decoy cop using the ATM machine across the street."

"You're kidding."

"Hardly. Three robberies in two weeks at this same machine, one ended in a stabbing. Now, tell me what's wrong."

"Why do you think something's wrong?"

"Because I haven't heard from you in two weeks, it's after midnight, and that creepy ex-husband of yours has crept back into town."

"Mike, how the hell do you know all that? Are you spying on me?"

"Relax, it's a coincidence, that's all. I stopped by the Blend for a double tall latte and spotted Allegro getting out of a cab."

"I hope you got your coffee."

"I did. Tucker makes a nice latte." There was a semi-long pause. "You make them better."

The pitch went slightly lower just then. The pleasure pitch. The pitch that made me conjure images of the lanky cop drinking his double latte in my bed.

I cleared my throat. "Thanks."

"Anytime. So what's the trouble, Clare?"

I spilled, telling him about the shooting. I described the murder scene, how I'd found Treat shot, then the shells on the beach. He asked me to describe the bullet casings and I did. I even mentioned the tracks in the sand, the flipper fins, and told Mike the name of the investigating officer.

"I never met this O'Rourke but I'll ask around."

"Thanks, Mike."

"Listen, Clare. I see two scenarios here. One is that the murderer is an amateur, not a true professional—"

"Because I found the shells the shooter left behind?"

"Because you found three shells. Did you see any other bullet holes? In the window, the walls?"

"No, nothing, but I'll try to find out if the police found anything."

"If there are no shots close to the window, then for a pro the shooter was a lousy marksman, which brings me to my second scenario."

"Which is?"

"The shooting was an accident."

"What! That's crazy."

"Think about it, Clare. It's the Fourth of July. Fireworks are going off all over the place. Some kid, maybe a teenager or even an idiotic adult with too much money and not enough sense starts shooting off a rifle for the hell of it. Most of the shots go wild, but one hits the mark and someone dies. It's happened before."

I remained unconvinced and told Mike so.

"Okay," he said. "There's a third possible scenario. That the shells were left behind on purpose. If that's the case, look for the gun to show up in a place where the cops can easily find it."

"Because the shooter is trying to frame someone else?"

"Exactly," said Mike.

"I've already considered that possibility. But all these theories don't answer my central question—who was really the intended victim? I'm convinced it's David, but he swears he has no enemies. He's convinced it really was Treat."

"If you want to eliminate this Mazzelli kid as the true victim, then you need to know more about him," said Mike. "What types of things was he doing off the job, who were his known associates. Who did he hang with, in other words. That said, if I had to make the call based on what you've already told me, I'd say your friend David is in danger."

"Why?"

"It's simple. Rich men tend to make more enemies than waiters."

Twelve

Mike Quinn's words stayed with me as I closed my cell phone. *I'd say your friend David is in danger.* I peered through the kitchen window at the shadowy lawn, the white dunes, and the ebony expanse of ocean beyond. Anyone could be lurking out on that shoreline, I realized, lying in wait for David if he were to return home along the beach. Once again he would be an easy target.

I opened the back door and stepped outside. The outer reaches of Long Island were always cooler than Manhattan. Tonight it was almost chilly for a night in early July—temperatures in the middle-seventies, with high humidity, a wet wind off the ocean. Cool and refreshing after long, sweaty hours in the crowded restaurant.

Listening to the dull continuous roar of the incoming surf, I strode across the cedar deck, scanning the grounds for any sign of the guard who'd startled me earlier. The young man must be up front, I concluded, because there was no sign of anyone in the back of the mansion. I followed the stone path down to the shore and crossed the beach. My sneakers were filling with sand, so I kicked them off and hung them over my shoulder by the laces.

Moving along the shoreline, I noticed bright lights farther down the beach. Square paper lanterns the color of fresh blood had been strung along a huge stone patio. They trailed all the way down to the water, lending the pale white sand a reddish hue. In the scarlet glow, I saw knots of people in relaxed poses. The smell of mesquite charcoal drifted toward me on the summer breeze, only to be scattered by a strong cold gust from the ocean. I walked closer and began to hear whiffs of laughter on the air, a tinkling piano.

I turned to scan the beach in the other direction. But all was dark and quiet. This was the only party on the shoreline that I could see, and I concluded this had to be the bash that David was attending.

Yet it didn't make a lot of sense on the face of it. Unless I was mistaken, this party was taking place on the grounds of The Sandcastle. But Edward Myers Wilson claimed David and Bom Felloes had waged an ugly war over the restaurant space. Since David had never mentioned Bom to me, I assumed things were still chilly between them.

So why was David going to a party at Bom's home? Was Bom trying to make up with David? . . . Or was there something more sinister in the invitation?

I was still fairly far from the whirl of activity, and I picked up my pace to get a better view. Apparently, I was not alone in my curiosity. As I drew closer, I heard a sound that was totally out of place. A click of metal on metal, like a rifle being cocked.

I stopped dead, straining my ears.

For a long moment all I heard was the lapping waters and the party's tinkling piano. I was ready to believe I'd experienced an audio hallucination when a dark silhouette moved out of some high scrub grass on the beach. In the uncertain light, I was sure the figure was wearing a full body wet suit so black it seemed to absorb the night.

The man carried something clutched close to his chest. I could not see his face because he was facing the party. I was pretty sure the stranger had not seen me on the dark beach, but I was too afraid to do more than stare, figuring that if I moved, I might attract his attention. He gripped something in his hands, but because his back was turned to me, I could not see what it was.

For a long time the man just stood there, his broad back to me. Finally he turned away from the bright lights and darted across the beach, toward the lapping water. I watched him dive into the surf, quickly vanishing beneath the dark surface of the churning waters. I hurried to the shoreline. Large finned footprints creased the wet sand.

The Creature from the Black Lagoon had returned.

I scanned the ocean, wondering where the mysterious swimmer was headed. I made out the dull white gleam of a pleasure boat bobbing perhaps fifty yards off shore. There were no lights aboard, even the running lights were dim in what I was certain was a violation of maritime law. In any case, the boat was barely a smudge on the horizon and I was not certain I'd properly judged the distance from the beach. But since I'd been swimming in these same waters for weeks, I didn't hesitate.

Dropping my sneakers on the sand, I waded into the churning surf until I was waist deep. Then I dived through the middle of a wave and started swimming. The water was chilly, but I generated my own heat, moving with strong strokes that pushed against a mild but persistent undercurrent.

Never one to miss the opportunity for a morbidly inappropriate thought, my mind began to replay the opening of *Jaws*—the scene where a young girl is eaten alive during a midnight skinny dip—and I began to worry whether there were any dangerous sharks in these waters. On the other hand, considering that I was probably chasing a professional hit man who had killed before, I realized that marine life probably should not have been my primary concern.

It took several minutes, but I was soon approaching the boat, which was anchored and seemingly deserted. Then a head popped out of the water next to the stern ladder, face covered by huge goggles.

Blowing against the waves breaking over my face, I watched the stranger grasp a ladder and drag himself out of the water. Yes, the swimmer was definitely a man, lean and hard-muscled under the form-fitting wet suit. He grasped the brass rail with one hand; in the other he clutched something I still could not see. Once aboard, the man dropped what he'd been carrying and moved toward the superstructure. Then I heard a hatch open and, a moment later, the engine rumbled to life. Finally the running lights came on and a tiny lamp illuminated the pleasure craft. I read the plain black letters on the bow:

Rabbit Run, Hampton Bays, N.Y.

The motor's rumble became a roar and the boat lurched forward. The roiling waves spilled over me as the craft began to move. In just a few seconds the boat accelerated until it was skipping across the waves, heading south. I bobbed like a cork in its wake, watching its lights fade in the distance.

Before the boat was gone, I began to shiver. I was in fairly deep waters, and the incoming undercurrent was practically frigid. Okay, I thought, now it's time to worry about sharks—or hypothermia. I suddenly understood why the intruder had worn a wet suit (beyond its obvious camouflage potential) and I wished I'd had one, too.

Treading water, I turned to face the shore. It was a lucky thing for me that the beach party was still in full swing, because it would have been very hard to judge how far away the dark shoreline was otherwise. The only source of light close by was the scarlet glow of the Japanese lanterns, alarmingly tiny in the distance. I struck out, swimming along with the incoming waves for what seemed like a very long time.

Finally I touched soft sand. Battling the sucking surf, I climbed out of the white-capped waves in my bare feet, my wet khaki skirt plastered against my naked legs, my Cuppa J Polo clinging to my cold, clammy flesh. A gust off the ocean whipped against my wet back. I wrapped my arms around myself and shivered again. My teeth were actually chattering now, and I was certain my lips had turned the color of a Hamptons' summer sky.

A dozen or so startled partygoers had watched me emerge from the crashing waves like some kind of bedraggled mermaid. I was vaguely aware that these people looked familiar—they wouldn't know me, but I knew their faces. A few had been at David's party. There were sports figures, TV stars, a famous model.

As I moved off the sand, and onto the vast green carpet of lawn, I heard snickers from the men, confused laughter from the women. Someone made a loud joke and pointed to a nearby garden table of wrought iron. Raw oysters and sushi surrounded the centerpiece of a life-size representation of Sandro Botticelli's *Birth of Venus*—the iconic fifteenth-century painting of a naked woman emerging from an oyster shell on the shores of the Mediterranean. Here the grace and delicacy of that masterpiece of Renaissance style was rendered in ice.

No, I wasn't as naked as Venus. Or as beautiful. But the carved-in-ice part—yeah, okay, that was me.

I shivered again and smoothed my clothes, trying to regain a shred of dignity by tugging at the clinging canvas skirt, folding my arms over my wet, skintight Polo. As I continued moving through the crowd on the lawn, a woman touched my arm. She was young and very beautiful, eyes wide on a too-perfect face (possibly sculpted like that chilly statue of Venus, but with a surgeon's instruments instead of an ice pick). Her blond hair was swept back to reveal a pert nose, high cheekbones, bee-stung lips, and a flawless forehead the color of ivory.

"What happened to you?" she asked.

I shrugged. "Got bored. Went for a midnight swim."

The woman blinked vacantly.

The young man at her side looked away, offering me his profile—handsome but boyish, with sideburns so long, they nearly went back in time, to early-seventies muttonchops. He appeared to be waiting for me to recognize him, but I actually didn't have a clue.

"By the way, have you seen David Mintzer?"

The woman's eyes grew wider. She shook her head. "I don't know him, but there are lots of people here I don't know." Then she blinked as if in surprise when a thought sprang into her pretty, pampered head.

"Wait a minute! Oh, gawd. I've seen that Mintzer guy on TV. He works for Oprah, doesn't he?"

"Ah . . . That's okay, I'll find him on my own."

Stepping off the lawn and onto the cold stone patio, I continued moving among the surprised partygoers—socialites and show business personalities alike—who parted at my barefoot, sopping wet approach as if I were carrying a tray of bird flu appetizers.

I recognized New York City's most public real estate tycoon—the one with the reality show and the trademark hair. I spied a popular young singer, a famous movie director who was now doing commercials for a brand of camera film, and that handsome movie actor, Keith Judd, who'd given Joy his cell phone number—*the creep*.

I even saw David Mintzer's lawsuit-happy neighbor, Marjorie Bright. The heiress stood chatting with a group of well-dressed men and women. While I watched, she dropped a cigarette butt and crushed it with an elegant sandal, even as she fired up a fresh smoke with a gold filigreed lighter.

In fact, the only people I didn't recognize were a group of graying, balding, pudgy men gathered around some lounge chairs, drinks and cigars in hand. Their conversation appeared quiet and sober compared to the festive people around them.

Earlier that summer, David mentioned such men to me at a similar gathering Cuppa J had catered. He told me these men only seemed anonymous and interchangeable. In truth they were the real movers and shakers of the business world.

"They don't appear impressive, but believe me these low-key, unglamorous little men buy and sell the billion-dollar talent around them like any other commodity. Like pork bellies or oil futures. Scary, isn't it?"

What was scary for me at the moment was that I had risked my life to follow a clue that could lead to David's mortal enemy, and now I couldn't even find David to tell him. Even worse, my bedraggled appearance was continuing to garner attention, which I tried to ignore.

I passed a table occupied by a local senator who appeared on the Sunday morning chattering-class news shows like clockwork. Unfortunately, I couldn't help staring for a few seconds—and this politician noticed me when his eyes met mine. We both froze, and I immediately looked away, but it was too late, the burly man not far away from the senator's side noticed me staring, as well.

By the time I approached a knot of people gathered

around an outdoor bar, to ask again about David, the senator's bodyguard came up behind me and grabbed my left elbow—and his grip was not gentle.

"Hey!" I cried. "Let me go. I'm a neighbor. My name is Clare Cosi—"

"Come with me, and don't make any trouble."

The bodyguard was a head taller than me and as wide as a Hamptons Hummer. His thick neck was stuffed into a too-tight collar, and I noticed a small radio receiver in one ear. The way the wire coiled out of his bullet-shaped head and down the collar of his finely tailored outfit, I was sure I'd just been accosted by an Armani-clad Frankenstein monster.

I tried to yank my arm free, only to have my other arm grabbed by a second man, another bulked-up guard in a dark suit, this one a redhead with a crewcut.

"You are not on the guest list," said Crewcut. "That means you're trespassing. Don't make a scene. You can explain it all to the police."

Frankie and Crewcut began to drag me away. Heads turned, conversations ceased as I resisted.

"Wait! Listen," I pleaded. "I want you to call the police. I saw a real trespasser. And I'm worried about the safety of someone who was invited to this party. David Mintzer. He's here somewhere. I'm a guest at his house, just ask him."

"Mr. Mintzer has left the party," Crewcut replied. "His manager, Mr. Papas, drove him home fifteen minutes ago."

"He's okay then?" I pressed. "David's all right?"

Crewcut responded in a monotone. "Mr. Mintzer was just fine when he left the premises."

"Good," I said, extremely relieved. "That's all I wanted to know. You can let me go and I'll be on my way."

Naively, I thought the crisis was over. In my mind it was . . . for David anyway. For me it was just getting started. When I yanked my arms to break free, Frankie refused to release my left one, and Crewcut actually tightened his hold on my right.

"Ow! You're bruising me!"

Crewcut's response was to tighten his grip even more. With his free hand, he flipped open a cell to call the police. He was about to bring the phone to his ear when another hand, a strong one, belonging to someone else, reached out and closed on his wrist.

"Let her go," said the man attached to the hand. "She's telling the truth. She is a guest of David's."

Crewcut looked down his nose at the interloper, a tall, handsome, well-built man in a gorgeous summer-weight Helmut Lang suit. The man I'd seen before—the suit I hadn't.

Crewcut angrily shook his wrist free of the interloper's grip. "And are you on the guest list?" he demanded.

With a smug grin, my defender nodded. "I'm on the list, along with Breanne Summour. You know who *she* is, certainly."

"Yes, of course," sputtered Crewcut, releasing my arm. "And you are?"

I faced my impeccably dressed defender with the chiseled features and Caesar haircut, saw the amusement in his dark brown eyes.

"I'm Matteo Allegro," he said flatly, "this woman's ex-husband."

THIRTEEN

～～～～～～～～～～～～～～～～～～～

"Clare, you're soaking wet," said Matt after the Incredible Hulks left us. "And you have seaweed in your hair."

I sighed, feeling around for the strand of soggy vegetation, "Hey, a girl's got to look her best." I pulled the slime off my head and flicked it away.

Matt's dark eyebrow rose as he checked out my skintight Polo, his gaze snagging on the wet outline of my full breasts. "I never said you didn't."

I felt my cold cheeks flush warm as he smiled and opened his mouth again—probably to say something I'd make him regret—when Breanne Summour walked over.

Tall and thin as a runway model, she wore a flowing white silk pantsuit with glittering silver sandals, her brown hair twisted into a tight chignon to show off the faceted rocks in her ears. Her elongated neck was still as annoyingly swanlike as I remembered, her forehead still as wide as an HDTV screen, but her lips looked a whole lot more bee-stung than I recalled. Probably pumped up with collagen for the party, I concluded.

"Clare, isn't it?" she asked, stepping between me and Matteo.

I nodded, resisting the urge to shield my eyes from the glare of her earrings.

Now it was her turn to look me up and down. Her reaction, however, was far from identical to Matt's. Not even close. "My god," she said, her revulsion undisguised. "I didn't know the drowned rat look was in season."

Well, Breanne, I thought, *if rats are all the rage, you ought to know.*

As the editor-in-chief of *Trend* magazine, Breanne knew all about what was in season and what was passé, partly because she was one of a powerful circle of media types who helped deem it so. At the moment, all things coffee were hot and trendy, so said her magazine. Was that simply because of the coffeehouse craze ignited by Starbucks and other newcomers to the java biz? Was it because of Lottie Harmon's super-hot line of Java Jewelry? Was it because of her friend David's brand new Hamptons restaurant, Cuppa J? Or . . . did it have something to do with my ex-husband, coffee buyer and co-manager of that New York City institution, the Village Blend?

Whether the woman had been into coffee first and Matt because of it (or vice versa), two things were true: Matt was overseeing the Village Blend's expansion into "hot, hot, hot" coffee kiosks in upscale clothing boutiques and department stores throughout the world, and Breanne couldn't get enough of him.

The two had been seeing each other, on and off for almost eight months now. Not that I was counting. I only knew because Esther Best, one of my part-time baristas back at the Blend, had an annoying habit of pointing out photos of Matt and Breanne. The typical shots, taken at black-tie charitable functions, gallery shows, or restaurant openings, appeared from time to time in gossip columns like *New York Post*'s Page Six.

Still, I could (almost) forgive poor Breanne for her nasty snipe. Anyone would have been embarrassed to see her date participating in the ugly scene that just took place. So, instead of taking the swipe I was dying to, I simply said—

"So nice to see you again, Breanne."

Although my words were civil, I just couldn't resist wringing out my shoulder length chestnut hair right in front of her. The water made a satisfying spat on the patio stones. A woman nearby gave me a dirty look and Breanne blanched whiter than her pantsuit.

Of course, Ms. Summour's attention span—not unlike her magazine's flashy, shallow articles—had always been as short as a gnat's life, and she was already moving on. (Okay, okay, so I'd pushed it with the hair wringing. But people like Breanne Summour were almost too easy to horrify.)

Anyway, seeing Breanne here made me wish my ex-husband had minded his own business. Not that I wasn't grateful to him for defending me. But spending the night in the Hampton Village jail with drunken college kids would have been a lot less annoying, in the scheme of things, than enduring Breanne's smugness under these circumstances.

Ms. Summour waved a manicured, beringed hand at a group of guests she apparently hadn't noticed before. Then, without so much as a "toodles," she and her diamonds were gone, sweeping across the stone patio to bestow a flurry of air kisses.

After she'd zoomed out of our airspace, Matt turned to me. The sexual amusement was completely gone from his eyes now. Something a lot less playful, a lot less *Matt*, had replaced it.

"Clare, what's going on?" he quietly demanded. "Why are you here, dripping wet?"

Clearly, he was taking his emotional cues from Breanne now—at least when it came to caring what people thought of his ex-wife at a public party.

"I could ask you the same question," I replied, gesturing to Breanne's back. "Except for the dripping wet part."

"What are you talking about?"

"Just this morning you told me you were totally jet lagged and heading back to the Village for a good night's sleep."

"I said a *few hours* sleep."

"Whatever! You never mentioned coming out to the Hamptons . . . with *her*."

"Bree knew I was back from the West Coast. She invited me to hop a chartered plane into East Hampton airport and join her for the weekend. I accepted."

"I can see that's not all you accepted, from *Bree*."

"Excuse me?"

I gestured to Matt's designer eveningwear, the kind of clothing that cost more than I grossed in a week—more than Matteo grossed in a week, too, because I saw the books.

When we'd been married, Matt's cocaine addiction had not only eaten through our savings, it had also evaporated his trust fund and left us in terrible debt. He was off the drug now. And he'd become a hard worker. But the Village Blend expansion was a financial risk, and we had a daughter to put through school. Neither one of us had money to burn. Not by a long shot. That was why Matt had refused to give up his rights to use the duplex above the Village Blend during his periodic layovers in New York.

His mother, Madame, still owned the Greenwich Village townhouse that contained both the century-old Village Blend coffeehouse at street level and the duplex apartment above it. When she'd convinced both of us to sign contracts to co-manage and one day co-own the Blend business and its townhouse, she'd neglected to let us know we were not partnering with *her* but with each other.

Now Matt and I were stuck. Unless one of us wanted out of the very lucrative deal, both of us had to learn to get along. So far, we'd been doing okay, attempting to remain civil business partners. And since staying a week or more in a Manhattan hotel every month, between his buying trips or other international business, was too much of an expense for Matt, we'd ended up occasional housemates again after a decade of separation.

In any event, that's one of the reasons I knew for a fact that my ex-husband had a finite set of fine clothes, every piece of which I'd seen already.

"So I have a new suit?" he said defensively. "It was a gift."

"From Bree?"

Matt's sour expression answered my question. He looked away. "She has relationships with top designers, Clare," he said quietly. "Because of her magazine. It's no big deal, you know?"

"What I *know* is that it means something when a woman starts dressing a man."

Matt stared at me, speechless for a moment, and I wanted to take the words back as soon as I'd blurted them. I had told myself that Breanne was just another thrilling new blend, Matt's flavor of the month—even though she was far from his typical young, bubble-headed bimbo fare (and, yes, I did wonder if maybe that was what bothered me about Breanne more than anything). But it was patently none of my business what her relationship was with my ex-husband, and Matt had every right to tell me to go to hell. But he didn't. He simply looked uncomfortable that I'd made the observation.

"Clare, I don't . . ." he said haltingly. "Bree and I . . . it's just a networking thing." He shrugged, looked away. "She needs an escort that knows which fork to use, someone to open doors for her, hold her coat, give her, you know . . ."

"Don't strain yourself searching for a euphemism. I know what it is you give her."

"It's not like that. We're just casual friends."

I was sure he was serving me baloney, but I bit my tongue, feeling stupid for having let our conversation get even this far. I had allowed myself to fall back into some cheated-on wife pattern when I was no longer his wife. It was embarrassing. And Matt was being more than patient with me.

I was about to apologize when a breeze blew up off the ocean, rustling the Japanese paper lanterns and making my teeth chatter. I hugged myself, shivering, and Matt shook his head. He slipped off the Helmut Lang evening jacket and draped it over my shoulders.

"Listen, Clare, changing the subject won't get you out of hot water . . . although it's obvious the water you just stepped out of was ice cold." His eyebrow rose again, a little of the old playful Matt back in his expression. Then he actually smiled. "Anyway, I still want an explanation from you. But first I'm going to borrow Breanne's car and drive you home."

"Matt, that's okay. You don't have to—"

"I want to talk to David anyway, tell him how the installations on the West Coast are going. I tried to get to him tonight, but there were just too many people surrounding him. I just need to tell Bree where I'm going. Back in a minute."

I couldn't argue, mainly because I was too chilly.

I watched Matteo cross the patio, put a light touch on Breanne's shoulder. She turned from her small circle of friends, smiling—a little forced I thought. They spoke for a moment. The smile disappeared. Her eyebrows rose into that HDTV forehead and she glanced in my direction.

I looked away, watching the rest of the party to pass the time. Matt was at my shoulder again before I knew it. He grabbed my elbow, not much gentler than the security man had a few minutes ago. I couldn't stop myself from observing—

"It's amazing what an uplifting effect Breanne has on you."

"Come on, let's go."

"Was Bree cranky?"

"I'm cranky," he growled, pressing me through the crowd. "Don't go there."

"Trouble in paradise?"

We entered the mansion's crowded first floor, and I gawked at the decor. The Sandcastle was the most extravagant home I'd seen yet. Gothic in style, the place had been fashioned to resemble a medieval castle, complete with a single stone tower. Constructed of granite, glass, cast iron, and heavy wood, the mansion's rooms (what I saw of them anyway) were huge.

Matteo led me through a split-level living room, the lower portion transformed into a dance floor complete with disco lights. Then we headed down a long hallway, lined with medieval-style tapestries, stunning reproductions of museum pieces. An anteroom held an actual suit of armor. Then there was another hall, this one lined with portraits of medieval knights, and finally we came to the mansion's grand entranceway.

The foyer sat directly under the castle's only tower. The area had a vaulted ceiling with graceful, carved stone arches that met at its center. The room was illuminated with tall iron braziers (actually gaslights behind glass, no open flames). Coats of armor hung on the bare stone walls.

A wide curving staircase descended from a second floor mezzanine constructed of carved oak, black with age. On the opposite side of the entranceway the huge front door was guarded by a mob of valets.

The door itself looked like something out of *Ivanhoe*, and I thought to myself that all this place needed was a portcullis, one of those iron gates that drops down from the ceiling. That, and a few actual knights with broadswords, of course.

Matteo approached a valet and handed the young man a parking chit. As we waited for Breanne's car to be brought around, I heard a commotion from the mezzanine. Then a pleasant voice cried out.

"Don't go, the party is just getting started!"

A handsome man hurried down the stairs. I recognized him immediately. Two women in maid's uniforms followed right behind. One clutched a fluffy royal-blue robe, the other a pair of matching slippers. The man practically shoved Matteo aside to reach me, something he could easily do because he was as tall as Matteo, with shoulders looking as broad as Mike Quinn's in his fine, buff-linen suit.

No older than thirty, olive complexioned, with a square jaw, a close shave, and neatly combed ebony hair, the host of the party regarded me through eyes of black onyx. For a long moment, he simply stared at me with an intensity that almost embarrassed me.

I self-consciously pulled Matt's jacket closer around me, worried, not for the first time, how much was revealed by my damp clothes.

"Please," he finally said. "You're soaking wet, allow me . . ."

He took the floor-length robe from the maid and held it open.

"We really should go," muttered Matt.

I slipped Matt's jacket off my shoulders and handed it back to him. Then I stepped into the soft, warm folds of the thick, Egyptian cotton robe.

"That's better, isn't it? And now the slippers." The man actually got down on one knee and placed the slippers on my bare feet.

"Th-thank you," I stammered, flabbergasted. The last time anyone knelt down to put a pair of shoes on me I'd been around ten years old, getting fitted for First Communion patent leather.

"My name is Bom Felloes," he said with his familiar British accent and a warm, open smile. "Welcome to my home."

His name was no surprise, of course. I'd already recognized the man from his Gourmet Channel show, *Elegant Dining*. A very charismatic mix of British and Portuguese ancestry, Felloes obviously had become quite wealthy from his show, the chain of restaurants bearing his name, and whatever else he did on the side.

"My name is Clare. Clare Cosi," I said.

"Yes, I know, my head of security told me. I do apologize for his manhandling you in any way. You're not hurt are you, love?"

I suppressed a laugh. Now I knew why Bom was being so solicitous. He was probably terrified I was going to sue the pants off him! Not that Bom with his pants off would be an unattractive sight, I realized. Seeing the man up close and personal gave me a whole new perspective on his villainy.

Could anyone this charming really be a contract killer?

"Yes, I witnessed it. Your head of security *was* pretty rough with her—" Matt began to gruffly respond.

But I quickly interrupted him. "No worries, Mr. Felloes. I'm the one who's sorry for crashing your party, and in such a state."

"Why you look perfectly charming, even sopping wet!" he declared. "A waif from the sea. An adorable little Venus."

"Yes, well . . ." I stumbled, embarrassed. "I did see your ice sculpture on the way in. I think she had a few less shreds of clothing on than me."

Bom laughed, his dark, intense eyes sparkling. "So you're my neighbor?"

"Yes, I'm staying with David. Something, uh . . . came up and I crossed the beach to find him. It was dark, you know? And I, uh . . . I was stupid . . . I walked too close to the water. A high wave caught me by surprise."

Bom frowned. "Well, it's a shame you missed David. He left a little while ago. His restaurant manager, Jacques Papas, arrived late, but he agreed to cut short his fun and drive David home. Alas, David claimed he wasn't feeling well."

Bom paused and then chuckled. "I hope it wasn't the company."

"I'm sure he had a fine time," I politely replied.

"And I'm sure you know . . . we've had our business rivalries in the past. But I invited David here to bury the hatchet, as you Americans say. So tell me, how do you know David? Are you two . . ."

He let the words trail off in implication. "We're just friends," I replied, quickly straightening out any misconceptions. "I'm his barista manager for the summer at Cuppa J. I'm overseeing the coffee service, managing the beans, putting together the dessert pairings, that sort of thing."

Bom's face lit up with boyish excitement. "So *you* are the 'coffee steward' everyone's talking about! Such a delight to meet you. Why the Hamptons are simply abuzz about Cuppa J this season. I confess that one of the reasons I invited David here tonight was to wheedle an invitation to sample his dessert parings for myself."

"Please do . . . I'd love to know what you think of what we're doing."

Matteo cleared his throat. "The car is here."

"Oh, no!" Bom exclaimed. He closed the distance between us, took my hand, folded it into his. "Please stay. I'm simply captivated by your charm and obvious experience, all wrapped in such a delightful little package."

Matteo was practically rolling his eyes. I ignored him.

"I'm sorry, but I really have to go. Matt's giving me a ride," I told Bom. "But you're very kind."

"On the contrary, I'm very selfish." He glanced at Matteo. "But I understand if you must leave."

"We must," said Matt, grabbing my elbow again and steering me toward the door. I felt like yanking it free but didn't want to cause a scene.

"Oh," I cried, stopping short. "Your robe and slippers."

"Keep them," Bom said with a wave of his hand. "Or better yet, return them later . . . when we can both chat—" he shot a pointed glance at Matt, "—privately."

I nodded. "Goodnight, Mr. Felloes—"

"Bom, Clare. Please call me Bom."

"Goodnight then . . . Bom."

I barely had the words out before Matt was hustling me through the mansion's huge front doors. I softly sighed as we stepped outside. Bom Felloes was successful, handsome, very wealthy, and apparently interested in me. I was crazy for keeping him on my suspect list. But I fully intended to.

Although I was flattered by his flirtation, I knew he still had a motive for hurting David. And, in the end, I knew wealthy, overly polished, perfect men ten years younger than me had never been my type anyway. (Honestly.) The rumpled, earthy, ironic toughs of the world were more my speed, men who'd been knocked around by life, who were somewhat rough around the edges. Mike Quinn and his crow's feet came to mind. Even Matt—before Breanne had gotten hold of him.

Outside the night had cooled even more. Landscape lighting had turned the mansion's castle-esque exterior and flowering grounds around it into a glowing wonderland.

Matt opened the door to Breanne's sleek silver Mercedes convertible now waiting at the bottom of the steps. I climbed in, sank into the fawn-colored custom leather, and faced The Sandcastle again.

Bom Felloes was standing there. He noticed my glance, smiled, and waved, looking as dashing and polished as a British lord.

I offered a tiny wave in return, not sure what I should be cursing more—his continued presence on my suspect list or my complete inability to reengineer my taste in men.

FOURTEEN

∿∿∿∿∿∿∿∿∿∿∿∿∿∿∿∿∿∿∿∿∿∿∿∿

WITHOUT a backward glance in Bom Felloes's direction, Matt climbed behind the wheel.

"Buckle up," he barked.

I barely got the strap over my shoulder when the engine under the silver Mercedes' hood sprang to life, a high performance purr. The radio came on with the engine. The "Music of Love," a sentimental ballad poured from the speakers. I actually liked the song, but Matt snapped it off with a sharp turn of his wrist, then shifted into first gear and stepped on the gas so hard the tires spun against the driveway's paving stones.

The Mercedes lurched forward, slamming me back into my seat. Matt steered the car around the horse circle too fast. It fishtailed for a second, and I thought we were going to end up in a flowerbed.

"You weren't very polite back there," I pointed out.

Matt shook his head as we left the front gate and turned onto the road. "Guys like that . . . they're a dime a dozen,

Clare. I've met them all over the world. Wannabe aristocracy. You can't trust him."

"Who do you mean?"

"You know who I mean. Who does he think he is with that 'let me put your slippers on' act, Cinderella Man?"

"Wasn't Cinderella Man that World Heavyweight Champion boxer? The one they made a movie about?"

"I meant *Prince Charming*, okay! But let me tell you, the charm turns into a pumpkin at midnight. And that British accent's about as real as the potted plants in a used car salesman's showroom. And what kind of name is that, anyway? *Bomb*? How can you trust a man named after a weapon of mass destruction!"

"It's Bom, Matt. B-O-M, the Portuguese word for good, and I know you know that. That's why his restaurants are called Good Felloes. And I know you know that too. You're just being difficult. And please slow down!"

Matt frowned, sighed, then slumped a bit in his seat as if giving up. His foot finally eased on the gas pedal, and it occurred to me he was now feeling the way I had when I first ran into him and Breanne at the party—jealousy, then confusion and embarrassment about feeling that way when you weren't supposed to anymore. Did all divorced couples feel that way? Possessive about a spouse they'd long since given up?

"So what were you doing at the party?" Matt asked, his voice calmer now, more reasonable.

"I told you. I was—"

"Looking for David, I heard what you said to Mr. Goodbar. I just don't buy it. In fact, what I really think is that you were looking for Mr. Right."

"Excuse me?"

"You're a smart woman, Clare. Too smart. I think you cooked the whole wet tee-shirt arrival up to make an impression on the celebrity chef. Well, I guess you got what you wanted. The act worked. He's interested."

In a word, I was furious. "I *was* looking for David. Something came up. I had to find him. Do you really think I risked pneumonia just to meet that man?" I lightly shook my still-wet hair to make my point.

"Careful," Matt irritably cautioned. "These leather seats were custom made for Bree."

"Oh, *were* they?" I narrowed my eyes, then shook my wet head again, this time with the vigor of a just-washed poodle. Water droplets sprayed the interior of Breanne's Mercedes. More than a few landed on Matteo's Helmut Lang suit jacket.

Matt smirked. "How immature."

"That's rich, coming from you."

Luckily, the trip to David's estate was too short for the two of us to continue our sorry little war.

"Turn here," I said, pointing.

As we swung into the driveway, the uniformed guard, who I'd met earlier, blocked our path.

"Who's this?" Matt asked.

"David has added some security," I said.

Matteo's eyebrow lifted with curiosity, but he didn't ask why.

I waved a greeting to the guard. "It's only me," I said as the young man approached, his flashlight moving from Matt's face to mine.

"I didn't know you left the grounds, Ms. Cosi."

"I went for a walk . . . and, uh, got a little wet."

The guard stared at Matt.

"This is Matteo Allegro," I quickly explained. "He's an associate of David's. He'd like to pop in and say hello, update David on some business they have together. David has come home, right?"

The guard nodded. "Mr. Papas brought him back about an hour ago, ma'am. Dropped Mr. Mintzer off and drove away."

"Good," I replied, relieved I did not have to deal with David's condescending and possibly dishonest restaurant manager. "We'll just pop up to the house. Mr. Allegro won't be long."

The guard paused, clearly wondering whether he should allow the Mercedes entry. "Come on," I coaxed. "I'll vouch for Matt."

Finally the man stepped aside and waved us forward.

Matt drove up and parked behind my Honda, which I'd left behind David's little sports car. The guard followed us up to the house and let us in with a passkey. Inside the lights were dim, the foyer deserted. No one was in the living room, either.

"Maybe David already went to bed," said Matt.

A moment later we found Alberta Gurt in the kitchen—in fact, we must have really startled her by entering because she dropped a crystal tumbler. An hour ago Alberta was fine; now she seemed agitated.

"Oh, my goodness! You gave me a scare!" she cried, grabbing a tea towel. She bent down to pick up the broken glass. "You really shouldn't sneak up on people like that!"

"I'm sorry," I said, although we really hadn't been sneaking and she should have heard our approach. I could only assume she'd been terribly distracted. But I didn't want to argue and make things worse. "Alberta, this is Matt Allegro, one of David's business associates. He's here to say hello. Has David retired?"

"He's in bed, and in no condition to talk," the woman said, dumping both the glass and the tea towel into the garbage. "Too many martinis, I thought. So I whipped him up one of my Fizzy Friendlies—"

"One of your what?" I asked.

"It's an anti-hangover drink David asks me to prepare

for him when he's partied too hearty, as he calls it. Usually the Friendly eases David's nausea and gets rid of his headache, and he goes right to sleep. But tonight it didn't help at all. He's moaning, in pain—David said he thinks he was poisoned—"

"Poisoned!" I cried.

"He's very sick," Alberta continued. "I don't know what to do. David's in a very bad mood. He says he wants to be left alone. I wanted to call Dr. Ramah, his physician, but—"

"Wait. I know Dr. Ramah. Isn't he in Manhattan?" I'd met the good doctor at a charity event connected to St. Vincent's Hospital in the Village. It was Madame's friend Dr. MacTavish who'd introduced us.

Alberta shrugged. "I didn't know who else to call. I don't know any doctors out here in the Hamptons."

"I'm going to look in on David right now." I headed out of the kitchen, Matt on my heels.

Alberta hurried to catch up. "He's in a very bad mood," she warned, her voice strained.

I kept walking. "You said that already, Alberta. But don't worry. I don't care if he fires me in a fit of pique. I already have another job."

When I reached the bedroom door, I could hear David moaning on the other side. I gently tapped on the wood, then opened the door a crack. Super air-conditioned air rolled over me.

"Why is it so cold in here?" I asked alarmed.

Alberta said she'd pumped up the temperature herself because David had always claimed that lying in a cold, dark room alleviated his migraine symptoms in the past. Still soaked under the robe, I shivered.

"David," I called, barely above a whisper. "It's me. Clare."

"Go away," David replied in a quivery voice. "I'm sick."

With the limited light streaming through the partially open door, I could see David lying under a tangle of blankets. He lay on his side, his back facing me, pillow over his head.

"I know you're sick, David . . . Alberta told us."

"Us?"

"Matteo is here too. He came to say hello. But if you're sick—"

David moaned. "God, Clare, I'm not up to socializing. I'm dying here . . . I think I've been poisoned."

"Poisoned! By whom?"

He moaned again. "That bastard Felloes. I knew I shouldn't have eaten anything at his party."

"You think Bom Felloes tried to poison you?" *Ohmygod, ohmygod*, I thought. *I was right. Felloes had the motive and the opportunity. He must have hired the contract killer that mistakenly shot Treat.* "We have to call the police. O'Rourke needs to hear that your neighbor is the one trying to kill you—"

"Kill me! God, no. No, no, no! Please, Clare, don't go off the deep end again! I'm not saying he poisoned me literally—or even intentionally. The man uses what I call 'poison' at that slop house he calls a gourmet restaurant, but I never would have believed Felloes had the nerve to feed his guests that vile stuff."

"Stuff? What stuff?" I demanded.

"MSG. Monosodium glutamate . . . I think I must have CSR—"

"CSR? My god, what's that?" Matteo asked. "It sounds lethal."

"It's Chinese restaurant syndrome," David informed him, moaning again.

"Are you kidding?" asked Matt, shooting me a skeptical look. "That can't be a real syndrome—"

"I assure you that's the shorthand term doctors use,

even though they acknowledge you can get it at any restaurant that uses the food additive, and in a lot of processed food, too. Cramps, headache—"

David gagged, flopped on the bed like a fish out of water. He settled in a moment, let out a painful sigh. "Just go away," he wailed.

I pulled Matt and Alberta back into the hallway and closed the door. "Where's the nearest hospital? I think David needs medical care."

"The only emergency room I know of out here is Southampton Hospital, and that's fifteen miles away," said Alberta.

Though he wasn't much bigger than me, it would be no easy feat getting David Mintzer out of bed and down to the car, and brother was I glad Matt was there to help. An ambulance would have made more sense, but David absolutely, positively refused to go along with that.

"We do this quietly, or not at all," he said, face pale from the pain, dark circles beneath his eyes. "Either I go to the hospital on my own power or I'll die in this bed."

I closed my eyes. *Again that ugly word . . . die.*

"We'd better take the Mercedes," I told Matt. "It's faster and more reliable than my clunky old Honda, and the three of us will barely fit into David's sports car."

"Hold on, the Mercedes isn't my car—"

"Don't be petty, Matt. A man's life may be at stake here. Now help me."

But instead of moving to David's bed, Matt took out his cell phone. "What are you doing?" I demanded.

"I'm calling Breanne. I'll tell her what's happened so she won't get stuck at Bom's bash."

I reached out and closed the phone. "You can't tell Breanne anything. Breanne will blab everything to her friends, to people at the party. David won't like it."

"Clare, don't be absurd. Bree wouldn't do that."

"Matt, she's a magazine editor. Her stock and trade is gossip. Gossip about the latest trends. Gossip about the rich and famous. She'd sell her best friend down the river for a ten-percent increase in circulation. Now put that phone away and help me!"

Matt rolled his eyes, slipped the phone into his jacket and helped me sit David up. Mintzer groaned and clutched his head, suddenly dizzy. He wore oversized red silk pajamas, which made him appear small, frail, and very pale. His skin felt clammy.

"We have to hurry," I said.

Alberta led the way, opening doors and clearing obstacles as Matteo and I half-carried, half-dragged the limp man down the stairs and across the living room to the front door.

The guard came over to help, and I took the opportunity to race to my room. Inside of two minutes, I tore off Bom's robe, stripped off my wet clothes, and threw on a fleecy jogging suit. My sneakers were on the beach, and I didn't take any time to look for another pair, so I ran back to the front door still wearing Bom's royal-blue slippers.

Outside, the guard had opened the car door for Matt, who was helping David into the back seat. Alberta brought a quilt and wrapped it around her shivering boss.

"I'll call if anything happens," I told the housekeeper.

Chewing her lip, Alberta nodded.

Matt started the engine and pulled away.

"Oh god, oh damn," David moaned. "I think I'm gonna throw up!"

"Not on Bree's leather upholstery!" Matt cried, hitting the brakes.

Unfortunately, his warning came too late.

FIFTEEN

~~~~~~

Dr. Richard De Prima, intense and thirtyish in a white lab coat, with prematurely graying hair and a golden golfer's tan, leafed through papers on a clipboard. His eyes scanned the pages then stalled on a long block of text. Finally the doctor looked up.

"Good thing you brought him in."

"How bad is it?" I asked. Matt and I were standing with the doctor just outside an ER examining room. David was still inside.

"Mr. Mintzer complained of a burning sensation in the chest, shoulders, abdomen, forearms, and back of the neck. He felt bouts of numbness in his face, along with fairly constant abdominal pains, which are still persisting. He's experiencing heart palpitations, and when he first entered the hospital he was wheezing, which indicates difficulty in breathing—and that indicates to me that Mr. Mintzer was very close to anaphylactic shock."

"Oh, god." I looked at Matt.

He squeezed my shoulder. "Then we did the right thing, bringing him in? Right, doctor?"

"Yes, of course," De Prima replied. "And the patient said he'd vomited on the way to the hospital?"

Matt sighed. "Repeatedly."

"That's actually good," De Prima noted. "We would have had to pump his stomach if he hadn't."

"What's wrong with him?" I asked.

"I administered an antihistamine, a standard precaution with such a powerful and dangerous allergic reaction—"

Matt blinked. "He nearly died because of an allergy?"

"A rather common sensitivity to MSG. That's mono-sodium glutamate—"

"Yes, yes, I know what it is," I said. "And so does Matt. But we didn't know until tonight that David had an adverse reaction to MSG. Apparently, he's known for a long time. That's why he's tried to avoid the additive."

Dr. De Prima offered me an indulgent smile. "Ms. Cosi, MSG is so prevalent in our modern diet that it is difficult to avoid completely. There are over forty different names to represent MSG found on food labels. It's called every-thing from the euphemistic 'hydrolized proteins' to 'natu-ral flavorings'—perhaps the biggest lie of all."

Matt cleared his throat. "Bottom line, please doctor. Will David be all right?"

The doctor nodded. "We're keeping him here overnight, mostly for observation. The danger's passed."

"You're sure?" Matt pressed.

"The effects last one to four hours, but in a dosage as high as Mr. Mintzer has ingested, it could last longer. The antihistamines should help. When the effects fade, Mr. Mintzer will feel weak and tired for another day or so—a feeling not unlike a hangover—but he should return to his old self in forty-eight to seventy-two hours."

"Can we see him?" I asked.

"Sorry, I can't allow that," advised the doctor. "He needs his rest. The trip here took a lot out of him."

"You can say that again," quipped Matt.

"Doctor, you said that David consumed a large amount of MSG. How do you know?" I asked.

"It had to be a large amount to elicit such a powerful reaction. The intensity of the allergy attack is directly proportional to the amount of MSG absorbed."

I shook my head. "But David said he just ate a little at the party he'd attended tonight."

"From his reaction, he consumed quite a bit," the doctor insisted. "In fact, it's a good thing you brought him in. He had so much MSG in so short a time that with his personal sensitivity to the substance, he could have died."

Matt and I said very little after we returned to the parking lot. I waited outside Breanne's Mercedes while Matteo cleaned the back seat with clumps of paper towels he'd grabbed from the hospital's men's room.

I offered to help, but he waved me off. So, while he held his nose and wiped out the back seat, I watched moths flutter around the parking lot lights. It was close to three in the morning and the only sounds I heard were the constant cricket chirps and the wind rustling the trees.

Matt slipped his jacket over my shoulders to keep me warm while he took the convertible's top down "to blow out the stink." A moment later, we were heading back to David's mansion, the wind in my salt-encrusted hair. As we drove in silence, I tried to process the events of this crazy night.

It was apparent to me that a second attempt had been made on David Mintzer's life—nothing I could prove, of course, but apparent to *me*. It also seemed, at least at first glance, that the identity of the culprit was obvious.

There had been years of bad blood between David
Mintzer and Bom Felloes, as much a battle of inflated egos
as anything else, but real nonetheless. And while the elegant young restaurateur maintained publicly that he'd invited David to his party to "bury the hatchet," Felloes may
have also used the opportunity to slip David an MSG
mickey large enough to induce anaphylactic shock.

In its white powder form, monosodium glutamate was
practically tasteless. A large amount of the stuff could have
been added to almost anything David was ingesting at
Bom's bash, from the martinis to the peanut sauce that
dressed the seafood satay.

While my theory sounded good, there was one major
hole. The killer had to know about David's ultra sensitivity
to MSG. How would Bom have known it?

I myself had known David for nearly a year. I considered him a good friend, but I didn't know about his allergy.
Sure, at Cuppa J, we never used MSG, but that was a matter of food and beverage policy, one I happened to agree
with. I never knew it had anything to do with David's sensitivity to it.

But Alberta . . . she probably knew. After all, she knew
a lot about David, personal information gathered over the
years. She knew his likes and dislikes, the details about his
health and his frailties. And Alberta was one of the benefi-
ciaries in David's will. With David Mintzer dead, she stood
to benefit. Even if David left her a fraction of his estate, the
business interests owned by Mintzer were so vast that the
value of the inheritance would still be immense.

But was a big cash payoff enough to motivate Alberta
Gurt to murder her employer? Maybe.

While I found Alberta a pleasant and likeable individ-
ual, I also found the growing pile of circumstantial evidence against her very troubling. For instance, she'd
mentioned a nephew named Thomas she was very fond of,

a young man David had come to know and help. He'd even made Alberta's nephew a beneficiary in his will. This "Tommy" was, by Alberta's own admission, a troubled youth who'd paid his debt to society, straightened out his life, and entered the military, where he certainly would have learned how to handle a rifle. That would explain the rifle shells.

So . . . could Alberta and her nephew have plotted cold-blooded murder together? Could Alberta's "Tommy" have been the shooter on the Fourth of July? And when the nephew made his mistake and killed Treat Mazzelli, did Alberta try again to kill David tonight? She could have easily slipped a little MSG cocktail into his "Fizzy Friendly" anti-hangover elixir.

Now that I thought about it, the woman had been surprised and agitated when Matt and I came upon her in the kitchen. In fact, she'd been at the sink, washing out a tumbler, which she'd subsequently dropped. Was she destroying the evidence, cleaning the very glass she'd used to serve the poison cocktail to David?

I thought back to the night of the shooting. About how David came down with a migraine before the fireworks display—yet he told Madame that he didn't recall ingesting any of the foods that exclusively caused him to suffer migraines. Could someone have added MSG to something David had ingested? Maybe it was someone he trusted? Someone like Alberta Gurt?

And there was another thing that continued to bother me. Why had Alberta been dressed so well last night? She'd had on makeup and jewelry too, but she hadn't come to the party. She'd apparently just been spending the night alone in her room.

I played the scene back in my head. Now that I thought about it, the television had been off when she opened the door to her bedroom suite. Yet, before she'd opened it, I'd heard voices talking. Could those voices have been Alberta and her nephew? Could she have been hiding him when I knocked? Or had she simply turned the TV off before coming to the door?

Just when I thought I had everything tied up in a neat little package, I remembered the flipper prints in the sand. I didn't yet have an explanation for those—or the mysterious trespasser. Who was the frogman I'd spotted on Bom's beach and followed out to his boat? And what the hell had he been up to, swimming back and forth to a boat with its running lights turned off?

The whole business brought to mind one of my dear old dad's adages: *Cookie, anyone who's got to operate in the dark is probably up to no good.*

Then there was Jacques Papas and his suspicious ten percent deal. Did Papas know about David's allergy? He'd been at the Fourth of July party. And he'd given David a ride home. And I couldn't forget Marjorie Bright lurking in the trees *and* at Bom's party. I still remembered her less than "neighborly" tone. If anyone had a death wish for David, it was the acid Ms. Bright. But how would she have known about David's allergy? As my head began to spin, I realized Mike Quinn was right. Rich men definitely made more enemies than waiters.

I sighed. *Well*, I thought to myself, *at least I know one thing for certain* . . . "Someone tried to kill David tonight."

"What!" said Matt.

I squeezed my eyes shut. It was late and I was tired. I'd let my guard down and muttered the last dregs of my thoughts. Or . . . maybe it was just Freudian. Maybe I was feeling tired and alone, and I wanted Matt to help me. Either way, I knew I was stuck now. Or so I told myself. I had to spill everything to Matteo, and I did, recounting the shooting of Treat Mazzelli, the frogman footprints, the sighting of an actual frogman outside Bom's home earlier in the evening, my suspicions about Alberta Gurt and her nephew, Jacques Papas, and Marjorie Bright.

Matt's initial response was understandable. "And you let my daughter and mother stay in that house!"

"*You* try moving them," I cried, throwing up my hands and nearly knocking Matt's large suit-coat from my shoulders. "The two of them, together and individually—they're nearly as stubborn, pigheaded, and apparently *amoral* as you are."

"Get a grip, Clare."

"You get a grip. Okay, maybe the amoral snipe was out of line—but only for them. Anyway, I'm the only one who believes David is in danger. And your mother. Madame sees the danger, too—"

"You dragged my mother into your little thrill ride?"

"It's not a thrill ride, Matt."

"Are you sure about that? You're talking to a guy who was hooked on cocaine for years! Clare, a drug impairs your judgment. And this playing detective is obviously getting out of hand with you. It's a thrill ride all right. It's your drug and I'm starting to think it's also your obsession!"

"It's not a drug. It's not a thrill ride. And it's certainly not my obsession! It's a matter of life and death is what it is! I didn't ask for this to happen, but it did. Now we're talking about David's life. You saw for yourself what happened to him tonight."

Matt shook his head. "And I can't believe you're involving my mother again."

"Your mother's staying at David's. She was in the middle of everything as it unfolded." I shrugged. "She couldn't be held back. You know how she gets."

Matteo had nothing to say about his mother because he knew her even better than me. However, he did zero in on a bulls eye of another sort—

"I'm guessing David doesn't see things your way, does he?"

"Nobody sees things my way," I replied. "Not the police, and certainly not David, who's worse than anyone. David's in denial, though he may not have that luxury much longer given tonight's close call."

Matt drove on in silence while he considered my dilemma, the road's hum filling the void. We were almost in sight of David's mansion when Matteo finally spoke again.

"So what are you going to do now?"

I was surprised. For once my ex-husband's voice lacked its usual accusatory tone.

"I'm going to stick around and do what I can to prevent any harm from coming to David," I replied frankly. "Not to mention our daughter and your mother, both of whom are too stubborn to leave the mansion. And I'm going to find out who's trying to kill him and reveal the assassin's identity to the police, if that's possible."

Matt swerved into David's driveway and rolled the Mercedes up to the house. The guard waved us forward, nodding his head in greeting. Matt parked the Mercedes behind my Honda and faced me.

"What do you want me to do?" he asked.

I opened my mouth to speak, but the chirp of Matt's cell phone filled the car. I realized after a moment that the cell was in the pocket of the jacket I still wore around my shoulders. I fumbled around in the pockets until I found the phone, handed it to Matt. The cell stopped ringing as he took it from my hand.

Matteo slipped the phone into his shirt pocket and waited for my answer. The cell phone beeped three times. Three missed messages, all from Ms. Summour, no doubt.

I slipped the jacket off my shoulders and popped the door.

"Thanks for vouching for me at Bom's party, and for helping me get David to the hospital . . . I owe you, Matt—"

"Clare!"

"You better get back now. Hurry. Bree is waiting."

Sixteen

~~~~~~

Another day in paradise.

The next morning came all too soon. The sun broke through my windows with more brightness than I could handle, and my clean canvas of forgetfulness, that momentary innocence at early awakening, was quickly splattered with black recollections of the days before.

Skipping my usual morning swim, I rose and showered fast, deciding the one good thing I could say about the horrendousness of the last evening was that I'd found my daughter home safe and sound when I finally dragged myself upstairs. After looking into her room and finding her sleeping peacefully, I knew I'd be able to do the same.

My mother-in-law, however, was another matter. She'd gone missing. I'd found her room empty, her bedcovers unmolested, but I'd panicked for only a few minutes. Her message on the cell phone, which I'd left in my handbag, explained it all—

"Clare, dear, just letting you know, I'm spending the night at . . ." Her voice lowered, ". . . a friend's. I did receive your earlier message, the one about Graydon Faas. I'll ask around about that young man as well as Bom Felloes, and see what I can find out for you. I'll see you tomorrow, dear. Good night!"

I was still shaking my head over Madame's message as I blew my hair dry. She was spending the night at . . . "a friend's"? Her attempt to be discreet was almost laughable, I thought as I pulled on jeans and a yellow vee-neck tee-shirt. *I mean, really. That's one mystery I won't need help solving.*

After slipping into a pair of leather sandals and grabbing my handbag, I headed for the quiet kitchen. By rote, I prepared a doppio espresso and drank it down, savoring the crema (the rich caramel-colored layer that defines a properly drawn espresso). Fortified for the day ahead, I climbed into my Honda in the mansion's driveway. I tossed a wave at the security guard on duty, a new one since the night before, then drove off the mansion's grounds, down the country lane and towards the main road. My destination was west of Southampton on Montauk Highway—

Hampton Bays, NY.

The words were practically burned into my brain. They were the exact words that had been painted on the bow of *Rabbit Run*, the boat I'd seen floating offshore near Bom Felloes's mansion. The name and location of that boat were the only clues I had to finding my frogman, and, before I reported for work today, I hoped to locate the boat and its owner.

David's Suffolk County phone book listed eight marinas in Hampton Bays. I tore out a page and took it with me on my drive, determined to check as many marinas as I could in the time I had.

Luck was with me, because I struck gold on the second try. Monroe's Marina had maybe sixty vessels moored in its slips. I parked my car in the small lot and walked the dozen or so long docks, reading the boat names. After about ten minutes of searching, I spotted *Rabbit Run*, a thirty-five-foot inboard of white fiberglass.

Gotcha.

In the light of day, I could see the "boat" was really a power yacht. The helm was weather protected under a hard top, and there appeared to be a salon and galley below the deck, maybe even a sleeping berth.

From the dock, I looked for any sign of human activity aboard, someone I could speak with, but the yacht looked deserted. And so did the marina. I squinted against the glare of the morning sun, spotted a middle-aged couple on a sailboat at one end of the marina and a young man emerging from a mid-size yacht on the other. But that was it for human activity.

At seven in the morning in a resort area like this, most people were still sleeping off their partying from the night before. Any serious fishermen would have already taken their crafts out at dawn. And judging by the expensive-looking yachts in this marina, I'd say nobody was actually "serious" about much of anything here except maybe their pleasure.

I checked my watch again and sighed. If I were a professional P.I., I could have waited around here all day for someone to show up and board *Rabbit Run*. But at the moment I was being paid for my barista-management talents, not my sleuthing ones, so I had only a few free hours before I'd be expected at work for the Saturday lunch shift, one of the busiest times of the restaurant's week.

I'd have to bite the bullet, I decided, and speak with the people running the marina. Certainly, they'd know who owned this vessel. The only question was—would they tell me? I'd have to concoct a good story for them to give away what they might very well consider to be private client information. But if I could persuade them, I'd have a name and a solid lead.

I walked over to the marina office, a squat gray building located between the parking lot and the water. I turned the handle on its front door, but it was locked up tight. There was no closed sign in the window, no hours posted. I peered in the window, knocked.

No answer. No sign of anyone.

With my morning caffeine still coursing through my molecules, spurring me on, I decided to take another plunge— so to speak. I walked back to the slip mooring *Rabbit Run*. With one more careful look around, I boarded her. If my luck continued to hold, I figured I could find some sort of lead on the identity of the man who'd been doing the frogman act (and, of course, swim fins and a hunting rifle with fresh fingerprints wouldn't hurt, either).

I stepped onto the polished wood deck of the stern, but didn't see any personal items. There was nothing telling in the helm area, either—just two leather seats, a steering wheel, and a whole lot of technical bells and whistles.

I went below, and I checked the salon and galley. There were some dried spills of liquids on the bolted-down coffee table, a few wrappers on the floor. I picked them up— Twinkies? A half bag of Doritos had been left in the small galley (reportedly Saddam Hussein's favorite snack, but I doubted very much the deposed Iraqi dictator was my frogman). I also found six empty Sam Adams beer bottles and a few Coke cans.

I found more trash in a small container below the sink. But there wasn't much in there, just a few more Twinkie wrappers, also the kind of thick cellophane that gourmet food stores use to wrap sandwiches, and some newspapers— yesterday's editions of *Newsday* and the *New York Times* sports section.

Nothing. I found nothing to indicate an identity of the owner or any reason someone would have been in diving gear at night near Bom's mansion.

I continued to move forward below the yacht's deck, opening up the door to the sleeping berth. There was a comfortable-looking double bed, portholes, but no personal items. I was about to inspect the small head when I heard voices outside. It sounded like two young women talking and laughing.

"Girls!"

The third voice was deep, a man's, coming from far away.

I knew I had to stay below, but I wanted to see who these people were. I moved back into the sleeping berth and peeked out the porthole to see if I could glimpse what was going on.

Two slender young women of about sixteen or seventeen wearing worn jeans and tee-shirts stood on the next dock over. Approaching them was a gray-haired portly man in khakis and a blue Windbreaker. I strained to hear what he was telling them.

". . . busiest weekend of the year, so don't waste any time. Here are the boats that came in late last night. Start cleaning them in this order and be quick about it."

After the portly man turned and stalked away, one of the girls gave an exaggerated salute behind his back. The other rolled her eyes. They consulted the list for a second then both looked up, straight at *Rabbit Run*.

"Oh, damn," I whispered, reactively pulling back from the porthole. Of course, my luck had just run out. They were heading right for me, and not slowly.

I knew I couldn't very well scramble onto the dock now. If I did, they would see me leaving the yacht. In itself, that might not produce any dire consequences. The girls were young, clearly just a couple of local kids hired to keep the rentals clean. They'd probably shrug off my exit, and I could get in my car and drive away without being charged with trespassing. But it would also mean I'd leave here without any good leads.

Come on, Clare, think of something!

But I couldn't. And the girls were getting closer—

". . . and he said he wanted my digits, so I gave them. I really thought he'd call me, you know?"

"You can't expect that anymore. Some guys just collect numbers. It's like little trophies or something to them. You know, to brag to their loser friends."

My imagination continued to fail me, but I knew Madame would have found a way out of this. My dear old dad would have, too, for that matter.

That's it!

I almost laughed out loud when I realized that each of them—the bookie and the grand Manhattan lady—would have resorted to exactly the same thing in this situation.

Bribery.

Digging into my handbag, I found two twenty-dollar tips from waiting tables the night before. I shoved them into a front pocket of my jeans then quickly moved to the cabin's salon and sat down on the built-in couch, crossing my legs like it was my plan all along to just wait here for the girls to find me. Their last snippets of conversation gave me the final bit of inspiration I needed—

"That's pretty shitty. I mean, why are guys like that?"

"Are you kidding? Romance is a joke. Guys are so cheap. It's like in their DNA—"

The girls had come down the stairs together, each carrying a bucket filled with cleaning products. But they pulled up short and gaped when they saw me just calmly sitting on the cabin couch.

"Excuse us," said the first one, a blond with a short ponytail and a light dusting of freckles across her nose. "We didn't know Mr. Monroe rented this yacht out already."

"He didn't," I told them levelly.

The blond exchanged a nervous glance with her partner, a brunette with ruddy cheeks and hair in a long French braid.

"Well . . ." said the brunette slowly, "should you be on here then?"

"No. I shouldn't. But I couldn't help myself. You see I'm only here because of true love."

The girls eyes widened. They exchanged glances again, but not nervous ones. They were clearly now excited and curious.

"You see, I was having a drink at Bay Bar, you know the one, in Southampton, where the boats can just pull up and dock?"

The girls nodded enthusiastically. No doubt they'd heard of it. I wouldn't have been surprised if they'd even gotten into the popular place using fake IDs.

"Well, there I was," I continued, "minding my own business when this man sent me a bottle of champagne."

Again their eyes went wide.

"He sent you a whole bottle?" the blond asked.

I nodded. "It was Cristal. It must have cost him five hundred dollars."

"And he didn't even know you?" the brunette asked.

"I think it was love at first sight," I said. "For me it was. The moment I saw him and our eyes met . . . I knew."

The blond's mouth gaped. "You knew?"

I nodded again. "I knew he was the one."

The two exchanged glances and sighed.

"I was about to ask the man to join me when I saw him answer his cell phone. I think it must have been a personal emergency or something, because he threw down some cash at his table and raced off to his boat. And that's the last time I saw him."

"You mean you didn't even get his name?" the brunette asked. Both girls look absolutely horrified.

"I followed him out to the dock, but by that time, he was already motoring away. The only clue I had to finding him was the name of this boat."

I did my very best to look devastated, and the two girls stared at me for a long, silent moment.

"I don't know how to tell you this, ma'am," the blond said, "but this is a rental. We don't know who the man is you met last night. Whoever he is, he rented the boat to go out late. And we just work in the mornings."

"She should just go talk to Mr. Monroe," the brunette told the blond.

But the blond shook her head. "Monroe will never give her that info. He always says all rentals are confidential."

The brunette shrugged. "Then I guess she's out of luck."

"Girls," I said softly. "If you would do me the favor of looking up the name of the man who rented this boat last night, I'd be so very grateful." I placed the two twenty dollar bills on the small coffee table bolted to the floor in front of the salon's couch.

The girls stared at the twenties. Then they looked at each other.

"It'd be really easy to look it up, Janice, you know that," the blond whispered to the brunette. "Monroe's always schmoozing outside with the owners."

"I don't know, Pam . . ."

"Come on, Jan, you heard the lady. It's, like, for true love!"

Inside of a minute, the girls had finished their debate and took me up on my offer. The brunette named Janice went topside and returned with news on her boss's whereabouts. As they'd predicted, Monroe was already out of the office, hanging at the other end of the marina, chatting with the young yachtsman on the deck of his boat.

Under the pretense of needing more cleaning supplies, the blond named Pam returned to the office and let herself in. She came back in record time, but the look on her face was one of defeat.

"I snagged the only notation I could find for yesterday under *Rabbit Run*. No address and no name. Just a phone number. Weird." She handed me a yellow Post-it note with the number scrawled on it.

"Sorry, ma'am," said Janice. "Guess that's the best we can do. Want your money back?"

"Not a dime," I told them. "This is perfect. This is all I need."

I climbed off *Rabbit Run* and didn't . . . *run* that is. I was tempted to, but I walked instead, very casually toward my car. I could see the portly owner at the other end of the marina, still chatting with that yachtsman. The last thing I wanted to do now was call attention to myself.

I got behind the wheel and pulled out. When I reached the highway, I looked for a spot to park and make a cell phone call. The phone rang once, twice, three times—

"Yeah?"

The voice was low and gruff. I'd slept next to the man long enough to know that I'd just woken him up.

"Sorry, Matt."

A yawn was his reply. "Uh . . . what time is it?"

"Who is it, darling?"

My spine stiffened, though not voluntarily. Over the years, I'd heard enough female voices in the background of calls to my ex-husband to have developed an autonomic response.

"It's nobody, Bree," Matt called, away from the receiver. "Just business."

"Oh, so now I'm 'nobody'?" I teased.

"Hold on a second," Matt told me pointedly.

A muffled conversation ensued in the background, concluding with the words ". . . I'll take it in the bathroom." A door closed. Then Matt's voice came back on the line. He was whispering.

"What's wrong, Clare? Something had better be wrong

for you to call me so early when you, of all people, should know how late I went to bed."

"Matt, I can only assume you went to bed. Whether you got any sleep is another matter entirely."

"What's that supposed to mean?"

"According to what you said last night, you and Bree were just casual friends."

"We are."

"So you're just casually sleeping with your casual friend?"

"Get to the point. Why are you calling?"

"I need your help."

"Again?"

"I'll owe you again."

"You're getting to owe me a lot."

"Matt, please. Considering what you pulled during our marriage, don't you think it's the other way around. I mean, remember the time when you—"

"Okay! Point made. What do you want me to do? Drive you to Nova Scotia for some salmon? Or maybe David's got a craving for an authentic egg cream. I should be able to drive to Brooklyn and back in about six hours. Or maybe—"

"That won't be necessary, but thank you for offering. What I need is for you to punch something into your PDA."

A frustrated exhale followed.

"What's the matter?" I asked. "Did you lose it?"

"It's in my suit jacket. In the bedroom."

"Where are you?"

"In the bathroom. I didn't want to disturb Bree."

"You mean you didn't want Bree to know you were talking to your ex-wife."

"I meant what I said."

"Ooooh, I get it. Talking to *me* is something that disturbs Bree."

"Bingo."

"Well, I can't help it, Matt. What I need involves your using your PDA."

"Which, like I said, is in the room where Bree is right now."

I really should have bit my tongue, but I couldn't stand hearing Matteo Allegro, fearless Third World coffee trader and extreme sport junkie, twist himself into a pretzel for that designer-draped python.

"What are you?" I asked, hoping at least to give him a reality check. "Afraid of her or something?"

"Clare, please. Just wait a minute, okay?"

I drummed my fingers on the dashboard and watched a gull wing its way inland. Finally, my ex-husband came back on the line.

"Okay. I've got it."

"Are you back in the bathroom?"

"Yes, as a matter of fact. Why?"

"I just think it's amusing. She's forcing you to do business in the place where you do your—"

"Yeah, very funny. Now do you want my help or do you want me to hang up?"

"Help."

"Fine," he said. "Shoot."

"Not literally, I hope."

"*Clare*—"

"I need you to go online and use the reverse phone directory," I told him. "I'll give you the area code and number. Punch it in and let me know what address you get."

"Jesus, Clare . . ."

"What?"

"Tell me you're not playing detective again."

"I'm not playing detective again."

"Then why do you want me to do this?"

"I'm following a lead."

"You're playing detective again!"

"Lower your voice, Matt. You'll disturb Bree."

"I'm not helping you, Clare."

"Why not?"

"Because I don't want to enable you."

"Enable me?!"

My mood had been relatively lighthearted up to that moment. I'd used my wits, took a chance that paid off, and found a solid lead. But that single phrase not only pushed my buttons, it sent me into outer space.

"For god's sake, I'm not a drug addict!" I practically shouted into my cell. "I told you last night, I'm trying to help David. Do I have to remind you what I put up with during those days when *you* were an addict?! *Enable me!* You've really got a lot of nerve laying drug psycho-jargon on me!"

"Christ, Clare, take it easy! I'll help you, all right. Just calm down."

I did. Then I gave Matt the phone number. He punched it into the internet site with the reverse directory. Easy as pie, the answer was there. He gave me the address attached to the number.

"That's very close to where I am now," I said. "Is there a name?"

"Only a first initial and last name . . . someone named S. Barnes."

"Thanks, Matt. Just one more favor . . ."

He groaned. "What?"

"Since you're still in the Hamptons, I'd like you to go by the hospital and check on David. You said you wanted to talk to him anyway, right? Give him the update on how the Village Blend kiosk installations are going on the West Coast?"

"Right."

"So go visit and hang around for a while. Keep an eye out for anything suspicious."

"*Suspicious*? Clare—"

"Please, Matt."

There was a long silent pause.

"Okay?" I pressed.

"Okay, Clare. You win. Okay."

Seventeen

~~~~~~~~~~~~~~~~~~~~~~~~~~~~~~~~~

S. Barnes lived on Gate Street, a tiny lane in the hamlet of Bridgehampton—population approximately fourteen hundred.

Back in its heyday, most of Bridgehampton's founding families were connected to the whaling industry. But today it's known for its stately traditional homes located on an elevated acre of the town's highly desirable Bridge Hill Lane area.

It was also known for its picturesque Main Street business district, but on the July Fourth weekend, traffic on that route was sure to be a horrorshow. So I did my best to avoid it, taking side roads through neighborhoods dominated by brick doll houses with modest yards.

Gate Street was located on the un-chic side of the highway, a secluded little lane lined with topiaries and post fences. A bubbling creek meandered out of a kettle hole and along the road until it vanished in a thick tangle of century-old trees, their roots partially exposed.

The address Matt gave me belonged to a small ranch, a

typical 1960s tract house (what canny realtors were lately referring to as "mid-century dwellings"). Surrounded by trees, it sat on a nice stretch of yard that sloped gently down to the edge of that pretty little bubbling creek.

I passed the house once, then circled the block for a second look. Lucky thing, too, because I came back in time to see the front door open and a man step outside. Before he noticed me, I swung into a parking spot between two SUVs, cut my Honda's engine and slid across the front seat to watch him.

He locked the front door, then checked the mailbox, running his fingers through a shaggy mane of copper hair. Tall, with long legs encased in scuffed denims, he had a rugged build with broad shoulders evident under an electric-blue diver's shirt. I spied a smudge of color on his muscled forearm—a tattoo? From this distance I could only guess.

The man crossed the lawn and little bridge over the creek, and mounted a motorcycle parked at the curb. A moment later, he sped off. I watched him head toward Main Street. Just around the corner I'd seen a newsstand, a bakery, and a diner. Was he going for a quick newspaper? A fast pastry? Or a long breakfast?

I waited ten minutes, until I was sure he wasn't coming back right away. Then I climbed out of my car, walked across the street and little bridge, and approached the house. The front door was locked, of course, but the man had left a large bay window open, its lacy curtains billowing in the ocean-tinged breeze. I scanned the neighborhood, saw absolutely no one on the street or lurking on a porch or yard, so I walked over to the window and peeked inside.

I couldn't see much because the interior of the house was dark. I strained my ears, but heard no sounds—no radio, no television, no footsteps or voices. All I heard were the bees humming around the pink and red rose bushes in the yard. I was fairly certain the man had left the house completely empty.

Cautiously, I followed a concrete path to the rear of the dwelling, past a coiled garden hose and a brick barbecue pit. There was no porch, only two concrete steps that led up to the back door. The screen door was closed, the wooden door wide open. I knocked, not quite sure what I would say if someone actually answered. Fortunately no one did, so I tested the screen door. It was unlocked, and I entered.

I knew I was taking a big risk. *Huge.* This wasn't a rental boat in an open marina, this was a private home. And the muscular man who'd left it didn't strike me as a softee who'd fall for a pathetic story about Cristal champagne and true love. If I were caught, the guy could have me arrested for breaking and entering—if he didn't decide to break my head first. Nevertheless, with the windows open, I reasoned I could hear the sound of the motorcycle engine approaching and slip away before I was discovered.

The back door led to a tidy little kitchen with French Provincial-style cherrywood cabinets, spotless white walls, stove, and refrigerator. My eyes were drawn to the familiar silver and octagonal shape of a stovetop espresso pot on the back burner.

"Okay," I reassured myself. "He makes his own espresso. He can't be all bad."

The sun streamed through a large window above the sink. A healthy spider plant hung above it. In a dish rack, three glasses and two dishes were lined up to dry. The only sign of disorder in this room was the overflowing trashcan. I noticed it was filled with fast food containers, crinkled up Dorito bags, and Twinkie wrappers. Lined up next to it were empty Sam Adams beer bottles, no doubt waiting to be recycled.

Well, now I've got a clue what this guy lives on.

I also knew this was the right address.

Still . . . something didn't add up. The scruffy rogue on the motorcycle who left Twinkie wrappers, Dorito bags, and beer bottles in his wake didn't strike me as the kind of guy who kept an immaculate kitchen and made his own espresso.

"Hello?" I called, still wary of being discovered. My voice sounded hollow in the empty house so I quickly moved to the next room.

If the kitchen seemed like it belonged to another tenant, the living room seemed to belong in another house. The space was adorable and very feminine, with shades of pink the dominant color scheme and ruffled everything. The chair, the sofa, the flowery wall paper, the wall-to-wall carpeting, the tablecloths and curtains, were all cast in tastefully combined hues of rose, salmon, pink carnation, and subtle reds. Scattered about the too adorable room were scented candles, sachets, colorful quilts, and empty vases ready to be filled with fresh cut flowers.

Now I started to wonder if I should introduce Motorcycle Man to my head barista, Tucker Burton. Either the guy was bucking for a spot on *Queer Eye for the Straight Guy*, or he was married to Homemaker Barbie.

I found the bedroom next, its door ajar. Once again, things didn't compute. The tidy order of the rest of the house was no longer evident. Was it possible, I wondered, for a hurricane to blow through just one room?

The queen-size bed was rumpled and unmade, clothing hung from chairs, and two posts of the four-poster bed frame. Two pairs of socks and sneakers were scattered on the floor, along with a pair of dirty boat shoes and another enigma. Magazines were stacked high against the wall with dumbbells as paper weights: *Teen People*, *Celebrity*, *Diva*, *Star Watch*, *Guns and Ammo*, and *Soldier of Fortune*. What kind of a person would subscribe to that schizo mix?

In the corner, I saw folding chairs and a card table had been set up. On the table were several digital cameras, a laptop computer, and a photo printer. Next to the printer I found two neat stacks of photographs. I picked up the first stack, which consisted entirely of shots taken at David Mintzer's Fourth of July party—celebrity photos mostly, though there were several pictures of David himself. The second stack were photos taken at Bom Felloes bash the next day, including several shots of Keith Judd. I put the photos down and continued looking around the room.

A second bedroom door led to a bathroom with a large glass-enclosed shower stall. Inside the stall I saw a tangle of rubber hoses, three large air tanks, two pairs of swim fins, and several pairs of underwater goggles. They'd been carefully cleaned. Sea salt and seaweed still encrusted the shower's drain.

For the second time in as many hours I thought—*Gotcha*.

I couldn't help feeling the rush. I smiled as I backed out of the bathroom, deciding I'd found the lair of the Creature from the Black Lagoon. For now, I'd seen enough. Unfortunately, I was about to see more than I'd bargained for.

At the distinct click-clock of a weapon cocking, I spun and found myself facing the business end of a very large handgun. Motorcycle Man had leveled it directly at my heart.

"Now ordinarily, finding a tight little package in my bedroom is not something a man like me would object to." His voice was low, even, and unexpectedly casual. "But since you're here without an invitation, you can understand why I'm a little bit peeved."

I didn't know how it happened. I'd never heard the rumble of his motorcycle engine. I'd never heard him opening the front door. Yet here the man stood with the drop on me that I'd been sure he'd never get.

"Please put the gun down. I'm unarmed."

He studied me, his brown eyes weren't so much angry as

curious. His fortyish face was weathered, his jawline strong but brushed with stubble, the day's growth of beard a shade darker than his shaggy copper hair. I noticed a small earring in his left ear, a dagger with a jewel in the hilt.

"Breaking and entering is a crime, you know?"

"You've got the gun." I spoke as calmly as I could, given the circumstances. I was plenty scared, but I knew if I wanted control of this situation, I'd have to start by controlling my own emotions. "You can just call the police. And they can cuff me and haul me off to jail. *Or* you can put that weapon away and we can talk like civilized people."

He didn't put the weapon away, or even lower it. "Sit down," he said, gesturing to the bed behind me.

I sat on the edge of it.

"Good. Follow my instructions and we'll get along just fine. Now you talk. And I'll listen. Got it?"

I nodded.

"Who are you?"

I saw no point in lying. "Clare Cosi. Who are you?"

His gaze went cold. "How quickly we forget. This is how it works, Clare. You talk, I listen. Remember? Now who do you work for?"

"I'm a barista manager and, technically speaking, also a coffee steward, at Cuppa J . . . that's a restaurant . . . in East Hampton."

He blinked. Obviously that was not the answer he expected to hear. "Wait a minute. That's Mintzer's new place, right? The one that's getting all the write-ups this season?"

I nodded, he frowned. "So you work for David Mintzer?"

I didn't reply.

"Listen sweetheart, take my advice, when a guy's got a gun on you, answer his questions."

I folded my arms, trying my damnedest to mask my fears with bravado. "When a guy's got a gun on me who hasn't shot me yet, I don't think he's going to."

Almost imperceptibly, the man's dark eyes widened. "You're willing to take a chance like that?"

"Mr. Barnes," I continued reasonably, "I'm trusting my own judgment. If you were going to shoot me, you would have done it already."

"Mr. Barnes, huh?" He smirked. "How the hell did you track me down?"

"I saw you on the beach last night, outside The Sandcastle. I couldn't see the name of your boat from the shore, so I took a little late night swim."

"You *swam* out to my boat?"

"Yes."

"Last night?"

"That's right, Mr. Barnes."

"Christ, I must have been sixty or seventy yards offshore. I'm surprised you didn't get hypothermia."

"I didn't say it was easy. Or smart for that matter. But I got the name of the yacht you rented. I found your marina, and bribed a couple of very sweet Bonackers."

"Where the hell do you get your nerve, Clare Cosi?"

"Eight to ten cups of coffee a day. At least."

The man actually laughed. Then, to my great relief, he lowered his weapon, put on the safety, and tucked it behind him, presumably into a holster fastened to his belt at the base of his spine—the same place my ex-husband carried when he went coffee hunting in Africa.

"That's better," I said, rising from the bed. "Guns make me nervous . . . especially when they're pointed in my general direction."

The man folded his muscled arms and regarded me, about a foot below him. "If I were you, Clare, I wouldn't let my guard down in a situation like this one." His dark eyebrow arched. "What makes you think I won't beat the truth out of you?"

"Oh, puh-leeze!" I threw up my hands. "This is the

Hamptons. What are you going to do? Flog me with a Louis Vuitton briefcase? Anyway, Mr. Barnes, my partner knows where I am and if anything should happen to me—"

"Spare me. You don't have a partner. That gambit is so tired, I doubt even you would buy it. Besides which, I saw you watching me from your Honda across the street. You were alone."

"You saw me?"

"And if we're going to talk like 'civilized people,' you can stop calling me Mr. Barnes because there is no Mr. Barnes—"

"What?"

"Sally Barnes is the woman who owns this place. She rents it out every summer . . . and for too damn much money if you ask me."

"Well, that explains it," I muttered.

"Explains what?"

"The Barbie-pink living room and rogue-male bedroom. The beer bottles and Twinkie wrappers and the neat kitchen and espresso pot. I take it you don't make your own?"

"Make my own what?"

"Espresso," I said. "Do you want a cup? I could really use one. Unless you really do know how to make your own, then by all means you can play host."

"Clare, I'm trying to follow you. But you're tempting me to go nuclear again—"

"Look, let me make you some coffee, okay? Then we actually can talk like civilized people." Before he could object, I pushed past him. He followed me out to the kitchen. I searched the cabinets and found a small vacuum-sealed bag of beans from a local gourmet store.

"Good. They're Arabica. Can't abide robusta. Arabica's the way to go—high grown, high quality."

"Excuse me?"

"Just talking out loud. It's a nervous habit."

I rummaged around some more, found a small grinder, burred the beans finely, then filled the bottom half of the pot with water, tamped the ground coffee tightly into the filter, and dropped the filter into place.

Motorcycle Man watched it all with intense fascination, arms folded, one lean hip resting against the counter. "It looks like you're making a bomb."

"Close enough. It's an Italian blast."

"Are you finishing anytime soon?"

"Just have to screw the two parts together." I did, sealing the pot's top to its bottom. I felt his eyes on me again and looked up.

He was smirking. "You screw very nicely, Clare."

I narrowed my gaze. "We're striving for civilized. Remember?"

The man snorted. He pushed his lean hips off the counter and took a seat at the kitchen table. His gaze stayed on me as I scrounged up two demitasses and a bowl of sugar.

The room filled with the heavenly aroma of the earthy, nutty beans, and I filled the cups with the hot, fresh espresso. I handed him one. He didn't ask for cream or milk, didn't touch the sugar.

"It's good," he said after a sip and then another. "Very good."

I gestured to an empty Twinkie wrapper. "Too bad I don't have time to make you my chocolate-walnut-espresso brownies. They pair much better with what your drinking now than your usual dessert, Mr.—"

He sighed as if surrendering. "It's Rand. Jim Rand." He reached his open hand across the table. "Nice to meet you, Clare."

I hesitated, but finally put my hand in his. We shook. The feel of his palm was rough. I began to pull away but he held on. His grip was powerful.

"What are you doing in my house?"

I swallowed, realizing how tiny my hand looked in his. "You said it wasn't your house."

"Tell me."

"I was snooping. You saw that."

"Why? Who are you really working for?"

"I told you. David Mintzer." I tugged my hand—hard. He let go.

"Clare, what you're telling me is nothing. Nothing that makes sense anyway. What were you looking for?"

I sat back, gulped some caffeine for courage. "I have some questions for you too, Mr. Rand. You're a professional photographer, right?" I said. "Or should I say paparazzi?"

"No comment."

"I'd also guess from your tattoo that you were in the Navy."

He glanced at the design on his arm, an eagle clutching a fouled anchor. "I was a SEAL, sweetheart, special operations. The night before I was mustered out, my SEAL team took me on a bender that started in San Diego and ended up in Tijuana, where I got this tattoo. I vaguely recall the event."

"I see."

"And I take it that you're a coffee-making private detective? Working for David Mintzer." He sat back in his chair, cup in hand, waiting for my reply.

"Now why do you think I'm a detective?"

"Because my partner in this business, Kenny Darnell, warned me that we'd occasionally get pictures that the rich and famous would not want to be made public."

"So private detectives bother you regularly, do they?"

Rand shrugged. "Not yet, but this is only my second summer doing this."

"Really?"

"In the Navy my specialty was reconnaissance photography. Now I'm pretty much making a year's salary in a few months, snapping exclusive photos of celebrities on or near private beaches and seaside homes for the tabloids, for newspapers, and gossip magazines. The rest of the year I spend in the Caribbean, diving, surfing, and generally having a life."

"And this is your retirement scheme?"

"Not mine," Jim replied. "My partner, Kenny Darnell, came up with the scheme. We were in the Navy together."

"He's a SEAL, too?"

Rand shook his shaggy head. "Kenny washed out during training, retired from the Navy soon after that. He's a great paparazzi, though. Started selling to the tabloids as soon as he got out of the service. But he wanted to expand, and to do that Kenny needed a partner to help with the capital, the equipment, the boat and house rentals. In case you haven't noticed, this part of Long Island is a tad expensive.

"I noticed. Where is your partner now?"

"Kenny went back to Queens. His mother's just had an operation, so he's taking two weeks off to help her out around the house."

We finished our espressos while Jim Rand told me more about his business.

"I'd like to see some samples of your work," I said.

"Like what?" he asked suspiciously.

"How about all the photos you took at David Mintzer's house on the Fourth of July?"

Jim wanted to say no, I could tell. But I also knew we'd made a connection. It seemed like he was beginning to trust me. Was he? Or was he just playing me?

"You're sure you're not a private investigator?" he asked skeptically. "You're too cute to be a shamus, but you never know."

I reaffirmed my prior claim and he rose, went back into the bedroom, and returned with the photos—more than in the original stack I'd found. I began going through them, not sure what I was looking for. More evidence maybe.

Halfway through the pile, Rand reached across the table, touched my arm. "Okay," he said. "I answered your questions. Now why are you here, Clare? Really."

I finally told him about Treat Mazzelli's murder, watched his face, his eyes as I gave him the highlights. The news still hadn't made the papers, though every Bonacker probably already knew the details. I told him about how I suspected David was the target, and how I was investigating the shooting.

Jim Rand didn't give much of a reaction to my tale. His sober face remained impassive. He simply listened and stared. "Wait," he said when I'd finally finished. "So you're claiming you're not a professional investigator, right?"

"Right."

"And you're not a cop?"

"Of course not."

"Then why are you involving yourself?"

"Treat worked for me. I was his manager. And David is my boss and my friend. I'm worried about his safety. I feel obligated to get involved."

Jim snorted again and shook his head. "You sound as gung-ho as my drill instructor. Or, as one of my former commanders used to say, 'you have an overwrought sense of justice.' Frankly, I find that . . ." He looked up just then, met my eyes, ". . . irresistible. You're not married are you?"

I looked away, then down at the photos and changed the subject, willing away a rather annoying primal reaction to the man's advances. He was ruggedly attractive, obviously intelligent, and my close proximity to his palpable maleness in this cozy little house was straining my nerves. But, given my discoveries in his bathroom, I had my doubts about Jim Rand. Major ones. My primary suspicion being the possibility of a hunting rifle stashed somewhere on these premises.

"You really didn't know about the murder on David's estate?" I asked, looking up again to gauge any sense of subterfuge, guilt, or nervous tension.

"God, no," Jim replied, apparently at ease. "Honestly, if I had known about the shooting, I would have stuck around to take photos of the police removing the body. I'm sorry about that kid. Nothing personal. But it would have been a helluva photo to sell, and the scoop with it. Unfortunately, I was gone long before the fireworks even started."

"Can I take these?" I asked.

Jim hesitated. "Are you really a barista?"

"Manager, yes. Are you really a scuba-diving paparazzi?"

Jim regarded me again with those intense brown eyes. "Why don't you come out with me tonight and see for yourself."

"Out? Where?"

"On the job. On the water. I miss having a partner out there. Kenny's been a real prick this season anyway, bitching night and day. It'll be fun, you and me. I'll show you what I do. After you see with your own eyes that I'm telling you the truth, you can cross me off your suspect list, and I'll give you any photo you like."

"Or you'll push me overboard," I countered.

"Guess it's the chance you'll have to take. But, you know, Clare, the edge is an exhilarating place to be." He smiled, his eyes bright. "And I think you know that or you wouldn't have risked coming in here."

I shoved the pictures across the table, stood up. "You're just like my ex-husband. And I'm late for work."

Jim scooped up the photos and followed me to the front door.

"Monroe's Marina in Hampton Bays. Midnight tonight," he pressed. "Come out with me."

"I have to work," I insisted. "Good-bye, Mr. Rand."

I walked briskly across the street to my Honda and slid behind the wheel. When I looked up from starting the engine, he was leaning on my car roof with one arm. My heart almost stopped, seeing him suddenly there. He'd followed me without casting a noticeable shadow. He'd stalked me without making a sound.

"Keep the hard copies, Clare," he said, passing the photos through the open car window. "I have the digital files."

I didn't thank him. I didn't say another word. I took the photos and pulled away without a backward glance. But half a block away, I couldn't resist a quick peek in my rearview mirror.

He stood in the middle of the road, legs braced, muscular arms folded, watching me go. Seeing him like that, I couldn't help comparing him to another man who'd watched me drive away less than twenty-four hours before—Bom Felloes.

Despite his polish, his fortune, and his absolute gentlemanly behavior, Bom had left me cold. Consequently, it had been easy to keep him on my suspect list. But Mr. Rand, however, was another matter entirely.

Regardless of my determination to remain aloof, I couldn't deny, at least to myself, that Jim Rand, with his scruffy masculinity and wry sense of humor, was most definitely my type. And that's why he was terribly dangerous for me to be around.

Rand was the most likely killer I'd come across yet, and I had an obligation to inform Detective O'Rourke about what I'd found. Which is why, with a final, regretful glance in my car's mirror, I once again cursed my inability to reengineer my taste in men.

Eighteen

~~~~~~

"**W**E'LL question him, Ms. Cosi. Thank you for the heads up."

"You're welcome."

The phone call with Detective O'Rourke had gone well, now that it had finally taken place. I had left a message for him well before our lunch shift. We were about to prepare for dinner and he'd just gotten around to calling me back.

During the call, O'Rourke had been vague and distant. But he'd also seemed genuinely intrigued to hear that I'd "accidentally" come across that diver who happened to admit being in the vicinity of David Mintzer's mansion the night of Treat's shooting.

Unfortunately, O'Rourke wouldn't reveal much about the progress of his investigation. He'd implied that because I wasn't a member of Treat's immediate family, he wasn't obligated to tell me anything. I countered with the reminder that I had found the body and was a key witness to some basic events including the recovery of the bullet casings.

The Suffolk County detective wasn't too happy to be pressured, but he did politely invite me to call back again— "anytime." I intended to do just that, especially to find out where their questioning of Jim Rand would lead them.

"Hi, Mom . . . *Mom*? You okay?"

I'd been sitting on the couch in Cuppa J's empty break room, staring off into space after my call to O'Rourke. On the coffee table in front of me were the photos Jim Rand had given me, the photos he'd taken the night of Treat's murder. When I realized Joy was standing there, I checked my watch. She'd arrived thirty minutes early for her dinner shift.

"Hi, honey," I murmured. "You're early."

"I wanted to make up for coming late yesterday." She shuffled her feet, crossed and uncrossed her arms. "Look, I'm sorry about fighting with you, okay? I don't want to argue anymore."

"Oh, honey . . . I'm sorry, too." I opened my arms. She sat down beside me on the couch and we hugged.

"I want you to understand how I feel . . . I really like Graydon," she said quietly. "And I really like it out here. It's so beautiful. I hate what happened to Treat, but it was my idea to come out here in the first place. Don't ask me to go back to the city before the summer ends."

I brushed my daughter's lengthening brown bangs away from her green eyes. "I'm just worried about you."

"Mom, you want to see my driver's license? I'm over eighteen. If I want to spend the night with Graydon or Keith Judd or any other guy, I will. I only didn't last night because I didn't feel right about it. I didn't want to do it to spite you. When I sleep with a guy, it's going to be because I want to, not because I'm trying to prove something."

I smiled. "When you sleep with a guy, I hope it's because you love him. But if you don't, Joy, remember what I always tell you: when you make your choices, you have to live with the consequences."

"I know, I know. Just like you did, right?"

"What do you mean?"

"You know the other night, the night Treat was killed . . . Grandmother finally told me why you and daddy got married."

I frowned. "She shouldn't have."

"Well, I was angry at you when you ripped up Keith Judd's number in front of everybody. Really angry . . . but she talked to me . . . she told me about your getting pregnant accidentally, said that's why you're being the way you're being. Because of what happened to you around my age—actually, you were younger, weren't you?"

"She shouldn't have told you what I did or didn't do at your age."

"Why not? Are you sorry you had me?"

"No, Joy. You're the best thing that ever happened in my life."

"So your 'mistake' wasn't so bad, really?"

"My mistake was marrying your father, but at the time, I never could have seen it that way. This isn't about me anyway. That's ancient history, which is why I never told you. I don't want you to take what I did as a license to do anything yourself. I don't want you to have to make the hard choices I did, to end up in a bad marriage or even a bad relationship. I don't want to see you hurt, Joy."

"But you will, Mom. Everybody gets hurt."

"There's hurt and then there's hurt."

Joy shook her head. "Come on, Mom, lighten up. You are just soooo uptight. Haven't you ever heard of a summer fling? Even Grandma is having one!"

"Don't remind me. Unlike you, your grandmother never came in last night."

"What?!" Joy cried in outrage, jumping to her feet. "Where was she? Who was she with? Was it that geezer who was all over her last night in the dining room, the one with the ponytail and beret?"

"Come on, Joy, lighten up," I said, unable to suppress the smile. "You're just *soooo* uptight."

"Oh, stop it," snapped Joy, putting her hands on her hips. "Look, *I'm* going to start restocking. *You* should give Grandma a call." Then she wheeled and marched out of the break room like a little determined general.

My god, I thought, watching her go, *when did my daughter become such a bossy, intrusive, know-it-all?*

Just then, my cell phone went off in my hand. I checked the incoming number on the digital screen before answering. "You must be psychic," I told Madame. "I was about to ring you."

"Hello, dear. How was your day?"

I sighed. "It's not over yet. Ask me then. How was your night?"

"Divine!"

"And are you still with the divine Mr. Wilson?"

There was a long pause. Madame's voice went low. "How did you know I spent the night with Edward?"

"You're kidding right?"

"Well, I'm trying to be discreet."

"I should think so," I said. "What would Dr. Mac-Tavish say?"

"My dear, the good doctor and I are not engaged. And the last time I checked my driver's license, I was over eighteen. Haven't you ever heard of a summer fling?"

"You have way too much in common with your grand-daughter."

Laughter was the response to that. "Open your eyes, Clare. Joy is bossy, whip smart, and loves to meddle. She's a carbon copy of *you*. So what's the news on the case?"

I was still alone in Cuppa J's break room. Lunch service was over and the dinner shift wouldn't be arriving for another twenty minutes, so I rose and shut the door for privacy. Then I updated Madame about meeting Rand.

"I just spoke with O'Rourke," I quietly explained. "The Suffolk County police are going to question Rand."

"Oh, my. And you think this Rand person is the killer?"

"Rand had no motive that I can see. But he is a mercenary where shooting pictures are concerned. And I'm betting he switched his camera for a rifle. The important question for David's safety is who provided the payoff for Rand to make the switch? Hopefully the detectives will break Rand and he'll admit who hired him. But if he doesn't crack, we're back to square one."

"You mean we still won't know who wants David dead?"

"Exactly. And until we do, I'm sure David's in as much danger as ever."

"Oh, yes, I see. So you do still need our information, don't you?"

"Information?"

"Yes, Edward and I were very busy today, collecting information about your Mr. Felloes. And while we were doing that, we happened upon a very enlightening discovery about Marjorie Bright."

According to Madame, Edward was a member of the exclusive East End Country Club, which is where they'd gone to ask around about Bom Felloes. "And while we were asking about Bom, we saw Marjorie Bright. She was skeet shooting, Clare."

"Marjorie Bright? Skeet shooting? Are you sure?"

"Positive. She was blasting clay pigeons, one after the other. I tell you those little platters were bursting in the air like David's Fourth of July fireworks."

A thought occurred to me. As Madame continued to talk, I picked up Rand's photos on the coffee table and began to look through them again. But this time I was looking for something very specific. I found several wide shots of the whole party that included the mansion's side grounds. The photos had been taken well before sunset, and there was enough light to make out the identity of the woman smoking among the large, old trees.

"Marjorie Bright," I whispered.

"Yes!" said Madame. "She's a crack shot, Clare. Edward and I decided to take a look in the club's trophy case. That laundry detergent heiress has won the club's annual skeet shooting tournament for the last three out of five years."

"Madame, listen. I'm looking at photographic evidence right now of Marjorie loitering on David's property. This evidence shows that she wasn't just 'passing through' after the party, the way O'Rourke and David had assumed. She was not using David's property to get to the beach. She was hanging around out of sight of the partygoers on the back deck. But why? For what?"

"The chance to shoot David!" Madame blurted out. "In the photo, do you see a weapon in her hand?"

"No," I said, "but she could have buried the rifle in the sand dune long before she needed it . . . if she was the shooter herself, that is."

"Well, you know one thing now, she would not have needed to hire Mr. Rand," said Madame. "And why would Mr. Rand have handed you those photos if they could be used against the woman who'd hired him?"

"Unless he was trying to double-cross her now. Or Jim Rand is what he says he is—which means there's another shooter . . ."

"But if Marjorie hired another person to do the shooting, why would she risk loitering on David's property? It only calls attention to herself."

"Unless . . ." I said, "like any demanding, wealthy customer, Marjorie Bright was simply anxious to see if what she purchased lived up to her expectations."

Madame and I paused at that notion. It did sound like the woman's personality type.

"There's only one problem," I said. "How would she have known about David's allergy?"

"Excuse me?"

"I'm sure that David was poisoned at Bom Felloes's party last night."

"Poisoned! My god, Clare, is he all right?"

"He's fine, he's fine. Matt and I drove him to the hospital and he's still recovering. Matt called me with an update an hour ago. If the doctor releases him today, he'll probably be driving David back to East Hampton this evening."

"Thank goodness!"

"But here's the thing. Marjorie was at the same party as David last night. I remember her chain smoking, talking with some other guests."

"So you think, since Treat caught the bullet meant for David, she might have tried to poison David the next night?"

"Yes. It's possible." I flopped back on the couch. "But she couldn't have."

"She couldn't have? Why not?"

"David was poisoned with a super-high concentration of MSG. But how would she have known about David's allergy to it? I didn't even know about it."

"Just a minute, dear," said Madame. Her voice became muffled and she called, "Edward, bring that magazine over . . ." I heard some paper rustling then Madame was back on the line.

"Clare, I'm sure Marjorie Bright knew about David's allergy. So did Bom Felloes."

"But how—"

"Edward and I were reading through his back issues of *East End* magazine, and—"

"He keeps back issues? How many?"

"Oh, well over ten years' worth. He writes for them—reviews on Hamptons' gallery shows, articles on the art world, you know. Now listen, Clare, this article we found is quite interesting. Edward remembered it because it carried a big splashy photo of David, Bom, and Marjorie Bright posing by the ocean. Here's the caption: '*Good Neighbors! David Mintzer and Bom Felloes pose together on the Bright land they recently purchased. Marjorie Bright, one of Elmer Bright's heirs, poses with her new neighbors.*'"

"So Marjorie Bright sold them the land?" I assumed.

"No," said Madame. "According to Edward, it was her older brother, Gilbert Bright, who made the sale. She was supposedly furious about it, but there was nothing she could do since the land was left to him. She posed for the photo because *East End* asked her to, and that magazine is read by everyone in East Hampton, Clare. *Everyone.*"

"It also sounds like David and Bom were pretty thick back then," I noted, "like they'd coordinated the land purchase together."

"This article may have been the beginning of the end of their friendship. Just listen to this section: '*Both men claimed separately to this reporter that they always dreamed of living in East Hampton and opening a restaurant here. But apparently not together . . .*'"

"Go on."

"They quote David as saying, '*I could never dine in Bom's eateries. The MSG flows like water and I'm severely allergic. It's a shame really. In my opinion, no self-respecting restauranteur would allow MSG to be placed anywhere near his cuisine . . .*'"

MURDER MOST FROTHY   195

"Ouch," I said. "I know David can be catty. But that's a terrible swipe to take in print. Maybe he was running off at the mouth with the reporter. Do you think he realized he would be quoted?"

"Yes, dear, I do. I think he was lobbying even then to win the restaurant war that ensued. And Bom was no better. Here's what he told the reporter: '*David's very successful, it's true. But what else can you expect from a twenty-four/seven self-promoter? Is he more style than substance? Some do call him the Prince of Hype, and if the shoe fits . . .*'"

"Ugly stuff," I murmured. "For 'good neighbors.'"

"I'm sure both Bom and Marjorie would have read this article since they're in it. So both would have known about David's MSG allergy."

"But neither were at David's July Fourth party," I pointed out. "Marjorie was loitering outside it. And Bom wasn't invited."

"Your point?"

"David had complained of a migraine at his own party, remember? That's the reason he went up to his bedroom before the fireworks started."

"That's right," said Madame. "And he was perplexed by it. He said he was certain that he hadn't ingested any of the foods that give him that reaction."

"But someone could have slipped MSG in his food or drink then, too. The plan could have been to get him to move away from the party, to go up to his bedroom so the shooter could target him there."

"But who would have done that?"

"I don't know."

"It's all so elaborate, Clare. Why would this person have created such a production? I hate to say it, but there are probably much easier ways to kill David Mintzer."

"That's what I'm afraid of . . ."

"Clare! Clare Cosi!" Jacques Papas's perpetually irritated voice called outside the closed break room door. "Where is that woman?"

The lilting Irish voice of Colleen O'Brien answered. "I think she's in the break room, Mr. Papas. Joy said she's making a private call."

Before I could even rise from the couch, the door flew open with such force it banged against the back wall. "Why is this door closed?!"

I calmly regarded the swarthy manager. "I'm making a phone call, Jacques."

"To whom?" He barreled into the room, his fleshy face reddening.

"It's private."

He spied the photos on the coffee table. "And what is all this?"

"I'll have to call you back," I told Madame.

"One more thing, Clare. I've been asking around about Graydon Faas, just as you requested, and you really shouldn't worry. The Faas family out here co-owns Taber-Faas pharmaceuticals. They're multimillionaires, dear."

"Okay, gotta go," I said and closed the phone.

Frankly, I didn't care if the Faases were multi*billionaires*. The fact that Graydon's family was rich told me nothing about the character of the boy himself, nor did it explain why he was working in the lowly job of waiter for the summer in an East Hampton eatery. But I didn't have time to discuss all that with Madame. Not with Cuppa J's crazy manager breathing down my neck.

By now, Papas was pawing through Jim Rand's photos. I calmly got to my feet. "Jacques, what I'm doing is none of your business."

He didn't seem to care. He continued rudely looking through the pictures. "These photos . . . they're from David's party."

"They're my business," I said, finally grabbing them back.

Jacques's beady black eyes narrowed on me. "What sort of business?"

"If you must know, I'm conducting a little, uh . . . investigation."

"An investigation!" Papas cried. He appeared appalled at first and then upset. "An investigation into . . . into what exactly? What do you mean?"

"I'm looking into some suspicious things that are happening around David, that's what I mean. I'm his friend and I don't intend to see anyone injure him."

"I don't understand you," Papas sputtered. "You're just a glorified barista. Who do you think you are?"

"Dial it down, Jacques. There's no need to become insulting. And, if you don't mind, I'm on break—"

Papas tapped his watch. "Your break was over five minutes ago, Ms. Cosi. And do you know what I think?"

"No, but I'm sure you'll tell me."

"I think you have an *attitude problem*, just like that Lopez girl. And I intend to inform David Mintzer of that fact. Now get yourself in gear. The dinner shift is arriving, and there's much to be done!"

Nineteen

∞∞∞∞∞∞∞∞∞∞∞∞∞∞∞∞∞∞∞∞

SATURDAY night was always the busiest night of the week at Cuppa J. The under-forty crowd packed the place, pumping up with caffeine to party until the wee hours. Papas had yet to hire a replacement for Prin, and I was stuck waiting tables again as well as managing the coffee bar.

When my next break came around, about eight o'clock, I didn't dare risk another scene like the one I'd had earlier with Papas. I walked through the kitchen and out the back door, got into my car in the parking lot and locked the doors. Only then did I place my cell phone call.

"O'Rourke here."

"Hello Detective, it's Clare Cosi again."

The unhappy exhale was hard to miss. "Yes, Ms. Cosi? What can I do for you?"

"I'm sorry to bother you, detective, but I have some more information for you. Did you know that Marjorie Bright is a crack shot? She's a champion skeet shooter."

"No. I didn't know. And now I do."

"You see why I'm telling you, don't you? She has the skill to fire a rifle and hit a target. I've also got photographic evidence that she was not just passing through David's property. She was loitering there during the party, skulking around for some reason, staying out of sight. Don't you think those two things make her a likely suspect?"

"Did she have a motive for murdering Treat Mazzelli?"

"No. For attempting to murder David Mintzer."

"Ma'am, Mr. Mintzer was not the man murdered the night of July Fourth, as you well know since you discovered the body. Now, I thank you for your information, but we have some very strong leads on our investigation and they do not involve Ms. Bright at this time."

"It's Jim Rand, isn't it? Do you have him in custody?"

There was a pause and another weary sigh. "Ms. Cosi, we did question Mr. Rand, but his alibi checks out. The man couldn't have shot Treat Mazzelli on the night of July Fourth. So he's not in custody, nor is he a suspect at this time."

"What alibi did Rand give you?"

"That's all I can tell you, ma'am."

"Wait, but—"

"Ms. Cosi, I will take your information about Ms. Bright under advisement, but I have to ask you to stop investigating this crime on your own. And if you break any laws doing so, I'll see that you're prosecuted to the fullest extent of the law. Do you understand me?"

"I understand." I gritted my teeth in frustration. "Goodnight, detective."

"No hard feelings, now, Ms. Cosi. Goodnight."

I hung up, suddenly feeling both angry and stupid. Here I was trying to stop a murderer. And I'd just been accused of being an outlaw!

* * *

"Joy, can I talk to you a minute?" I asked after returning from the parking lot.

My daughter had been talking with Graydon Faas and Colleen O'Brien by the dessert prep area. I waved her over to the back door.

"I'm off at eleven," I told her, "but I know you're here until closing."

"Yeah, so?"

"So I thought I'd be going straight back to David's, but I have some business to take care of first."

"At eleven at night? What sort of business?"

"It's no big deal, honey. I just want you to stay available by cell phone. Don't power it down. Let me know what you're going to do, where you're going to be. Okay?"

"Graydon and I are just going out for a little while. We're both going to surf in the morning, so I won't be in too late. If my plans change, I'll tell you."

"You have your birth control?" I whispered.

Joy rolled her eyes. "Yes, Mom. *If* I need it, I have it! Please don't worry so much!"

A few hours later, at fifteen minutes to midnight, I was sitting behind the wheel of my Honda in the parking lot of Monroe's Marina.

The phone call to O'Rourke hadn't just frustrated me. It had made me angry. And, okay, maybe that anger had impaired my judgment just a little bit. I'm sure Matt would have said as much. But at this very moment, I wasn't emotional. I was calm, cool, and trying to think as logically as I possibly could.

Detective O'Rourke believed Rand had given a solid alibi the night of Treat's murder. But I trusted O'Rourke to catch the killer about as much as I trusted Rand, which is to say not at all. Consequently, I couldn't get Jim Rand's invitation out of my head.

"Midnight tonight . . . Come out with me. . . . After you see with your own eyes that I'm telling you the truth, you can cross me off your suspect list, and I'll give you any photo you like."

"Or you'll push me overboard," I muttered, remembering my earlier response to his invitation.

I got out of the car and slammed the door. With more than a few nerves fraying, I walked down one of the marina's many long docks, and right up to *Rabbit Run*. The yacht was still in its slip, completely dark. There was no sign of Jim Rand anywhere. In fact, there was no sign of anyone on board.

"Damn you, Rand," I muttered.

It was obvious he had been pulling my leg about the invitation. *I am such a fool. He was playing me.*

"Excuse me, ma'am, may I help you?"

I turned to find a young man walking towards me along the dock. He had short brown hair, a baby face with a very serious expression, and he wore a navy blue Windbreaker with the words MONROE'S MARINA SECURITY emblazoned on the front. The Windbreaker was unzipped and I noticed a picture ID clipped to the pocket of his shirt. I read the name beneath the picture.

"T. Gurt."

"That's my name, ma'am. What are you doing out here?"

"Oh, I was supposed to meet someone. But he's clearly standing me up."

"Sorry about that. Can I help you call a taxi?"

"No, no, I have my car in the lot. I was just leaving."

"All right, ma'am. Good-night," he said, and started to head back down the dock.

"Wait," I called.

The young man turned back. "Yes, ma'am?"

"Do you have an Aunt Alberta by any chance?"

The young man nodded. "Yes, ma'am, Alberta Gurt."

"I know her. She's a very nice woman. So you must be Thomas?"

"That's right."

"She said you had a security job here in Hampton Bays."

"I do, during the day." He checked his watch. "And at midnight, I have another job to go to. Sorry to cut you short, ma'am, but I'm due to change the shift."

"I understand. Nice to meet you."

"Likewise."

As Thomas Gurt headed back to the marina office, I recalled what Alberta had said about Thomas having trouble in his youth, but then straightening out after enlisting in the army. With all those "ma'ams" it wasn't hard to believe he'd been a GI.

I hadn't forgotten my suspicions of Alberta. She had motive to murder David, and Thomas was obviously comfortable with firearms. Still . . . the baby faced kid seemed so earnest.

"Murderers come in all temperaments, Clare. All shapes, all sizes."

Mike Quinn's words came back to me then. And I knew I shouldn't let a momentary good impression persuade me one way or the other. In the end, I wasn't ruling out anyone as a suspect. Which led me back to the reason I'd come here in the first place.

As I strode back down the dock and into the parking lot, I checked my watch. It was exactly midnight now. If Jim Rand had played me, I figured he'd also played the authorities—cooked up some bogus alibi to send the cops in another direction. But I wasn't going to give up on Rand as easily as O'Rourke apparently had.

I decided to question the frogman myself. If he was telling the truth, I wanted to hear it with my own ears, find it believable with my own brain. But if he was protecting the person who hired him, I would find out who that person was.

I decided to drive over to Rand's house in Bridgehampton, and if he wasn't home, I would simply wait in my car until he showed. *But one thing I am not going to do*, I told myself as I yanked open my car door, *I am not going to blow an opportunity to nail him.*

"Giving up so soon?"

I turned to find Jim Rand standing no more than two feet away, his arms folded casually, his cocky confidence evident in his posture and expression. He'd cleaned up for our meeting. He'd shaved, exchanged his diver's shirt for a seafoam green button-down. His blue jeans looked new.

For a second, I didn't think I would find my voice. The man had approached me from behind, like a silent shadow in the dark marina parking lot. Somehow I managed to keep it together long enough to say—

"Yeah. You were a SEAL, all right."

"I didn't scare you, did I?"

"Were you trying to?"

"No. But a little payback is probably in order. You were trying to scare me, weren't you?"

"When?"

"When do you think, Clare? When you sent the Suffolk County police to my house."

I swallowed uneasily, didn't expect to be put on the defensive. "I had to, Mr. Rand. You must have known that I would."

"That's why I'm very surprised to see you here. I'd already convinced myself you'd been playing me."

"Funny, I was just thinking the same thing about you."

He smiled. "Guess we think alike, you and I."

"So are you going to take me out?"

He waved for me to follow him. We approached the rows

of docks. But we didn't go down the one I'd just left. Instead, he gestured to a lit boat on the far side of the marina.

"That's not *Rabbit Run*," I noted as we walked up to the slip.

"I never rent the same boat two nights in a row."

"Why not?"

He shrugged. "Throws off the scent."

We boarded tonight's rental, *Rabbit Is Rich*, and headed out. This yacht was about thirty-five feet, too, but unlike *Rabbit Run*, the helm on this vessel was open to the air. It was a nice night, warm and clear, and the smell of the ocean was strong as we motored slowly out of the marina then picked up speed on the open water.

"It's a nice night." I had to speak loudly, over the sound of the rushing wind. But I knew it was important to start the conversation. Any conversation. As Quinn once put it, *"The best way to get a suspect to talk, is to get him to talk."*

Unfortunately, Rand had no reply to my riveting weather report. So I tried another subject.

"You know, *Rabbit Run* and *Rabbit is Rich* . . . those are both titles of novels."

"Yeah, I know," Rand said. "Updike."

"Have you read John Updike's *Rabbit* novels?"

"Do I strike you as the kind of guy who reads suburban angst novels?"

"Uh . . ."

"Don't strain yourself. I read nonfiction. Geopolitical history mostly."

"So who's the Updike fan?"

"Byron Baxter Monroe, he owns the marina, he's also a former college professor. He named all his rentals after favorite Updike novels and short stories."

"You know him pretty well?"

"The guy's bi-polar and mildly depressed, which he remedies via what he calls 'self-medication,' usually alcohol. The man likes to belly up to the bar and pontificate about the vacuity of the conventional upper-middle class suburban existence in general and Updike in particular. Why do I know this? Because as long as he's buying, I'll listen."

"So you 'self-medicate' too? With alcohol?"

"I down the occasional beer. But risk is my kick. I'm an adrenaline junkie. Like you."

"Like me?"

"Don't you remember what you told me this morning? You get your nerve from eight to ten cups of coffee a day. Caffeine's your drug, isn't it?"

I bristled. "It's a legal one."

"And what I found you doing today in my rental house. That was legal, was it?"

Shit.

"You know, Clare, I could have told the police about what you did."

"Why didn't you?"

"Because . . ." He smiled. "I knew if they arrested you, then you wouldn't be able to keep our date."

Date. My god. Was he being sarcastic? Or playing me again?

I watched him drive the boat for a few minutes. We were paralleling the shore now. I could see faint lights from the Hamptons' mansions on our left, which meant we were heading away from Manhattan, toward the tip of Long Island. If we kept going much longer, we'd be away from all land. We'd be out to sea.

"We're traveling east, right?" I asked, trying to keep the nervousness out of my voice.

"Northeast." He tapped the compass, just one gauge on the fairly dizzying array in front of us. There was sonar, global positioning, and a host of other technology I could only guess had something to do with communications and weather.

"Northeast," I repeated. "And your fuel tank is full. That's about all I can recognize on this dashboard, besides the steering wheel."

Jim smirked. "Dead reckoning is more your style, right? Or, judging from what you've involved yourself in, maybe just the dead part?"

I didn't know whether the man was making a bad joke or a threat, but I took it as the latter. "Don't menace me, Rand. Ten people know I'm with you right now."

Jim said nothing. He continued to drive for a few minutes and then he cut the engine. We slowed on the water; I could feel the waves lapping the boat, the vessel gently bobbing.

Is this it? I half wondered whether he was going to throw me overboard now.

"I'm not trying to menace you," he said softly. Then the ex-SEAL stared straight ahead, into the dark water, as if thinking something over. He rubbed his clean-shaven chin. There was a faint scent of citrus and soap about him. Now that his stubble was gone, I could see his jawline was magnificent. Sharp angles chiseled from marble. Twenty years ago, I would have been itching to sketch it.

He abruptly turned to face me, caught me staring.

"You ready to watch me work?" he asked.

"Does it involve firearms?"

"No guns, Clare. Just shooting."

Rand suited up in the cabin below, exchanging his blue jeans and button-down for a black wet suit. His camera was an impressive piece of equipment, waterproof with an incredible zoom lens. It pained me to realize it, but his body was an even more impressive piece of equipment. The wet suit was skintight, revealing every lean muscle.

It's official. The man's a Greek statue.

"Here. This is for you," he said, handing me yesterday's newspaper. It was a popular paper, widely read on this part of Long Island.

"What's this?"

"Page one. Read the photo credit."

The front page was dominated by a spectacular shot of fireworks taking place above Bay Bar in Southampton. Everything that was wonderful about a Hamptons Fourth was in the shot. Beautiful yachts docked next to a popular watering hole. Attractive couples embracing, gazing up at the explosions of color high above them. The photo credit read *Jim Rand.*

"This is some shot. How did you get it?"

"From the water. I was in the water, that is. But the real question you should be asking me, detective, was *when* did I get it. See the date on the paper."

"I see. You shot this July Fourth. They published it on the fifth."

"You can see I was in Southampton at the time of the fireworks over Bay Bar. Right? You following?"

I nodded, understanding what he was showing me. "It's your alibi. The police know the time of death for Treat Mazzelli. You were nowhere near David Mintzer's mansion at that time."

"That's right, Clare. Like I told you. All of my shots at Mintzer's were before sunset. That's why I gave you all of the photos I took. Do you believe me now? Or do you want to see the complete set of digital shots I took in Southampton? There are only about a hundred or so that put me there from the beginning of the display to the end."

"Mr. Rand, please understand, someone is trying to hurt my friend."

"I hear you. But I'm not your man . . ." He smiled, one eyebrow arching. "At least, not when it comes to your criminal investigation."

The flirtation was hard to miss. My reaction was visceral. I ignored it. "Did the police ask you if you saw anything suspicious that night, while you were on David's beach?"

"Yes, of course. And, no, I'm sorry to tell you that I didn't. Look . . . we'll talk when I get back, okay? I just didn't want to leave the boat here and find you'd lost your nerve with me, motored away, and left me to fend for myself in the Atlantic."

I couldn't help laughing. "You know I had that same scenario down for me. I was half convinced you were about to throw me overboard."

"Trust is a beautiful thing, isn't it?"

Dammit, Rand, don't make me like you.

The ex-SEAL moved to gather the rest of his gear, an oxygen tank, and goggles. He strapped on an impressive-looking dive watch. Then he picked up a pair of binoculars, handed them to me, and pointed.

I scanned the shoreline. There were a few mansions lit up. One was having a big party on the beach. "I guess that party's your destination?"

"You guessed right."

I watched him jump off the stern. A chill went through me as he disappeared into the dark waves. The moonlight cast a silver hue to the ocean surface, but Jim Rand had disappeared completely beneath the black glass.

I watched patiently through the binoculars, waiting for him to emerge again. Finally, I saw him on the beach. I didn't even notice him come out of the water.

Shadows kept him invisible. Then he used topiaries and scrub grass to keep himself camouflaged. He stayed there for a good forty minutes. The party guests moving in and out of the mansion, never seeing him, never suspecting. Couples and groups moved into his frame without knowing it, then out again. Eventually, he moved. With smooth stealth he was back in the water again. Soon, he was back on the boat.

"Still here, I see," he quipped after removing his goggles and oxygen mouthpiece.

"Still here for good reason."

"You finally trust me?"

"I don't know how to start the engine on this tub."

Jim smiled. "Give me a chance to change and maybe I'll give you a lesson."

Ten minutes later, he was topside again. "You want to see some of my shots? They turned out great."

"You have the pictures already?"

"It's digital media. Come on down."

In the cabin below the open deck, Jim had set up a laptop and printer on a bolted down table. On the screen were thumbnails of the photos he'd just taken. He sat me down in a folding deck chair, then he leaned over my shoulder, and clicked on a few to show me the results.

I shook my head in amazement.

Jim noticed. "You can't get over the technology, can you?"

"I can't get over how many parties Keith Judd gets invited to on this tiny strip of land."

"Keith Judd? Oh, yes, there he is in the background, surrounded by pretty young jail bait, as usual. My focus wasn't on him for that shot. See here—that's Radio Brenner, the baseball star. He's got his arm around Gina Sanchez, the pop diva. In March they started their relationship. But nobody's gotten a photo of them together this summer. Now my client does."

"I see."

Rand heard the stiffness in my voice. He turned his gaze away from the laptop's screen to look at me. "You see but you don't approve."

"It's not my place to approve or disapprove. It's your living . . ."

"But?"

"But why don't you just do the kind of photos you did at Bay Bar? Why don't you just do legit stuff?"

"I do legit stuff. My partner, Kenny, does too. He even does accident scene photos for the police around here. You'd be surprised how many traffic smash-ups there are during the season."

"After driving around here this summer with the displaced, impatient Manhattan elites, no, I actually wouldn't be surprised."

"Well, those jobs don't pay enough. And I want my own boat by the end of summer. I want to make enough to retire on before I'm too old and too fatigued to dive anymore. Life's short, Clare. I've witnessed that first hand, I can tell you." He shrugged. "You've got to make the most of it while you can."

"Like I said . . . it's your business . . . it's just creepy, invading people's privacy."

"Oh? You mean, like when you invaded my privacy today?"

He wasn't wrong. I'd justified breaking and entering, telling myself it was for a higher cause. But it was still an invasion of his privacy. It was still breaking the law.

Jim rose, unfolding himself so high, his head nearly brushed the cabin's ceiling. "Clare, the places I've been . . . the things I've seen, the poverty, the suffering . . . fuck it. If the worst thing that ever happens to these filthy rich people is that they have their candid photo put in a magazine, I'd say they're still coming up winners on the global lottery . . . You want a drink?"

I nodded, surprising myself. But I suddenly needed something to sooth my nerves, my feelings of guilt about being a voyeur. And from the look on his face, so did Jim Rand.

He went to the galley fridge, pulled out two cold bottles of beer and opened them. He handed me one and went topside again, taking a seat on a padded bench near the stern. I stood against the rail. We both drank in silence for a few minutes, the waves lapping the hull, the boat gently bobbing on the dark water.

"So why did you leave the SEALs?" I asked. "Age?"

"Injury. It happened during . . . a training exercise."

"Oh, wow, that's bad luck. I mean, it wasn't even on a secret mission or anything."

Jim laughed.

"What's so funny?"

"Clare, no SEAL is ever allowed to say he's injured on anything but a 'training exercise.'"

"Oh? . . . Oh! I see. Sorry . . . so what exactly is your injury?"

"Decompression injury. In laymen's terms, the bends. It messed up my inner ear, my joints. If I go any deeper than recreational diving—about one hundred feet—I'll probably suffer severe bone damage."

"And this work you're doing. You don't dive any lower than—"

"Twenty feet tops. In the Caribbean, during the winter, I'll go deeper. Fifty . . . but no more."

"I see . . ."

I moved to the padded bench and sat down next to him. His dark, shaggy hair was wet and slicked back, dampening the green collar of his button-down. The scent of soap and citrus was still there on his skin, along with the faint briny smell of the open ocean. I liked it. I didn't want to like it, but I did.

Together we continued to drink our beers and watch the play of moonlight on the water. At least I thought that's what he'd been watching. When I glanced up, however, I found his eyes on me.

A sudden gust of wind tossed my chestnut hair around my face. Jim's brown eyes seemed to liquefy. For long, silent minutes, he didn't move.

That's when I realized that being this close to Jim Rand

was like being too close to a lightning strike. I could practically feel his coiled energy, the burning below his surface. He wasn't bothering to mask anything now. I could see what he wanted, and if he had touched me just then, it would have been over. I would have melted like chocolate in a five hundred degree oven. So I stood up before he got the chance—

"Jim, I need your help."

"You need my help?"

"David's in danger, and I need to find out who wants to hurt him."

Jim looked away, took a long swig of beer. "You need my help?"

"That's what I said."

He turned back to me, met my eyes. "Will you be grateful?"

"Yes."

An eyebrow arched. "How grateful?"

"Depends."

"On what?"

"On whether we catch the killer."

A smile spread slowly across Jim Rand's face. "I'm game."

WITH patient silence, Jim listened to all of my theories and suspicions. Then he suggested we go below and use his laptop again. He thought he might get somewhere examining the party photos on screen since he could zoom into any image. His idea was to locate David in every photo and analyze what was happening around him.

There were about seventy photos in the file. We didn't see anything suspicious for the first twenty-two. On twenty-three, however, I saw something that put a chill through me.

The main image was of a beautiful young movie star laughing. But in the background, something caught my eye.

"Can you zoom in on David back there, make the image bigger?"

"Sure." Jim moved the cursor and clicked. "What do you see, Clare?"

"David is talking to his restaurant manager, Jacques Papas. And look what Jacques is doing."

"Looks like he's handing David his drink to taste."

"Go to the next photo in order."

There was another shot of the starlet a few seconds later. "Zoom in again on David."

"Ohmigod. David is handing the drink back. Jacques had David sample his drink and hand it back."

"So?"

"So someone slipped David a small dose of MSG at his own party. And I think we just witnessed it right here."

"You think Papas tried to murder David?"

"I think Papas had a motive to have David murdered. And I think what we're seeing here is David being set up with the headache that sent him to his bedroom—where the shooter was supposed to take him out."

"I follow you. But what's Papas's motive?"

"Embezzlement. And I think I can prove it. Even if Detective O'Rourke won't buy the MSG mickey, I know he'll buy a book of accounts that shows a scheme to embezzle money from Cuppa J and David Mintzer. And I know Papas keeps that book locked up in his office desk."

Jim Rand leaned back in his chair, eyeballed me. "And how are you going to get this book?"

I folded my arms, tapped my chin in thought. "When you were a SEAL, did you have to break into things quietly?"

"Yes, Clare."

"So you know how to pick a lock?"

"Yes, Clare."

"Then the question, Mr. Rand, isn't how am I going to get the book. It's how are *we* going to do it."

"You're determined to pull me into your outlaw ways, aren't you, Cosi?"

"That's rich. Coming from you."

Jim laughed. "Just remember one thing."

"What?"

"You promised if I helped you catch the killer, you'd be grateful."

"First things first, Rand. First things first."

Twenty

I drove back to Cuppa J in my Honda, watching the lights on Jim's Harley in my rearview mirror. By the time we arrived at the restaurant it was nearly three o'clock in the morning. The building was dark and deserted, the parking lot empty. As I climbed out of my car, Jim rolled up next to me and cut the motorcycle's engine.

Together, we walked up the dark path to the restaurant. Through the glass of the front door, I saw the tiny red light on the alarm console, warning intruders that the system was activated.

Jim, hands shoved into his denims, leaned against the door jam. "So, do you want me to pick this lock?"

I shook my head. "I have the key. The lock I want you to pick is inside. Anyway, there's an alarm system. Even if you got through the door, you'd have to deal with the keypad. You don't know the code."

"Alarms have never been a problem for me."

"Okay, now you're just bragging."

I slipped the key into the lock and twisted it. After opening the door, I had ten seconds to punch in the security code or the alarm would go off, both here and at the police station. I tapped the code into the key pad. A single beep, and the tiny light switched from red to green.

"All clear," I called over my shoulder.

As I stepped into the restaurant's dining room, I knew at once that something was wrong. At first the air seemed heavy and close, then I detected a familiar odor. Jim came up behind me, gripped my shoulder. He smelled it, too.

"Gas," we said together.

"The pilot lights must have gone out!" I cried. "We have to fix it—"

I hurried forward, but didn't get more than two steps before Jim, his hand still digging into my shoulder, yanked me back.

"Clare, no. We have to get out of here."

"No, wait."

I struggled against him. But in a few seconds, I felt dizzy then woozy. I blinked, saw stars, felt my knees giving way. Jim snatched me up and carried me out of the restaurant. Choking, he stretched me out on the hood of my Honda, which felt warm against my back. I coughed and gasped for air.

"We can't let the place blow up," I cried between hacks. "We can't."

Jim pushed himself away from the hood, faced the building. I followed his eyes and noticed he'd left the front door open. Then, before I knew what was happening, he'd stripped off his button-down.

"Jim, what—?"

He dug into his pocket, thrust a cell phone into my hand. "Call 911." He wrapped his shirt around his nose and mouth and tied it behind his head. Head down, he ran back inside the restaurant.

I punched the numbers and the call went through immediately. I reported the gas leak, the address, and the fact that someone was inside the building.

I heard noise from inside the restaurant—the French doors opening, the sound of breaking glass. Still shaky, I hopped off the hood of my car and hurried to the entranceway. My head was throbbing and my feet seemed to take forever to obey my brain.

Just as I got to the front door, I saw Jim emerge from the kitchen. His shirt was still wrapped around his face, and his gait looked steady. I stepped inside to help him, but he rushed me at the door.

"Go back, Clare. I stopped the leak." His voice was muffled by the cloth, but his words were clear.

"Are you okay?"

"Jesus, Clare, are you forgetting I was a SEAL? Any one of us worth his salt can hold his breath for three minutes."

"What did you find back there? The stove is supposed to have a safety device. If any of the pilot lights go out, the gas should be automatically cut off—"

"The stove wasn't the problem. The lines were sliced."

"What?!"

"The hoses leading from the main to the stove were flapping loose and they looked sliced to me. I had to turn off the main. On the way, I opened those French doors—sorry, I had to break some of them. Are there any other outside windows in this place?"

"There's a big window in the employee break room."

"Which door?"

"The gas is already dissipating, Jim. Let me take care of it."

"Okay. I'll prop the fire doors."

I took a deep, fresh breath, ran to the break room, and opened the door. The gas smell wasn't so bad in here, probably because the closed door kept most of the vapors out. I began to walk to the window—then I screamed.

A body was sprawled on the couch, a woman clad in jeans and a flowered blouse. A pair of sandals lay on the floor. On the pillow, I saw loose auburn curls dangling from a disheveled ponytail. I grabbed the body's shoulder, rolled it over. Colleen O'Brien's skin had a faintly bluish cast, the freckles across her pug nose looked dark as blood against her deathly pale skin.

Frantically, I began shaking the girl. "Wake up! Wake up!"

Jim appeared at my side, pulled me away and bent over her, resting his ear on her chest. "She's breathing—barely. We've got to get her outside."

Jim hauled her off the sofa, cradled her in a fireman's carry. It took only a moment for him to cross the dining room and exit the restaurant. He laid Colleen across the hood of my Honda, which was getting more action than a hospital gurney.

"You know her?"

"Yes! She works for David."

"Think she was trying to kill herself?"

I blinked. "No . . . . I don't know . . ."

I remembered how distressed she'd been the night Treat had been shot, and I realized it was possible.

Jim checked her mouth and throat for foreign objects. Then he began administering CPR. He was at it less than a minute when Colleen's eyes opened. As she started sitting up, she began to heave.

Jim glanced at me. "She'll be okay, once she empties her stomach."

I held Colleen's hair while she threw up all over my car—cosmic justice, after what had happened to the back seat of Breanne's Mercedes. But I didn't care. I was so relieved that she was alive.

"Jim, why did you ask me if it was a suicide attempt?" I whispered.

"Someone cut those hoses to the stove, Clare. It was either suicide or vandalism."

Colleen held her head. "What happened?"

"There was a gas leak," I lied. "Why were you in the restaurant?"

"Well, the truth is . . . I've been sleeping there for days," Colleen said, "but don't tell anyone."

Jim snorted. "I think that ship's already sailed."

I silenced him with a jab of my elbow. "Colleen, why would you do that?"

She tried to stand up. I put a firm hand on her shoulder. "Stay still," I commanded, wondering where the hell the fire department was. I still couldn't hear any sirens. "Tell me why you stayed at the restaurant, Colleen."

"The jerks running my share house raised the rates midsummer without warning," she confessed. "I got angry. I didn't want to give up every dime I made to those people, and I didn't want to lose my job here, so I decided to sleep the rest of the season on the break room couch."

I stared at her blankly. "How did you pull it off?"

"Oh, that was easy. I'd hide in the restroom until Jacques or the designated closer locked up every night, then I'd hide again in the morning when the chef arrived so no one would see me. And there were a few times Jacques had me close up—like the other night when he went to Bom Felloes's party. Nights like that, I had the run of the place."

On the highway, I heard the single blast of a horn. Scarlet lights flashed in the trees. The fire department was on the way, sans sirens. I realized only then that they ran silently so as not to disturb the wealthy residents of this exclusive community. Jim faced the road, slipping back into his shirt as he waited for the authorities to arrive.

"Colleen, listen to me," I said. "This is important. Who closed up tonight?"

"It was Jacques. I thought he would never leave. He stayed in his office very late. But then I heard him lock up. I saw him from the break room window, driving away about two-thirty. I went right to sleep after that."

The village fire truck rolled into the parking lot, lights flashing. A police car and an ambulance pulled in behind it. The doors opened and two paramedics leaped out and ran to us.

The fire chief and several firemen with oxygen secured the area and entered the restaurant. As Colleen was helped into the ambulance, I approached the police sergeant and introduced myself.

"This was no accident," I said. "The gas lines appear to have been deliberately sliced, and the last person to have access to them—according to this young woman right here—was the manager of the restaurant, Jacques Papas. I believe he was trying to sabotage this place to cover up the fact that he's been embezzling from the owner, David Mintzer, and some of the vendors."

The officer shifted uneasily. "That's a heavy charge, ma'am."

"I know," I replied. "But Colleen here was sleeping inside the restaurant. She can testify that Jacques was the last one to leave. And I came by tonight to take a look at the contents of his accounting book. I believe the deals he made with vendors were never approved by the owner and the result of those deals would have been the extortion of money by Papas."

"We'll need a statement," the sergeant said.

"I'm happy to provide one," I said, then I dropped the bomb. "I also believe Jacques Papas has been trying to kill David. I think Papas may have had something to do with the murder at David's house on July Fourth."

The sergeant swallowed hard. Clearing the crimes I'd just outlined was probably above his pay grade.

"Wait here, Ms. Cosi," the sergeant said. "I'm going to put in a call to the Suffolk County police. Detective Roy O'Rourke is handling that case."

Jim appeared at my shoulder.

"Think you solved your mystery?" he asked.

"I hope so."

"You believe Jacques tried to burn down the place to hide his crime?"

I nodded. "Think it through. At the end of the summer, a bunch of vendors are going to be expecting the rest of their bills to be paid along with the ten percent Jacques had promised them. Blowing the place up would have created enough chaos to let him get away clean, jump a plane back to Europe—with the other half of those vendor payments. He was probably betting on David throwing in the towel and declaring bankruptcy."

Jim rubbed his jaw, considering my words. "So why blow the place now? He could have continued running the scam through the rest of July and August."

"I think that's partly my fault."

"How do you figure?"

"After Prin found out about his crooked deal, Papas was able to fire her without David getting wise. But then I got suspicious. Papas knew I was under contract, so he couldn't fire me as easily as Prin. And he knew I was aggressively snooping around his office the other day . . . and just this evening, he stumbled upon me making a private call while looking over your photos from David's party. I had to admit I was conducting an investigation. The man looked positively green when I told him. And speaking of green . . . I'm suddenly not feeling too steady . . ."

The world began to look a little fuzzy and I wobbled in place.

"Whoa, steady, Clare." Jim put his hands on my shoulders. "Sit down."

I sank onto my car's front bumper, put a hand to my forehead. "I guess Jacques panicked. I made him worried and frightened that he was going to be found out. And because of that an innocent young woman almost died."

"Come here." Jim pulled me up against him, and I held on, my head alongside his chest, my hands gripping the corded muscles of his arms.

"I feel sick," I muttered. "The gas—"

"It's not the gas, Clare," Jim said. "It's the adrenaline seeping away, making you feel unsteady, disoriented. My old team leader back in the SEALs had a saying. It was true in combat, and I guess it's true in life too."

"What's that?" I asked weakly.

Jim shrugged. "After the thrill, comes the crash."

Twenty-one

〰〰〰〰〰〰〰〰〰〰〰〰〰〰〰

I literally crawled out of bed the next morning, a hint of gas still tainting my palate. I threw a robe over my pajamas and shuffled downstairs to the kitchen. On the way I passed David in the great room of *Otium cum Dignitate*, also wrapped in a robe. He was so intent on his telephone conversation he hardly noticed my passing.

Like me, David had been up most of the night. He'd been called to the restaurant to secure his property after the gas leak, and the fire department declared the premises off-limits until the utility company could make repairs. I assumed David was on the phone doing just that.

Our collective lack of sleep called for desperate measures, I decided, and I reached for the canister holding the caffeine-loaded Breakfast Blend.

As the nutty, earthy aroma began filling the sunlit kitchen, David entered and slumped down into a chair at the big table with a long, dramatic sigh. "It's going to be hell finding a new manager in the middle of the season."

"Better no manager than someone like Jacques Papas," I replied.

David shook his head. "And he came so highly recommended."

"I can see why. He was efficient, demanding, and punctual. He *was* a good manager . . . except for the embezzlement thing. Why do you think he did it?"

David sighed. "I turned him down. I shouldn't have, I guess. He wanted to go back to Greece and open his own place. He wanted me to put up the money for him at the end of the summer. But I wasn't interested in backing a restaurant overseas."

"So he decided if he couldn't get the money from you one way, he'd get it another?"

"I suppose so. Oh, Clare, I hate to put you out, especially after all you've done for me, but until I do get a new manager, I'm afraid I'm going to need your help."

I nodded. "You know you can count on me."

"I'd like you to take over, manage Cuppa J full time for the next two weeks—perhaps longer if my search doesn't go well. That means long hours, and it means renegotiating the lousy deals with the vendors Papas made in my name. But I'll pay you well, Clare. You can count on that."

"I'm happy to do it, David. I'm sure I can ask Matt to postpone his next trip and take over managing the Village Blend for that long. But what about Chef Vogel? Wouldn't you want to consider asking him to take over the management duties before me?"

David sighed. "Chef Vogel enjoys creating menus. He does so admirably. What he does not enjoy, however, and he's made it abundantly clear, is payroll, employee schedules, personnel problems, and customer service. He'd be a lousy manager and he'd hate it, as well."

"All right then, I guess I accept."

David put his hands together in silent applause. "Thank goodness. Now let's have some of that delightful brew!"

I poured, and we sat together at the table, enjoying the warmth and much needed caffeine.

"My god, I can't stop thinking about that poor girl," said David, shaking his head. "Colleen almost died in my restaurant. I just . . . I just can't thank you enough for saving her life. And for saving the restaurant, of course. But, really, if that poor girl had died I never would have forgiven myself!"

"What about Treat?" I said evenly. "He's dead too."

"Yes," said Madame, strolling in. "Mr. Mazzelli was somebody's son, you know."

David nodded. "Yes, he was, somebody's drug informant son."

Nothing like dropping a bomb in the breakfast room. "What?" I said. "What do you know?"

"I just got off the phone with Detective O'Rourke," David said. "He tells me the police have found the murder weapon."

I felt my guts twisting. "Where?"

"In the trunk of a car belonging to a young man from Manhattan. He was arrested for drug dealing in the wee hours of July sixth. The authorities ran ballistics tests and checked Treat's background. When Detective O'Rourke was sure, he called me."

"Sure of what?" I asked.

"O'Rourke discovered that Treat was a former cocaine dealer—arrested and charged, but never convicted. He was cooperating with the D.E.A, acting as an informant in exchange for immunity."

The news to me was stunning. It certainly didn't fit with any of my own theories.

"Officer O'Rourke says forensics can now tie the bullet casings from the beach, as well as the bullet recovered from Treat's head, to the rifle. And since the weapon was found in a known drug dealer's car, O'Rourke concluded that Treat was the sole target of the hit man."

"Because Treat was informing on drug dealers for the D.E.A?"

"Yes. Now that O'Rourke has the murder weapon, the case is closed. That piece of evidence is incontrovertible."

"It's also circumstantial."

David blinked. "I don't see how."

"For starters, why target Treat in the middle of a party and use a hidden sniper? Wouldn't it have been easier to wait for Treat to leave the mansion, gun him down on the road, in front of his house—anywhere but in the middle of one of the biggest social gatherings of the season?"

"A moot point, Clare," said David.

I shook my head. "Don't you see that the murder weapon could have been planted? That maybe that's why the casings were so casually left behind on the beach. No professional hit man would have made such a mistake—"

"No one said the arrestee was a professional hit man," David argued. "He was probably just a punk."

"And I'll bet there are no fingerprints on that gun, either," I shot back. "I'll bet the killer wanted that weapon to be found by the police—he probably even tipped them—so that someone else would be charged with the crime."

"Give it up, Clare," David warned in an irritated voice. "O'Rourke says it's over. So it's over."

"One more question, then I'll let it rest."

He sighed. "Ask."

"Where did they find the gun and pick this perp up?"

"The wrong side of the highway," David replied. "Somewhere in Hampton Bays, I think. Anyway, I'm simply relieved to hear that Treat's killer has been caught.

I can pay off the security firm and be free of people in uniform staking out my house at all hours."

I was alarmed. "Why drop the security?"

"It's no longer necessary."

"Please. There's been a murder in this mansion. Your restaurant manager just tried to blow up your business. Can't you keep the security in place for a few more weeks? For my sake?"

Madame raised an eyebrow. "You know, David, Clare's right. Given what just happened with your misjudgment of Jacques Papas, don't you think you should listen to my daughter-in-law?"

Ex-daughter-in-law, I thought. *And considering Matteo's relationship with Breanne Summour, things are getting ex-ier every day.*

David's gaze moved from me to Madame and back again. Finally he threw up his hands. "I know when I'm outnumbered!" He set the empty cup on the table and rose.

"Now I have to dress," he announced. "I've got a round of social calls to make, and I have to convince the gas and the glass company to send people immediately to repair the restaurant, or Cuppa J doesn't open tonight."

Fortunately for all concerned Cuppa J did open on Sunday, though not in time for its famous brunch. By four o'clock, however, on that sunny afternoon, the glass company had come and gone, the utility company had affected repairs, and the village fire marshal had declared the premises safe.

While Chef Vogel handled preparations in the kitchen and Suzi Tuttle set up the dining room for the evening rush, I was on the break room's couch going over the vendor list, wondering which of the restaurant's clients I would have to charm on Monday in order to get our supplies delivered without the added ten percent markup negotiated by Jacques Papas, who was now cooling his heels in the Suffolk County jail awaiting a bond hearing.

I was making little progress when Suzi interrupted me with another crisis. "I think the espresso machine is broken."

I followed Suzi to the coffee bar and quickly discerned the problem. Though the machine was plugged in, the electric outlet it was plugged into had shorted out. Running a high-voltage extension cord along the wall from the kitchen to the coffee bar temporarily solved the problem until an electrician could check out the socket in the morning. Crisis resolved, I returned to retrieve my notes in the break room.

I paused just outside the door when I heard the voice of Graydon Faas. He was alone, talking to someone on his cell phone.

Now, as a rule, I don't eavesdrop on private conversations (unless, of course, I'm investigating a crime). But Graydon Faas was dating my daughter, which I felt gave me certain latitude as a parent. Also, Madame's revelation that Graydon was the member of a family with a pharmaceutical fortune had piqued my curiosity. Here was a young man who was worth—quite literally—millions of dollars, yet who was waiting tables at a Hamptons restaurant rather than summering in luxury with every other member of his smart set.

I guess it's ironic that, after all my concern over David Mintzer's safety and well being, it was concern over my daughter that prompted me to listen to the one-sided conversation.

"I kept up my part of the deal, Bom." I heard him say.

Bom? As in Bom Felloes? I crept a little closer to the door, careful to stay out of sight.

"Sure I could use some more," said Graydon. "You

know it, dude. But I don't know . . . the last time what happened afterwards really freaked me out."

A glass crashed to the floor in the dining room, startling me. Graydon ignored the sound, kept right on going with his conversation.

"Okay, if you say so. What time? . . . Okay, dude, eleven-thirty it is. You're the bomb, Bom. See you later."

I whirled and literally ran to the other end of the kitchen. Graydon emerged from the break room a moment later and went to help Suzi Tuttle lay out the silverware.

I didn't know what business Graydon Faas had with Bom Felloes, but I suspected it was something shady. Even worse, I suspected it had something to do with the failed attempts on David Mintzer's life.

When everyone else was busy, I cornered Chef Vogel in the kitchen. "I need to leave early tonight, okay? Can you cover?"

"Sure."

"Thanks, I owe you. Just don't mention the fact that I'm leaving early to anyone else, okay?"

The chef offered me a conspiratorial wink. "Have a blast," he whispered. "After all the hard work you've put in this summer, you deserve a little fun."

I smiled and thanked him. Then I hurried back to the break room to retrieve my notes and make a cell phone call of my own—to the one person I knew wouldn't question my "outlaw ways."

Twenty-two
᳁᳁᳁᳁᳁᳁᳁᳁᳁᳁᳁᳁᳁

The night was fairly still, even on the water. This eve-ning's rental, *Rabbit Redux*, had an open-air helm, an en-closed cabin below, polished chrome rails, and a wooden deck that looked better than the parquet floor in my Village duplex.

We were at anchor, rocking gently on the placid tide. The craft was moored about fifty yards offshore from The Sandcastle, Bom Felloes's faux-medieval multimillion-dollar estate. Bom's split-level living room faced the ocean; its interior was visible through the mansion's massive glass wall, a brilliant rectangle in the darkness.

I glanced at my watch, illuminated by the dull glow of the helm's light. It was twenty minutes after eleven o'clock. "Almost time," I whispered to Jim, who was watching the estate through a pair of expensive-looking binoculars. His jaw was set, his body tense under the tight black wet-suit.

"What are we looking for exactly?" Jim asked, his eyes never wavering from the target area.

"Anything suspicious," I replied lamely.

Laughing, he lowered the binoculars. "The *world's* suspicious, Clare. Everybody's guilty of something."

"You don't understand. Bom Felloes has been feuding a long time with David. David got the restaurant Bom wanted here in the Hamptons, which is worth millions of dollars in lost revenue to Bom. But the real damage is to his ego. And that kind of damage is the worst kind to men like these."

"That doesn't necessarily make him a killer," Jim said, still looking through the binoculars. "But it does make him . . . well, well, well—"

"What?"

". . . a drug user."

My spine stiffened. "Let me guess. Cocaine?"

"He's either doing lines or trying to clean his coffee table with his nose and a straw. Oh, yeah. He's got a nice size bag of white powder. Okay, now he's poured some out on the table and he's cutting it with something—"

"Cutting it? Do you mean—"

"He's mixing the coke with some neutral substance. Could be something like baby powder, for instance, something that stretches the mix and diminishes the quality."

"Why would he do that? He's filthy rich."

"Why indeed," said Jim. "Doesn't make sense after I saw him do a couple of lines of the pure stuff, unless he plans on cheating someone, or . . ."

"What?"

"He's taking the stuff he cut and putting it into another bag, wrapping it up. He set that bag aside, now he's putting everything else away except for a couple of straws."

Jim shifted the binoculars. With my naked eye I saw headlights pulling up to the house's entrance, below the stone tower at one end of the structure. I couldn't make out the type of automobile, but Jim read my mind.

"It's a Mini Cooper—"

"That's Graydon."

Jim nodded. "Gangly kid in his mid-twenties, right? I can see him getting out of the car . . . the kid's not alone—"

"What? Who's with him?"

"A pretty girl is also getting out. Dark brown hair, shoulder length, kind of like yours. Curvy like you—"

"Let me see," I cried, snatching the binoculars. I peered through the lenses, focused, and my breath caught. "Oh god. Oh no. That's my daughter!"

Jim Rand took the binoculars from me, gazed through them, at Bom's living room. "Felloes is getting up to answer the door himself, which means no servants are around. And that means he wants this meeting to be private."

Jim faced me. "Call your daughter. Right now. She has a cell doesn't she?"

I nodded, fumbled for my phone, flipped it open. I didn't need to toggle to her listing in my speed dial menu. She was the very first number. "What do I say?"

"Jesus, Clare. You're her mother. If you don't know how to rattle her cage I can't tell you."

Of course! I pressed send and the call went through. The cell rang once, twice, three times—I held my breath, fearing Joy had turned her own cell off against my express wishes. Just when I gave up hope, I heard my daughter's voice.

"What is it, Mom?" she answered, clearly annoyed.

"I'll tell you what it is, young lady," I replied, my anger countering her irritation. "You're at Bom Felloes's house with Graydon. You're there to pick up a bag of cocaine, which you and your surfer dude boyfriend will then consume!"

"Mom . . . I . . . I . . ."

"Don't speak because it will only be lies. I know where you are right now, young lady. You just drove up to The

Sandcastle in Graydon's Mini Cooper, and I know what you're doing—"

"Ohmigod, Mom, how do you—"

"Listen to me. You leave that house and go to David's at once or I *will* call the police. I'd rather bail my daughter out of jail than let her destroy her life with the very drug that ruined her father!"

Jim was watching me, clearly impressed. In the shifting light, I saw him nod and give me the thumbs up. But I wasn't finished yet. It was time for me to deliver the coup de grace. "Joy . . . You know I have Detective O'Rourke of the Suffolk County Police on my speed dial now. Don't make me use it!"

Before Joy could stammer a reply, I hung up. For all she knew I was dialing the detective right now.

"What next?" I asked Jim, my blood pumping with adrenaline.

He observed the mansion. "I'd say your daughter will be leaving in about . . ." He grinned. "Yep, there they go."

With my naked eyes I saw the Mini Cooper's headlights spring to life. Jim shoved the binoculars at me, started the boat's engine. A moment later, we were cutting through the surf on the way down the coast to David Mintzer's section of beach.

"Look over there!" I cried.

Jim followed my finger, saw the power boat bobbing on the waves in front of David's mansion. No running lights were visible, it was not even a smudge on the water. I only spied the boat because it was silhouetted against the pool lights on David's patio, which were shining brightly. Usually the house was dark by this hour of the night.

"Whoever it is on that boat, they don't want to be seen," Jim said.

"I know, and that's usually your MO, isn't it?"

Jim's eyes narrowed. He glanced in my direction. "Yeah, Clare. I'd call that suspicious."

He cut the engine and swerved our boat. Its momentum pushed us silently to shore. "Hold on," he quietly warned, and we ran aground with a lurch. Then Jim went below and I heard him fumbling around. He emerged chambering a bullet into his handgun.

"My god, Jim—"

"Clare, get below deck and stay there." His voice was quiet, but its tone had gone hard, sharp.

"But—"

"Now!"

I went down the short stairs, waited until I heard Jim leap off the deck and splash into the shallow water. Then I crept back up to the deck again. I moved into a crouch, my head low. I could see Jim on the shore, playing his flashlight in the sand. Then he extinguished the lamp and vanished into the shadows.

Fearful I'd lose sight of him, I crawled down the side of the boat and slipped into the water, my sneakers sinking into the cold, shallow tide.

I moved across the sand, to the place where Jim had vanished. Despite the pool lights in the distance, I couldn't see a thing. I wished I had a flashlight, too, then I remembered the tiny blue glow of the cell phone screen. I whipped it out and flipped it open.

With the faint illumination I saw tracks in the sand. Webbed tracks. Flipper prints. As far as I could tell in the gloom, they led up to the rolling dunes fronting David's mansion. I followed, stumbling along in what I hoped was the same direction Jim took.

Among the dunes, I glanced toward the pool and saw the reason the lights were on. David was lounging in the bubbling hot tub, a drink in his hand. I thought about calling a warning, but David was too far away to hear me— the rhythmic tumbling of the surf would surely swallow my voice. All I would accomplish was to warn the stalker that he was being stalked.

I crossed an empty stretch of sand, then entered another row of dunes and stopped abruptly. Silhouetted against the glare of the deck lights, I saw a figure rise up, rifle with a scope clearly visible. I watched in horror as the figure aimed the weapon at David.

"No!" I shouted at the top of my lungs.

The gunman turned to face me, bringing the rifle around too. But before he could aim, Jim dived over the dune and slammed against the stranger. A loud crack split the silence as the rifle fired into the air, its flash bright among the mounds of sand.

Jim knocked the rifle to the ground, grabbed the intruder by his shoulders and turned him around. When Jim saw the man's face, he cried out, "Kenny, what the hell are you doing!?"

Kenny? Kenny Darnell? Jim's paparazzi partner threw a punch at Jim, and the two began to fight.

I cried out for help, but a uniformed security guard had heard the shot and was already cresting the dune, flashlight beam pinning the struggling men.

"Freeze!" cried the guard, pulling his gun.

Kenny panicked. He broke away from Jim and stumbled across the sand.

"Freeze or I *will* shoot you!" the guard shouted.

"For chrissakes, Kenny!" Jim shouted, "Stop! It's over! This guard will shoot you in the back. Give it up!"

But Kenny kept running toward the water. I saw the guard drop into a firing crouch and take aim.

"No!" Jim cried, throwing himself in the path of the bullet.

Cursing, the guard lifted his weapon and Jim took off. He caught his partner halfway across the beach, tackling him.

The guard ran across the sand, yelling, "Stay down, stay down or I'll have to fire."

A moment later, the guard dropped to his knees in the sand next to Jim and cuffed Kenny. I arrived a moment later. Jim was breathing hard. He tossed me an unhappy, borderline pissed-off look.

I folded my arms and raised an eyebrow. *This is the thanks I get?*

He shook his head. "I told you to stay on the boat."

"You also told me I was a thrill junkie. How could I miss my fix?"

"Up and at 'em," said the guard, hauling Kenny off the sand. I blinked in surprise, finally recognizing the baby-faced guard. "Thomas Gurt? Is that you?"

"Yes, ma'am," he said, his pale smooth skin gleaming with sweat. "My aunt asked me to take this shift. She thought something funny was going on. She told me she thought David was being menaced."

"Alberta said that?"

"Yes, ma'am. She sure was worried about Mr. Mintzer."

I was glad it was too dark for everyone to see me redden. *And I thought Alberta was a suspect. Some amateur sleuth I turned out to be.*

I moved to Jim's side. He was glaring at the man in handcuffs. We followed as Thomas led him back to the house.

I looked at the shooter, then at Jim. "So this man, he's—"

"Meet my partner, Kenny Darnell. Apparently his mother made a miracle recovery and he's back, shooting bullets instead of photos."

Alberta and David met us at the edge of the mansion's lawn.

"I've called the police," Alberta told us. "They'll be here in a few minutes."

David followed Jim, the guard, and their prisoner into the house. I lingered behind to speak with Alberta.

"You suspected David was in trouble all along, didn't you?" I whispered.

Alberta nodded. "Yes, ever since that poor young man was shot in his bathroom. Then David got sick and I was certain someone was trying to do him harm." The maid leaned close and whispered, "David is frail, but he's not that frail. I knew someone was trying to poison him."

"Why didn't you say something to me? To David?"

"Well, I'm sorry to tell you, Clare, that I was suspicious of you all along."

"Me? Oh, goodness."

"And as far as telling David what I thought . . . well, you don't know David like I know David. The man is just stubborn. If you want to do something to help him, you have to do it behind his back. David hates sentiment, probably because he's more sentimental than most of us. All along, I felt so guilty, Clare. David is like a son to me, and I felt I'd let him down—"

"How?"

"I wasn't there, at the Fourth of July party. I wasn't there for him. I had a date, you see—"

"A date?"

"Shhh!" Alberta said. "I don't want David to know. He never would have approved my entertaining a gentleman overnight in the mansion. It's nothing serious, really. Only a summer fling."

"So that's why you were dressed so nicely, with makeup and jewelry? That's why I heard voices in your room?"

"Please don't tell him, Clare."

"Alberta, my lips are sealed."

From inside the house I heard a struggle, then Kenny's voice. "Let me go, you asshole!"

I entered the kitchen, which was more crowded than I'd expected. Joy and Graydon Faas had arrived. They'd come to the kitchen, drawn to the commotion, no doubt.

"Why did you do it?" Jim demanded of his partner.

Before I could step in, Jim Rand lashed out, slapping his partner hard across the face. Kenny Darnell reeled from the blow. Then he stood tall, spit blood, and sneered. "Screw you, Rand."

"Now, now," David fretted, wringing his hands.

Thomas Gurt continued to grip the cuffed prisoner by the arms, his face remained impassive.

Jim saw my shocked expression. For a flashing moment, he looked sheepish. "He won't talk."

I stepped forward, until my eyes caught Kenny Darnell's. He was a good-looking man with dark, curly hair, a squarish face, and an even tan. His defiant blue gaze met mine.

"Jim," I said, holding Darnell's gaze, "you don't have to make him talk. I've already figured out what's going on and I'm going to tell Detective O'Rourke everything."

"You don't know shit, bitch," Kenny replied.

Jim stepped up and raised his hand again. I put myself between them.

"Oh, god," David moaned, stroking his temples.

"Listen to me, Kenny. I know you lied and told Jim that your mother was sick in Queens. It gave you an alibi for being far away from the Hamptons when the shootings occurred. You knew your mother would lie for you. You also needed someone to frame for the murder." I turned to face Jim. "Who better to pin it on than you, Jim Rand, his own partner. By using your MO, the wet suit, the flippers, Kenny knew he could implicate you in the crime. He was probably planning on hiding that rifle among your personals. Some friend, huh?"

"Shut your mouth—" Kenny began.

"You shut yours, Darnell," Jim warned. "Or I swear to god—"

"Two problems arose," I quickly cut in. "First, Kenny killed the wrong man. Then the storm swept in on the night

of the murder and washed away the flipper prints. The cops had no evidence beyond the casings Kenny deliberately left at the scene. Now Kenny had a problem. He still had to kill David and pin it on you, Jim, so for Treat's murder he had to go to plan B and frame someone else."

"You mean, this man framed that drug dealer the police arrested?" David asked.

"Yes," I said and turned to Rand. "Jim, didn't you tell me that Kenny took photos for the police—traffic accident photos, right?"

"Yeah, that's right, Clare."

"So Kenny knows the score out here with the cops," I said. "He probably has friends among them, so he knew what was going on with the investigation into Treat's murder. He knew they wanted to solve the crime fast, pin it on a shooter. He also knew from his policemen friends that Treat had drug connections. I'm guessing it was Mr. Darnell himself who tipped the police about the rifle in the drug dealer's trunk—the guy in Hampton Bays. It was you who tipped them, wasn't it, Kenny? What did you do, make an anonymous phone call?"

Kenny sneered. "You think you're so smart."

I nodded. "Smarter than you, it seems to me, because I never thought Treat's murder was solved. The police did. They dropped their guard. So did David. Now you could strike again and get the job done right."

I faced Jim Rand again. "Tonight, Kenny used your MO like last time, only this time, he made sure to do it on a night with no storm. And, as I said, he was probably going to stash tonight's rifle among your belongings."

Jim shook his head. "Why, Kenny? We had a good thing going."

Kenny's face twisted in disgust. "We had nothing going. This business was my idea from the beginning. I brought you in. But you were always expendable."

"You were a washout, you prick. In the SEALs and out. You ran up debts with your sports betting, couldn't get a loan from a bank, or don't you remember? I was the one who put up the capital for the equipment, the rentals."

"Yeah, well, this business was my idea," Kenny said, "and I decided I didn't want to split my profits anymore."

"You punk, you ran up sports betting debts again, didn't you?" Jim said, closing in on his partner. "You were desperate for money. So desperate you had to do something like this."

Darnell looked away. "I didn't know how the hell I was going to get rid of you without making you my competitor. So I decided to kill two birds with one stone. Make a little extra money and send you away for a while. So I put an ad in *Soldier of Fortune* and I got a bite—to kill David Mintzer."

"Oh, gawd," David moaned.

Despite David's distress, I could see this interrogation was actually going pretty well. The only thing I needed to hear now, the only thing we all needed to hear, was Kenny confess who had hired him. I folded my arms, shook my head, and began to pace.

"Kenny, the only thing I can't figure out," I said, "is why your first attempt was during a big party. You could have killed David on the beach, on the street, anywhere—"

"Oh, gawd," David moaned again.

Kenny smirked at me. "So you're not so smart."

"I don't know, Kenny. Doing your hit at a big party like that. All that room for error. The chance of getting caught?" I turned to Jim. "Maybe your partner washed out of the SEALs for a reason. Maybe he's just stupid."

"Shows what you know, bitch," Kenny spat. "It's what my client wanted."

"So Bom Felloes was the stupid one?"

"Yeah, it was his idea to shoot David at his own party. He wanted to kill two birds with one stone too. David would be dead. And the public shooting would start rumors, ruin David's businesses by making it look like someone from organized crime wanted him dead. Like he was mobbed up."

"OOOOOOH!"

Alberta rushed to David's side, to comfort him. It was obvious the reality check was just too much for the man.

"Too bad you failed to kill the right guy," said Jim. "You had to come back and try again. Guess you weren't up to the mission, after all, eh, partner?"

"Go to hell, Rand. I would have done the job just fine. If it wasn't for you, this asshole would be dead now."

Jim snorted. "You give me undo credit, pal. It wasn't me who nailed you." His eyes found mine. "It was Clare."

I sighed, relieved beyond belief we'd gotten a confession without more bloodshed. Hadn't David Mintzer been through enough without having to endure more crimson stains on his beautiful floors?

Unfortunately, the interrogation wasn't quite over yet.

I turned to Graydon and Joy, who'd been watching everything in wide-eyed silence. I didn't take pleasure in involving my daughter in all of this; but, as it turned out, she had already involved herself. *Please, please, my darling daughter, learn this now: when you make your choices, you have to live with the consequences.*

I stepped up to Graydon Faas, looked him in the eye, and asked, "Why were you talking to Bom Felloes this afternoon, Graydon? And why were you visiting his home tonight?"

Graydon appeared defiant for a moment, until he saw the way my daughter Joy was watching him with a mixture of horror and disgust. Suddenly his chest sank.

"I needed money," he said.

"But your family is wealthy."

"Richer than you know," Graydon said. "But they disowned me several years ago, when I dropped out of college to be a surf instructor. They said they didn't like my lifestyle choices, so I told them to shove their money."

"How did you hook up with Felloes?"

"I met Bom at a club. He already knew I was waiting tables for extra cash at Cuppa J. He set me up with some good coke and a stack of Benjamins for doing him one little favor on July Fourth. I slipped David Mintzer something that would give him a migraine. Payback for losing the restaurant—that's what Bom told me. I had no idea anyone was going to get shot. After it happened, Bom told me it was just a weird coincidence that someone wanted to murder Treat. He called me every so often for more information on David . . . I was so worried about Bom blackmailing me, getting me into trouble, I just gave him what he asked for. When he called today, I thought he wanted more info. Instead, he just offered me more cash and coke for helping him. I drove over to get it, then Joy freaked out and we came here—"

"You're lucky," I told Graydon. "After tonight, Bom wouldn't have needed you anymore for information on David, and I think he was trying to make sure you never talked to the police."

"What do you mean never talked—"

"She means he was going to kill you, stupid," Jim snapped. "That cocaine he was going to give you? I watched him cut it with something. It was probably laced with enough PCP to fry every molecule in your brainpan. Smarten up, kid."

"Oh, my god," said Joy.

I heard sirens screaming—despite the disturbance to the neighbors. I glanced at Jim. "The police."

* * *

TWO hours later, things had calmed down again at "Leisure with Dignity." The police had taken Kenny Darnell and Graydon Faas into custody. Thomas Gurt went with the cops to assist in pulling Bom Felloes out of his luxurious Sandcastle and depositing him behind bars (the metal kind). We all gave our statements and were told the detectives would follow up with us the next day.

Madame had come home by now, and she was sitting with Joy, David, and Alberta in the mansion's great room, hearing the tale of Kenny's capture from beginning to end. Everyone was agitated and upset and would likely be up half the night.

Jim Rand hadn't said much during the hours the police were here. Now that they'd gone, he stepped through the back door of the mansion, onto the cedar deck. I followed him outside.

"Jim? Are you okay?"

He rubbed the back of his neck, shook his head. "The DA will want the big fish. If Graydon and Kenny testify against Bom, their sentences will be plead out to relatively minor time, and that's better than that son of a bitch partner of mine deserves."

"I'm sorry."

"You're *sorry*?" He turned to look at me. "Wow, Clare. That's disappointing."

I blinked. "Disappointing?"

"Hell yeah." A slow smile spread across his rugged face. "And here I thought you'd be grateful."

Epilogue

~~~~~~~~~~~~~~~~~~~~~~~~~~~~~~~~

"**You** know, I'm going to miss the way you smell," said Jim, nibbling my ear.

"How do I smell?" I asked.

"I never told you?"

"No."

"Like freshly roasted coffee."

"Oh, *that's* a surprise, I mean, given the hours I spend in the Village Blend roasting room. But that's just one of the perks of my job."

"Clare, that is so bad."

Jim Rand had his arms wrapped around me. We were happily naked, in the double bed of his yacht's cabin. He'd finally made enough money by the end of summer to have bought his own.

It was early September. The summer season was officially over, and I'd already moved back to the city. But Jim had convinced me to drive out from Manhattan to enjoy one more Hamptons sunset with him—and sunrise too.

We had seen many sunrises together since Treat's murder was solved. After the wave of publicity had passed and things had calmed down, Jim had shown up late one night at Cuppa J. He'd ordered an espresso to go, then asked me to go with it. I did, deciding at last to have a summer fling of my very own.

But the summer was over now.

"You know what I never got about that whole Mintzer thing?" Jim said. "What was the deal with your wanting all these close-ups of Marjorie Bright lurking around the man's mansion on July Fourth?"

"David's trees," I informed him, tracing the outline on his SEAL tattoo. "They partially blocked her view of the ocean. In my opinion, she was smoking like crazy, trying to burn them down with one of her butts. Probably figured David would think a stray spark from one of the fireworks caused it."

"How neighborly."

"Well, as it turned out, your recon photos helped resolve that little war."

"How's that?"

"David's lawyer showed shots of Marjorie lurking around David's property to Marjorie's lawyer. He threatened to charge her with trespassing and attempted arson. So she pulled back her lawsuits against David and his trees. And in return David agreed to trim the tops and sides of the things."

"What's wrong with looking at trees?" Jim asked. "Trees are good, aren't they? They attract birds . . . when they're not migrating."

I sighed. "That's what you're going to do, isn't it? Migrate? I mean, now that the celebrity shooting season is officially over, you're heading south for the winter just like the birds, right?"

Jim caressed my shoulder, kissed the nape of my neck. "I'd ask you to come with me, but I know you won't."

I laughed. "You won't ask me to go with you because you're worried I might. You're just like my ex."

Jim didn't hesitate. "Come with me."

"Can't. I have a life in New York. But you can send me a postcard from paradise."

"Maybe you'll visit? I'm going to miss your coffee, you know?" He nuzzled my hair.

"Well, you know where to get a good cuppa," I reminded him. "Manhattan is a port city, too."

"Okay, that's a deal. Just remember one thing, okay?"

"What?"

"I'm guessing solving murders is a bad little habit you're not going to give up anytime soon. So if you get into trouble—"

"Just whistle?"

"No." He sat up, reached for his jeans on the back of a nearby chair. After fishing in a pocket, he pulled out his card, pressed it into my palm. "Use the cell phone."

I laughed. Frankly, I didn't know what good a cell phone call would be to a man one thousand miles away, but I tucked the card into my wallet anyway, like a souvenir. On some gray winter day, I'd probably pull it out by accident and suddenly remember the time I'd spent on this desirable bit of acreage, this irresistible little plot someone like me could visit but never own.

I smiled at Jim, snuggled under the covers, and pulled his arms back around me. What was owning anyway? I found myself wondering. You couldn't own a person. You couldn't even own land, really. The Earth itself was just a rental. Our time on it was basically one big share. I thought of Bom and David, Kenny and Jim, Marjorie and her ocean view, even myself and Matt.

"Why so quiet all of sudden? What are you thinking?" Jim's voice sounded tense.

"Oh, it's nothing. I was just wondering if the quality of our lives doesn't simply boil down to whether or not we can all get along in the same house."

"Excuse me?"

"Forget it," I told him. "Explaining would take too long. And we only have a few more hours until sunrise."

After a pause, Jim whispered, "Clare . . ."

"Yes?"

"Now that I'm leaving . . . are you sorry? Sorry we got together?"

There was defensiveness in his tone, as if he expected me to turn on him now. As if he'd gone through some ugly good-bye scenes with women in the past, and he expected the same from me.

He wasn't going to get it.

There comes an age in life when you realize that blaming and regretting are a waste of precious time. Some thrills were worth weathering the inevitable crash. And in the end, as Madame and Joy had tried to tell me all season long, a summer fling didn't have to be a crime.

"No, Jim, I'm not sorry," I said. "After what we've both been through, don't you think the time we have, whether long or short, is something we should just make the most of?"

"I do, Clare," he said, turning me in his arms. "I do."

RECIPES & TIPS
FROM THE VILLAGE BLEND

CLARE'S TIPS ON
FROTHY COFFEE FRAPPÉS

Refreshingly chilly and smooth, laced with energizing caffeine, iced coffee drinks can be a satisfying pick-me-up in the sweltering heat of a city summer. Here are a few ways to make your favorite coffeehouse frappés at home.

The Village Blend's
Chilly Choco Latte

Yield: 2 servings

1 cup espresso or strong coffee (let cool)
¼ cup chocolate syrup
1 tablespoon vanilla syrup
1 cup milk
6 cups crushed ice

Pour all of your ingredients into a blender and blend on high until the ice is thoroughly crushed. Divide between two chilled glasses. Drink as a midday treat on a hot, sunny day or serve as a dessert coffee on a warm summer evening by topping it with whipped cream and chocolate shavings.

Tropical Coffee Frappé
(Rum and Coconut Coffee Smoothie)

Yield: 2 servings

1 cup espresso or strong coffee (let cool)
1/4 cup rum
1/2 cup milk
1/2 cup coconut milk
6 cups crushed ice
Simple sugar syrup to taste (see recipe later in this section)

This one's a great cocktail for summer parties. Pour all of your ingredients into a blender and blend on high until the ice is thoroughly crushed. Divide between two chilled glasses. For a cool, smooth dessert drink, substitute a scoop of ice cream for the 1/2 cup of milk.

Frothy Seafoam Frappé
(Cocoa-Mint Espresso Smoothie)

Yield: 2 servings

1 cup espresso or strong coffee (let cool)
2 tablespoons chocolate syrup
2 teaspoons crème de cacao
½ teaspoon crème de menthe
1 cup milk
6 cups crushed ice

For people who love the taste of coffee, chocolate, and mint. Pour all of your ingredients into a blender and blend on high until the ice is thoroughly crushed. Divide between two chilled glasses. The perfect drink to share on a lovely summer evening by the sea.

Old Fashioned
Iced Coffee

The best tip for making plain old-fashioned iced coffee is to remember that adding ice to regular coffee is not the way to do it! The ice will melt and simply water down your coffee. Either brew your coffee double strength first, or better yet, create ice cubes out of brewed coffee, then add these iced coffee cubes to your already cooled coffee. Now you won't have to sacrifice the flavor for the chill.

Simple Sugar Syrup

Want to sweeten an iced coffee drink? Do it the way iced tea drinkers do! Create this simple sugar syrup.

1 cup sugar
1 cup water

Combine the water and sugar in a saucepan. Simmer over low heat until the sugar is totally dissolved—probably no more than five minutes. Cool thoroughly, then store the mixture in a jar in the fridge.

Clare's Café Pousson
(8 layered chocolate-almond espresso)

This one's hot, literally. The eight-layered espresso is a complicated balance of physics—a careful pouring of heavier syrups and lighter liquids to create a beautiful-looking layered drink. This is my own version of a café pousson (translation "push coffee"), the multi-layered cocktail of liquors of different colors and densities that originated in New Orleans. These portions are enough for you to share this drink with a special friend on a cool evening by the seashore. For a more petite version, just cut these portions in half.

4 tablespoons chocolate syrup
4 tablespoons almond syrup
¾ cup (12 tablespoons) steamed milk
1 cup hot espresso

In a tall clear, tapered glass, (one of Jim Rand's pilsner glasses would work quite well), layer these liquids in the following order. Put this one together slowly and carefully—it's a challenge! Good luck.

Step 1 – Pour 2 tablespoons chocolate syrup into bottom of glass.

Step 2 – Carefully layer 2 tablespoons almond syrup on top.

Step 3 – Very slowly add 6 tablespoons steamed milk.

Step 4 – Pour slowly, into middle of glass, 2 tablespoons chocolate syrup.

Step 5 – Pour slowly, into middle of glass, 2 tablespoons almond syrup.

Step 6 – Slowly add 6 tablespoons of steamed milk.

Step 7 – Slowly pour the 1 cup of espresso into the middle of the glass.

Step 8 – Layer the foam of the steamed milk on the very top.

Clare's Chocolate-Walnut-Espresso Brownies

I had no time to make these for Jim Rand the day I met him. But they really are a quick and easy treat. Pair them with a darkly roasted coffee (like French or Italian roast) or a warm, earthy cup of espresso.

1 box of your favorite brownie mix
2 tablespoons instant espresso (or instant coffee crystals)
¼ cup espresso (cooled)
1 cup semisweet chocolate chips
1 cup chopped walnuts
1 teaspoon vanilla

Prepare brownie mix according to package directions. If water is required in mix directions, reduce the amount by half. In a separate cup, dissolve instant coffee crystals in the espresso, add vanilla. Mix until well blended. With a spoon, stir in the chocolate chips and walnuts. Transfer the batter to a greased pan. Bake according to package directions.

Garnish idea: After the brownies have cooled, try a glaze. Here's a walnut glaze, but you can easily create your own— a chocolate, vanilla, or coffee glaze would all work well. Just alter the extracts and flavorings as you like. For the walnut glaze here's what you do. Whisk together in a medium bowl 2 teaspoons of walnut extract and 1 teaspoon of vanilla extract with 2 tablespoons of water. Into this liquid mixture whisk 1½ cups powdered sugar and 1 tablespoon unsalted butter (well softened). Pour this glaze over the brownies and lightly smooth with a rubber spatula. Refrigerate the pan well, until the glaze is set, and then cut into squares.

Almond Torte

A lovely summer dessert! Here's a good tip for serving—make it the night before so it has plenty of time to chill in the refrigerator. Serve with a medium roast coffee from the Central or South American regions and a dollop of fresh whipped cream on the side.

Yield: 1 torte (serves 6)

¾ cup blanched almonds, toasted
2 tablespoons sugar
⅓ cup flour
½ cup sugar
1 stick butter (softened)
1 tablespoon vanilla extract
1 teaspoon almond extract
¼ teaspoon salt
3 eggs

Preheat oven to 350° F. Grease and flour a 9-inch round cake pan. Grind the blanched, toasted almonds and 2 tablespoons of sugar to a powder in a food processor or blender. Mix in the flour. Set aside. Using an electric mixer, beat together until creamy, the butter, the rest of the sugar (½ cup), the vanilla and almond extracts, and the salt. Add eggs one at a time and beat in well. Add the dry ingredients to the wet ones and spread this batter into a well greased pan. Bake 40 minutes or until top is golden brown and the top of the torte springs back when lightly touched. Wrap the cooled cake in foil and refrigerate overnight before serving.

Quick garnishing tip: Let the torte cool in the pan at least ½ hour. Then remove from pan. Lightly brush the torte's top with the simple sugar syrup (recipe elsewhere in this section) and sprinkle generously with almond slices for a pretty garnish. Then don't forget to store the tightly wrapped torte in your refrigerator overnight!

Flourless Chocolate-Kahlua Cake

A deliciously decadent dessert for summer with a hint of coffee flavor. Ripe raspberries or plump farmers' market strawberries make a great side garnish for this dessert, best served after being thoroughly chilled.

2 cups semisweet chocolate, coarsely chopped
2 sticks unsalted butter, cut into pieces
¼ cup Kahlua
8 large eggs
¼ cup sugar
1 tablespoon vanilla
½ teaspoon salt

Preheat oven to 325° F. Place the chocolate, butter, and Kahlua in the top of a double boiler and melt the mixture, stirring constantly, until it's smooth and creamy (this takes about 5 minutes). Combine eggs, sugar, vanilla, and salt in a large bowl and whisk with an electric mixer until frothy and almost doubled in volume, about 5 to 10 minutes. Fold this mixture into the chocolate mixture slowly, a little at a time. Pour the final batter into a springform pan (see tips on prep below).

Place the cake pan into a larger pan (a roasting pan would be best). Carefully pour enough boiling water into the roasting pan to rise about halfway up the sides of the springform pan. Bake until the cake has risen slightly and edges are just beginning to set, about 40 to 45 minutes, depending on your oven. Remove the springform pan from the larger (roasting) pan and cool on wire rack to room temperature. Then cover and refrigerate overnight.

Springform pan prep tip: You'll want to grease a 9-inch springform pan and line the bottom of it with parchment paper. Using aluminum foil, wrap the outside of the pan, covering up the bottom and sides so that no water will leak into the cake batter when you bake it in the roasting pan water bath.

Serving tip: About a half hour to an hour before serving, take the springform pan away from the cake's sides. Invert the cake onto a plate and peel away the parchment paper on the bottom. With your serving plate, turn the cake one more time, back onto its right side. A nice garnish would be a dusting of powdered sugar with some fresh summer raspberries or strawberries on the side.

Don't Miss the Next
Coffeehouse Mystery
DECAFFEINATED CORPSE

*A cuppa Joe without caffeine? In coffeehouse lingo, that's
called a "why bother?" Solving a mystery that's too hot to
handle? That's* no bother *for Clare Cosi. Join her for a double
shot of danger in her next coffeehouse mystery.*

Get cozy with a cup of coffee and
a delicious mystery.

The Coffeehouse Mystery series

by Cleo Coyle

On What Grounds
0–425–19213–X

Through the Grinder
0–425–19714–X

Latte Trouble
0–425–20445–6

"CLEO COYLE IS A BRIGHT NEW LIGHT
ON THE MYSTERY HORIZON."
—BEST REVIEWS

PC098